MARCUS

THE GUZZI
LEGACY BOOK 6

BETHANY-KRIS

www.bethanykris.com

Editor: Elizabeth Peters

Proofreaders: Tracy A., Mia B., Tori W. and Felicia F.

Cover Design © Under Cover Designs

Interior Design: Under Cover Designs

ISBN: 978-1-989658-06-2

For the fans

PROLOGUE

Black everywhere.

A sea of black, really.

Cella Marcello felt like everything had become painted with the color. *Tainted.* Maybe that was the better word for this day and what was happening. Everything was tainted with blackness because wasn't that the only appropriate hue for grief?

Especially grief like this.

One so hollow.

Empty.

Lonely.

From the suits and dresses surrounding her, worn by people with faces she recognized and—some—she loved to even the clouds above her head. Her emotions. The hole in the ground. The shiny granite headstone with her husband's name carved with white lettering.

All black.

She saw other colors, of course. The green of the grass, and the gray of the sky. The light rain from earlier in the day left a mist in the air, curling up from the ground and disappearing all around her. A few people dared to wear shades of gray and even navy blues for the day instead of the standard black clothing that accompanied funerals. The silver bangles on her wrist jingled with her trembling, and it didn't seem to matter how tight she held her child, the shaking didn't relent.

If anything, it became worse.

How much longer could she hold it in?

How long would it be before she could breathe?

"Want me to take her?"

Cella looked to the side, peering through the black veil that hung down from the rim of her large hat, finding her mother trying to offer her a smile. It didn't reach Jordyn's wet eyes, and there in the glistening tears, she found her own reflection. She looked like her mother—soft-featured, round face, a small, sloped nose, high cheekbones, and full lips shaped like a curvy bow. All her sisters, the two of them, took after their mother whereas their brother, John, looked far more like their father.

Except right then, all Cella saw in the reflection was her sadness. How despite the fact that her eyes felt so dry, as though she'd cried far too many tears and couldn't produce more, wetness still coated her cheeks. She found pain there.

Only pain.

"Cella?" her ma asked again.

She shook her head and tightened her hold on eight-month-old Tiffany when the baby squirmed a bit under her thin cotton blanket. Surely, the girl didn't need a blanket in this August heat, but with the occasional rain and slight breeze, she didn't want to take a chance. So, she wrapped her up.

Because that was the thing.

It didn't matter her husband was dead.

It didn't matter that she didn't want to get out of bed.

That her heart broke.

She was empty.

Life had *stopped*.

None of that could matter to Cella when she was still a mother. Her child depended on her constantly. Sure, Tiffany didn't understand why when she called out for *Dada* in the mornings, William wasn't there to pull her from her crib for their daily routine, but she made do with her mother. No doubt, she thought her father would be back—he would never be back—but she still had her ma.

And that left Cella to do everything when all she wanted was to do nothing. Except life didn't work that way. And this wasn't Tiffany's fault.

So, she put on her fake smile for her child day in and day out. She tried not to cry in front of her as much as she could, because then the baby would wipe away her mother's tears, and nothing felt worse than that.

She kept on going. Moving forward. The world continued turning. It was just hers that felt dead now.

"Pretty girl," Cella's older sister, Liliana, said as she reached out to fluff the bottom of her pretty summer dress that had peeked out from beneath the blanket. "Just a few more minutes, Tiff, okay?"

She refused to put her daughter in black. Little *Tiffany*. Named for her father's sister who had passed as a young girl from childhood cancer. With her head of golden curls that she took from her father, and big blue eyes she took from her mother—compliments of Cella's own mother, Jordyn—Tiffany wore the brightest yellow dress Cella could find in her closet that would make anyone smile who looked at her. She even added a headband with a big yellow flower to the girl's head.

Because *God* …

At least, she thought, if today couldn't be a day that she smiled … then she wanted others to find a reason to do it. Her husband would have appreciated that. Respected it. *Loved it*, honestly. William, with his heart of gold and his easy disposition, always tried to make someone laugh first and foremost. He made friends easier than most, and it was hard not to want to be in his presence.

Everybody thinks lawyers are boring, he told her once, *so I like to surprise people.*

It was exactly why she fell in love with him.

Why she started this life with him.

And then someone took it away.

A handful of dirt was tossed into the hole in the ground, dragging Cella from her thoughts with a vicious intent. She was just close enough to the edge to be able to see her husband's casket resting down below, yet another item that gleamed black that day.

Still so fucking black.

Like her heart, now.

She found it easier to stare at anything else except things with that color. It was why she missed the priest's final words as her husband was laid to rest in his grave, and the reason for her distraction as people started flooding out of the graveyard. She heard their condolences, sure, saw their familiar faces as they stopped to give their sympathies before leaving, but it was all just background noise to her grief.

The pain lingered.

Even when she was alone.

More so when she wasn't.

Still, she tried to thank people. She attempted to put on her brave face with each of their *I'm so sorrys* or the *please call me if you need anything*. The platitudes didn't mean anything to her, but they made them feel better, she supposed.

And besides, this was *their* way.

The Marcello way.

Even when her soul felt like it was being ripped out of her chest, even if her husband's young life had ended far too soon all because of the lifestyle all these people here today chose to live when William hadn't even been a made man, she was a Marcello daughter at the end of the day.

A *mafioso principessa*. And so, she would smile like one. Say thank you like one. *Die quietly inside like one.*

Because there wasn't a soul in this graveyard who cared to hear how Cella blamed *them* for this—for her heartache, and her daughter's loss.

She never wanted to marry a made man. So, she didn't. Her husband died anyway.

It taught her a lesson she wouldn't forget: one couldn't be *not in* with this life. There was no *from a safe distance* when it came to her family. She was who she was. And she sacrificed for it, too.

"Mrs. Gagnon? It's Cella, right?"

Cella turned her attention away from the spot she'd been focusing on over the top of her daughter's head to find yet another person had come to say goodbye and give his condolences. His face seemed familiar with all it's strong, classically handsome lines, and his dark brown eyes only reflected empathy when he stared at her.

Another day, and she might have recognized him.

Today, she only said, "And who are you?"

"Marcus Guzzi—I came in place of my father to pay respects."

Ah.

Another crime family. A Canadian one, this time. Funny how they all gathered at times like this.

"Well, thank you," she whispered. "And it's Marcello. Cella *Marcello.*"

She'd decided that if only because going back to her maiden name felt less painful than having to explain to each new person she met that her last name belonged to her dead husband.

Marcus nodded once. "My apologies. And my sympathies on your loss, as well."

"Of course."

Someone called the man's name, and he was quick to give her an apologetic smile before stepping away. She might have watched him go, but her attention was back on the hole in the ground and her mind strayed to the man resting in his casket.

Here she was ... *twenty-five*. A mother to one. Widowed and broken. Would it ever get better?

Not for a long fucking time.

CHAPTER
1

Four and a half years later

"How old are you?"

That question had Marcus Guzzi raising his brow. He didn't even bother to answer the man as he sat across the table from him. The room quieted all the way around the board; the men surrounding them turned their attention on the two people at the table like this meeting had just become slightly more interesting.

"Well?" the large man demanded.

The stark contrast between the vice president of the Quebec chapter of the Riders—a one-percenter motorcycle club that had a heavy hand in dealing with illegal pills and prostitution between Quebec and Ontario—and Marcus in his three-piece suit was never more obvious than in those moments. Here they were, dining in a five-star restaurant Marcus had closed down to the public for this goddamn meeting, and the VP came with his men in tow, on bikes, wearing their denim and leather.

The disrespect started there.

And it had yet to end.

"*Excusez-moi?*" Marcus asked, choosing French to reply to the man because he knew the biker—Glen, he went by—was French-born first. His last name, Cote, a testament to his heritage. "What does my age have to do with this conversation we're trying to have here? Because I am pretty sure the answer is nothing."

Glen grinned, but it came off as more like a sneer. His French accent heavily colored his words when he replied in English, "I'm wondering if you should even be here sitting at this table, or if I should have waited for something with a few more years and a bit of … *understanding* about this business of ours, *oui*?"

Marcus had every urge to grind his teeth right down to the fucking roots because that right there was a low blow, and he didn't doubt the other man knew it. In the world of mafioso, where Marcus had been born and bred from the moment he took his first breath, if a man sat at the table … it was because he earned his place there. Questioning it only meant more disrespect, and *shit*, hadn't he taken enough of that from this asshole today?

He thought so.

"We're not here to discuss my age," Marcus said, leaning back a bit in his chair to get back to his previously unbothered, calm disposition before the asshole across the table tried to change the subject. "We're here to discuss the fact that your *club* has decided to take issue with the Guzzi organization taking over the maple syrup farm—"

"In our territory."

Marcus arched a brow. "Let me ask you a question, yeah? Indulge me, you know, in all my *ignorance* because of my age and whatnot. Would you?"

Any man Marcus had brought into this meeting would have known right away that statement was nothing more than bait. Only a stupid man would take it because once it was thrown out there, it meant Marcus had come to *really* play. As the underboss of his father's Cosa Nostra, he didn't have time to play very much. Everything was serious. Walk the fucking line, type of deal. Three-piece suits every single day, up before the sun rose and walking the streets to do the kind of business, he'd been doing for most of his life.

He was made.

Mafia.

Guzzi.

So, when he took a minute to play, if a fucker was stupid enough to take the bait, he was going to reel them right in. Until he could snap their goddamn necks. The idiot across the table from him included. As he thought, the man took the bait.

Because *of course.*

"Sure, why not," Glen muttered. "As if we all have time today, ask me a question, Marcus."

His jaw ticked.

It'd been *Marcus* from the moment he walked in the door. Not *sir* or *Guzzi* or even *mister.* As though they were on a first name basis, despite the fact that Marcus repeatedly and clearly corrected the asshole every time he used his first name. Something else to add to the pile of disrespect. He wished he was shocked.

But *nope.*

"Do you assume when I put this suit on and get in my black Mercedes you saw me arrive in that I suddenly become a man who doesn't know how to nail your head to the wall with a well-placed bullet?"

Glen stiffened, his tattooed arms bulging when they flexed at his chest. "Is that a threat, Guzzi?"

Ah, so now it was Guzzi, huh?

"My age—it's three months shy of thirty, by the way—makes zero fucking difference to the fact that if your club doesn't stay away from the Guzzi's newest maple syrup farm we're going to end you. I've been kind enough—or gracious enough, depending on how you want to look at it—to give you opportunity after opportunity to make the right choice here. That farm being in the club's territory doesn't change the fact it is in *our* hands. Like every other farm now in Ontario and Quebec, and if you think you're going to slide in on the profits just because your clubhouse is six miles away, I have news for you."

Silence echoed in the restaurant.

Good.

That's what he wanted.

He felt all those eyes on him, waiting for what was going to come next.

"See, I feel the need to remind you now that compared to your fifty or so members within your club, the Guzzi organization is far larger, and our reach extends across this country and beyond. And don't get me wrong, *Glen*, I understand that this effort of yours to put your foot in the door with our mafia is your way of proving yourself to your president, it still comes at the expense of my boss's bottom line, and we just can't have that. Find someone else to make your patch there worth keeping because it won't be us."

Marcus leaned forward a bit, clasping his hands together on the table as he smiled, met the man's stare, so Glen knew he wasn't the least bit fucking scared of him, his *club*, or whatever threat the man might try to answer this with as he asked, "Do you understand me, or would you like to go back to taking cheap shots about my age? Either way, I'm good."

Glen's cheek twitched like he was chewing over a response before finally settling on saying, "You're essentially running a maple syrup cartel in Canada—you get that, don't you?"

"And?"

Because Marcus didn't see the problem.

Not only did the Guzzis have a legal venture in harvesting, manufacturing, and selling maple syrup, but it also served as a perfect front for all their illegal business. It was a great way to hide their dirty money and launder it until it was clean. And if this asshole thought just because his little clubhouse and gang were a few miles away that it meant they were owed a piece of that, well …

No.

Simply put, *no*.

"Listen," Glen tried to say, "we only think it's fair that—"

"What's fair is I let you leave here alive today, and that is all you will get from us." Standing from the table, Marcus ignored the stares of the men from across the other side of the table. Bikers in their cuts, clearly agitated and ready to roll. Thing was, he wouldn't be giving them anything to roll with from here on out. "This meeting is over, and it is the only one you will get unless you force my hand. I assure you that isn't what you want to do. *Voyages sécuritaires, mon ami.*"

Glen glowered up at Marcus, his bald head reddening from the clear dismissal of a man about half his age. "We're not *friends*. How about you remember that?"

Marcus nodded. "So be it."

Without another word, Marcus turned away from the table, not at all concerned about turning his back to the man. He brought a small army of made men with him, as well, for this meeting. He wasn't stupid, and before someone could even try to pull a gun on him, they would be dead by his guards.

He walked out of that restaurant knowing this wasn't the end. For now, though, it was one thing off his list. A list that never stopped growing.

So was the life of a Guzzi *principe*.

Especially Marcus Guzzi.

Duty always called.

It never ended.

And he didn't want life any other way.

* * *

"Did you see this *merda*?"

Marcus was already bitching before he'd even entered his younger brother, Christopher's, restaurant office in downtown Toronto. He wasn't all that shocked to find Bene, his other brother, sitting with Chris at the man's desk. Of course, on the other side of the desk. No one but the man who owned the space got to sit behind it.

That was all about *the respect*.

"See what?" Chris asked, never looking away from his computer screen.

"This."

Marcus tossed the Toronto-focused magazine to his brother's desk with a grunt that spoke of his utter *disgust*. The damn rag liked to write *all the shit* about things they knew nothing about. Usually regarding people they considered to be high society in Toronto, and all of that nonsense. And of course, because the Guzzi family happened to be very rich with a name that carried an interesting, if not murky, legacy … well, the five brothers, their wives, and even their parents were often topics of discussion in the articles whenever the rag thought they could get away with it.

This month, Marcus got to be included.

"I'm getting Dad's lawyer on their asses—they need to get my fucking name out of their mouths."

Bene sighed, reaching for the magazine before Christopher even bothered to look away from his computer screen. Soon enough, their younger brother had flipped to the article in question about Marcus which was really just noting that he had attended a charity gala where he danced with a young woman who happened to be the daughter of a prominent Canadian politician.

Except they couldn't just stop at *that*.

No, never.

"Oh my God," Bene muttered, trying and failing to keep his laughter under his breath. "They suggested she's your fiancée and *everything*. Where do they come up with this trash? *Marcus Guzzi was clearly enamored with—*"

"That's quite enough, reading it once was fine for me. I don't need someone else to read it to me, too."

"Yeah, I bet."

Bene tossed the magazine to the desk where Chris finally decided to pick it up as well.

"It can't be that bad," Chris said.

Right.

Yeah.

"You only say that because now when the society rags write about *you*, they talk about your wife. Same with Bene, or Beni. It's only Corrado they give a bit of shit about and that's because after a few years, they still don't understand how he can fuck two people at the same time."

"Easy," Chris murmured.

"I'm just saying. It's true. I'm the only single brother left, and they put me in that trash every goddamn weekend. I can't even go out and show my face at a club without them writing about how I am either lonely because I'm alone or marrying some stranger whose name I don't even know."

Chris quieted as he read the article, but his eyes slowly widened as he took in the rest of the piece. "Oh, wow. *Sources confirmed …* We all know that's fucking bullshit there."

Marcus ground his teeth harder than was healthy and gave Chris a look from where the man sat in his chair. "*See?*"

Wasn't it bad enough that he was three months shy of his thirtieth birthday, and all the made men around him constantly watched him? As though they were waiting for the moment when Marcus would announce a marriage because that was the obvious, required next step in this life of his. For his whole life, he'd been told he would be the next Guzzi boss. He'd be the one to take over after his father was finally finished, which only meant one thing for Marcus.

He needed to be married.

To an *appropriate woman*.

Which was fine because Marcus fully understood his duty to his family and this legacy. He accepted it long ago, but that didn't mean he was at that place yet. And it didn't help to have fucking magazines writing bullshit about him every single time he left his place to go out and have a good time.

The bigger problem was that since Gian, their father, had taken a step back in the public eye as the boss heading the family after his arrest years ago to deflect attention, even more of it was placed on Marcus. Constantly. His brothers liked to joke that Marcus was boring. He didn't do anything —stayed in, walked the line of their rules, never bending them even the littlest bit, and always doing everything that was expected of him.

That wasn't entirely true.

Everything he did was judged.

Dissected.

Interpreted.

And Marcus refused to give people more shit to talk about.

Simple as that.

"Ignore it," Chris said with a sigh, finally tossing the magazine back to the desk, done with it. Marcus wished he could do the same but shit just wasn't that easy for him. "We'll get the lawyers to send them a warning, and they'll back off for a bit."

Yeah, but for how long?

That was the real question.

"Vanna gets a kick out of it," Bene said, pulling his phone out to read something on the screen when it buzzed. "Makes bets with me about how many lies she'll find each week."

Marcus's jaw ached. "I'm so glad my frustration is her amusement, Bene."

His brother shot him a look, arching a brow. "Hey, it's not like *that*."

Yeah, he knew.

Marcus was just … a little sore about the topic.

"And watch your fucking tone about my wife," his brother added.

He had all he could do not to roll his eyes, but Marcus held it back. Because that's not what twenty-nine-year-old men with the status of an underboss did, even if that's all he fucking wanted to do in that moment.

"You know it's not about Vanna," he said quietly.

Bene shrugged. "Yeah, I got it."

And it wasn't.

Truly.

It took a while, and the first Guzzi son of their generation being born to Vanna and Bene, given the same name Marcus held because that was their *tradition* … but Marcus moved past what happened all those years ago.

And he loved his godson.

Like nobody knew.

"How'd the meeting in Quebec go?" Chris asked.

"Could have come along, being a Capo and all."

Chris smirked. "Yeah, but they don't even wear suits, so …"

"Alessio doesn't wear a suit," Marcus returned, referring to Chris's twin's one spouse, "and you sit down to dinner with him all the time."

"I also don't want to kill Les, you know?"

"Fair enough. And it went fine. I assume they're going to keep pushing the line, but as long as they don't jump all the way over it, then I will ignore them for the time being."

"You think that's smart?" Bene asked.

Marcus dropped into the chair beside the man. "They're not worth anything else."

"For now."

Right.

That couldn't be forgotten.

Bene waved his phone. "Someone sending out reminders about the meeting tonight at the mansion. What's that about, anyway? Since when does Papa call meetings in the middle of the week anymore?"

"Don't know."

Both his brothers' gazes turned on him.

"What?" Chris asked.

Yeah, he was just as confused as to why he didn't know what their father's meeting with the made men of the Guzzi organization was about.

"You heard me," Marcus said, "I don't know what the meeting is about."

Bene frowned. "Huh."

That's about how he felt, too.

Just *huh.*

And it wasn't a very good feeling to have. Marcus hated not knowing. Especially in this life.

"But don't be fucking late," he said, standing from the chair and readying to leave. "Never be late when the boss calls, yeah?"

Another thing off his ever-growing list. Checking in with his brothers. He had to do that. Always did it. Who else would? Marcus took care of his family, no matter what. It's just what he did. No excuses.

"You're just like dad," Chris called at his back.

Marcus waved a hand over his shoulder.

Was that supposed to be a bad thing?

* * *

His father was ignoring him.

Marcus was sure of it.

Although, he didn't have time to call his father out on the fact because Gian kept moving from man to man at the dinner party—he thought throwing elaborate dinners was the best way to bring all his men together—always out of reach of Marcus, not even giving him the option to ask him for five minutes alone to talk. Not to mention, Marcus also didn't have the time, considering with all the made men in the family in the same room, everyone seemed to have something to say to him. Or a request to make. A complaint to be let known.

With Marcus being the underboss for the family, he was usually the one left to delegate the men. Whatever they needed or their nonsense, it was left to him to handle it however he deemed fit best for their organization. Usually, he didn't mind that so much. That was easy shit for him—he handled it no problem.

Tonight, however, it irked him. Because it kept him away from his father.

Who was clearly ignoring him.

"Did you listen to a word I just said?"

Marcus frowned, cursing himself internally for not paying better attention to his mother. A sin in and of itself in the world of Guzzi men considering Cara might as well have been the religion their father preached to his army of sons all their life. It didn't matter that they went to church every Sunday and prayed in the pews at mass … their mother was their whole world. When she spoke, the rest of them tended to listen.

"Sorry, Ma," he said, giving her a smile from the side that he hoped charmed away any of her displeasure. "My mind is …"

"On other things?"

"Everywhere, really."

"Can it be back here with me for a minute?"

He did just that, no questions asked. Placing his drink to the decorative table along the wall, he turned to face his smiling mother to give her every single bit of his attention for the moment. He could go back to dealing with all these men, their issues, and the reason for his father ignoring him later.

His mother needed something. That came first, *always*. Love, then duty. It was their way.

"What, Ma?"

Cara's bright eyes showed her amusement as she smoothed back some of the wayward strands of her bright red hair. In her navy dress, surrounded by the wealth of the mansion they stood in, she looked like every inch a queen.

As she should, like their father would say.

"Chris mentioned something about a magazine—"

He made a noise under his breath. "It's nothing, we'll handle it."

"Well, that tells me all I need to know."

"Which was what?"

"That it bothered you."

"Of course, it bothers me."

"But why … because they speculate, or because they tell lies? Either way, it's easy to ignore it, Marcus."

Right.

If only shit was that simple.

"It bothers me because they don't know my life, but they

act as if they do. And that is what I don't appreciate, Ma. Yes, I can ignore it … I often do, but then I see another one, or like today, someone jokingly shoves it under the wiper on my car, and it just pisses me off all over again."

Cara reached up and patted his cheek with her warm palm. "I'm sorry."

"We'll handle it."

"Right, well … they're only trying to get readers and sales, so be easy."

Mmhmm.

He'd try.

"No promises," he murmured.

At the sight of his father slipping back into the dining room, Marcus was quick to give his mother a kiss on her cheek before he excused himself. He followed after Gian with the intent of finally getting the chance to speak to him about this meeting, which so far had been for nothing, and why his father seemed to be ignoring him.

But by the time he got back inside the dining room, his father was already at the front of the room, heading it like a proper boss should. Lowball glass in hand, he raised it just enough so that the *ting* of his knife hitting the side of it echoed throughout the space. The noise quieted all the chatting men. Just like that, every gaze in the room turned on the boss who was ready to speak.

They needed to listen.

Marcus stayed back near the entrance, knowing better than to move around when his father spoke to the rest of the men. He didn't want to take attention away from the boss just because he felt the need to take a seat at the table with the others. Besides, he could stand just fine, and his legs worked perfectly.

He wasn't paying attention to whatever his father said, instead scanning the faces of the men at the table because that's what he usually did. It wasn't that his father became unimportant to him, but quite the opposite. He would learn what his father said later, although he usually already knew exactly what would be said at these meetings. And so, that allowed him the chance to observe the men around them and look for any possible issues while he did so.

It was habit, nothing more.

And so maybe that was why when the gazes of the men at the table suddenly turned on him, like they all knew he was watching them, Marcus looked to his father for an explanation. Gian, still talking, finally had his words heard by Marcus, and his reason for this meeting came into sharp clarity all around the board.

"I will be taking a step back from being the *active* boss of this family, if only because it's time, and I think it's time for someone else to step up—Marcus, of course. I will still make the final decisions when I decide I need to step in until everything becomes final with a new boss taking over, but from here on out, Marcus heads this family."

He wasn't quite sure what happened after that or what the others had to say. He was still trying to catch up to speed, and what it all meant.

No. That was a lie.

Marcus understood perfectly well what it meant. So did his father.

Gian nodded his way, saying, "And this gives him time, *oui*? Time to figure out the details he needs to satisfy this family, and our expectations. There is not a deadline on this; we're beginning the process, that's all."

Yeah, he heard him loud and clear.

So, why did it feel like a timer had started?

Marcus didn't have time to think about it. Men started talking, and Gian moved away from the table. Someone came into his line of vision, a hand reaching out to clap him on the shoulder. Soon, his brothers, the ones that remained in their organization, Chris and Bene, were there too, ready to chat and give their congratulations.

It wasn't until much later that Marcus finally got the chance to speak with his father. Long after the men had left the mansion, and the dinner party was over. He sat on one side of his father's desk, and Gian rested behind it. The two stared at each other for a long time, neither willing to speak first.

Eventually, Marcus murmured, "You could have given me a heads up."

"For what, something you knew was coming?"

"Or that you planned to do it *tonight*."

Gian chuckled. "Someone has to keep you on your toes, Marcus."

He loved his father.

He *did*.

People often said they were twins, and considering Marcus was the only one of his brothers that didn't have an identical twin, it really said something. Right now, though, he thought in moments like these he was nothing like his father.

"You'll have time to get everything settled," Gian said, "I give my word."

Marcus nodded. "All right."

"I know you have a lot going on—"

"I'll handle everything."

He always did.

Gian smiled a bit. "I have no doubt, *fils*. On another topic, though, could you do me one more favor?"

"What else is there?"

"Something for your mother."

"Not for business?"

"No, something just for her … our anniversary, but I

can't be too close to the project, or she'll find out. She always does."

Marcus had every reason to say no. All his duties, this big shift in the family, too, that would surely change his entire life even more than it already had. He could have said no, and he doubted his father would complain about it.

Still, he said, "I'll do whatever you need, Papa. You know that."

It's who Marcus was.

He didn't know how to be anything different.

CHAPTER 2

"Knock, knock."

Cella grinned at the familiar voice of her older sister, finding Liliana standing in the doorway of her office at her design studio. "Finally made it to my side of town, huh?"

After her husband's death, Cella relocated to Rochester, which was a good six hours away from her parents' home. So, when her sister made the trip in from Chicago to visit, sometimes her and Cella passed each other by more often than not when six hours was a long drive to make just to visit for an hour or two. She understood, and never blamed Liliana, but she wished the two of them got together more often than they did.

"Still loving Rochester more?"

Cella shrugged. "Really, I just don't want to relocate my studio again."

Not entirely a lie.

It would be a lot of work, and more than she could currently afford to do what with her long list of clients—and the waiting list she had recently started—for her interior design business. She specialized in everything from personal spaces, to commercial. And when she needed it the most, her work had been there to give her an escape from the grief that seemed ever-present for those first couple of years after William's death. It helped that here in Rochester, there weren't memories she shared with him.

Essentially, she started over.

Hit a restart button.

If only it had been *that* easy.

"Did Joe come with you this time?" she asked.

Liliana smiled. "He had something to take care of in Chicago … last minute, and all."

"Too bad."

Joe, her sister's husband, was a quiet man. Very *there*, in presence, considering his large size, the fact he was covered in tattoos, and just his stare alone could quiet a person. Yet, with her family, he turned into a different man, kind and welcoming. Tiffany *adored* her uncle, who was also her godfather. She didn't get to see him nearly enough.

"Tell him no excuses, he needs to see Tiff before she starts kindergarten in the fall," Cella warned.

"Will do. I think he's planning a weekend trip, anyway. We'll let you know the details."

"Great."

"Hard to believe you're going to have a kindergartener in what, five months?"

Cella blew out a heavy breath, staring hard at her sister. "Thanks for reminding me."

"What? I thought you'd be excited for that."

She was.

God.

She honestly was.

At the same time … "It's been me and her for so long. It scares me to think for six hours a day, she's going to be away from me."

"She's in daycare *now*."

"Not the same," Cella said, shaking her head and causing the wavy strands of her newly styled, long balayage to fall over her shoulders. "This feels like … well, like she's growing up."

"Kind of the point, isn't it?"

Cella laughed. "You know what, I can have feelings about her starting school. Just let me have them, Liliana."

"Who else points out to you when you're being totally ridiculous?"

No one.

And she liked that just fine.

"Anyway, we're doing lunch, right?" Cella stood from her desk, one she used *only* for paperwork and things of a similar nature. Most of her work was done on her smart design board that covered an entire wall in a connecting room of her studio, or on one of her illuminating tables when she really needed to nail things down in a specific way. "So, let's stop wasting time. God knows when we're going to get the chance to do this again because I have to get home in lots of time to pack for this weekend."

Liliana gave her a look as she grabbed her purse before crossing the floor to stand with her sister in the doorway. "Well, that answers that for me, I suppose."

"What?"

"Ma said she didn't know if you were coming to the showing at Lucia's gallery this weekend, so I hoped that meant you probably were but hadn't found time to let them know."

Yeah.

"Can't make it," Cella said. "I had a client come in as a favor to Dad, although all I was given for it was an address and time to be there—in *Toronto*. The check cleared, a very nice check, so I am inclined to take the job. I let Lucia know, and she doesn't mind. Just hadn't thought to mention it to Ma."

"*Boo.*"

Cella followed behind her sister as they headed for the front entrance of her ground floor studio. In the large building, there were several different businesses set up. Upstairs, a ballet studio for young dancers stayed open for most of the day, but she swore they were so light on their feet at times that she didn't hear a thing. Besides, even if she could, she loved her studio and wouldn't be giving it up for nothing.

"And you don't know who the client is?"

She didn't respond until the two of them had stepped out onto the street, she locked the studio's front doors, and the late April breeze brought with it the scent of spring clinging to the air. "Dad assured me everything is on the up with it … and it's not entirely unusual for big name people to contract me for a design job through third-parties, but especially if they want to make sure everything is going to stay quiet."

"Are you taking Tiff?"

"Yep."

Her daughter hadn't been to Canada yet—Tiffany would love all the trees.

"So, you're not avoiding anyone, then?"

Cella gave her sister a side-eye as the two of them headed down the street toward her car parked at the corner. The only goddamn spot she had been able to grab that morning as she came in later than normal, and that always meant she had to fight for a parking spot that was remotely close to her studio. It was the only thing she hated about the current setup.

"What does that mean?"

Liliana shrugged. "Well—"

"When do I avoid people?"

"Sometimes, you just do it. I don't even think you mean to, but you *do*. I think it's whenever you're having a rough time, maybe because of life, or William … either way, you tend to hide away from the rest of us. John, I could understand because—"

"I don't avoid John."

And she didn't.

Not anymore.

Oh, sure, she had blamed her brother for a long time because of what happened to her husband. It had been because of things that happened with John's involvement that made those people attack William, after all, but her feelings *then* had been a by-product of her grief, and very little else. She tried not to react from that because she still occasionally felt herself slipping back to a grieving state of mind whenever she thought about her dead husband.

It happened.

No one was to blame but the people who pulled the trigger.

And they were gone.

Her father and brother made sure of that.

"Anyway," Cella said, "enough about me. Are we eating, or …?"

Liliana grinned. "Yeah, let's find a place to eat."

* * *

"Why is there a camera up there, Ma?"

"To make sure everything is okay in the elevator."

Tiffany, in all her blue-eyed, blonde-haired sweetness, peered up at the camera in the corner of the elevator with curiosity. "Oh."

"Any other questions?"

Because her kid asked about a million of them. Her daughter's desire to know everything about anything and anyone who stepped in her path just couldn't be contained. The constant flow of *whys* that came out of Tiffany's mouth were never-ending. Some people tried to deflect the girl onto another topic, but Cella never did.

She loved it.

And thankfully, Tiffany's curiosity made the two-hour

drive from Rochester to Toronto fly by in a blink of an eye. From why they had to stop to talk to the border control agent before they could be let across into Canada, to why the speed signs changed from miles per hour to kilometers. The questions came one after another.

"Who lives here?"

"Not sure," Cella said, digging in her purse to find her phone as the elevator jerked. She was supposed to send a message through to the contact on her phone when she arrived at the address provided—which she just found out downstairs was the penthouse in this very *old* but prestigious apartment skyrise in Toronto. "But I am sure—"

She didn't get to finish her statement before the elevator finally came to a stop, and the doors spread wide to welcome them inside the penthouse on the very top floor. She swore stepping into the place, the gleaming marble floors beneath her clicking under her three-inch stilettos, that it was like jumping back in time about twenty or thirty years.

Oh, it was *beautiful*, to be sure.

Back then, she bet the white décor and gold chandeliers dripping with crystals would have been what was most in style. The choice in floor surprised her, but it seemed like the marble ended toward the far side of the hallway. Art covered the walls, and a few pieces of furniture greeted them at the front door like the decorative table with one drawer to pull out, stained with a deep, cherry red. She didn't bother to use any of the hooks, or even the small closet, to hang up her coat or purse. She removed Tiffany's shoes before the two of them headed deeper into the place.

"Hello?" she called out.

Her voice echoed back.

"Is it *empty*?" Tiffany asked.

A dark chuckle answered that question. They didn't even make it to the end of the hallway before a man came to stand there. Dressed in a three-piece suit, shoes gleaming against the floor where light hardwood met the marble, he smiled at them with an easy disposition, and his hands stuffed loosely in his pockets.

"Cella Marcello, *oui*?" the man asked.

His dark brown hair, slightly peppered with gray at the temples, had been slicked back, likely by his fingertips, if she were to guess considering the messiness of the strands. Although, it worked for him. The hard lines of his features gave him a very classically handsome appearance, and his warm smile only added to the appeal. The lines around his eyes as he grinned spoke of his age, which she thought was likely closer to her father's.

And right away …

Instantly, Cella knew who he was.

"Gian Guzzi."

She only recognized him because a few times growing up, the man had made his way to New York for different business that he had with her father's crime family. Through the grapevine, and the inevitable whispers that followed his presence, like it did for the men in her life, she learned he was exactly like them.

Mafia.

Made.

And in fact, the boss of a Cosa Nostra faction in Toronto. A well-respected, and very powerful man, actually. They hadn't spoke except for polite conversation and hellos at the dinner table when he joined them on rare occasions, but it was always good to keep up with who was who in their world.

Despite living far away from one another, their world was still quite small. No one wanted to cause trouble with another family. It never ended very well.

"That's me," Gian said, still smiling in that welcoming

way of his. "Thank you for coming today, and also … well, for following along with my little demands about not getting a name of your client."

Cella kept a hand on her daughter's shoulder, determined to keep Tiffany in one place while she spoke to the man. If she let her go, it was very likely the girl would run off to explore. Which wouldn't be a problem, except she didn't know if that was okay here.

"I trust my father," Cella said simply.

"As you should. It was a little more than *who* I am why I asked for it to be kept quiet, however."

"Oh?"

"I'm trying to keep this a surprise for my wife—Cara. Have you met her?"

"No, but I have heard of her."

Again, through the grapevine.

From her sister, too, whom Gian's wife had counseled after a bad incident with an ex-boyfriend who now rotted underground where he belonged. Cara Guzzi had also been the therapist for Cella's cousin, Catherine, after a particularly rough patch in her life. From all accounts, the woman was wonderful.

In fact, after the death of her husband, Cara's name had been brought up repeatedly to Cella by literally everyone and anyone who knew the woman. It wasn't that she didn't think Cara would be able to help with her grief, but rather that she wasn't ready to invite someone else into her life to see her through it. She did better alone.

Still, everyone spoke highly of Cara.

She'd just never met her personally.

"Ah, well, my wife has certainly heard *a lot* about you."

That piqued Cella's interest. "Has she?"

"Adores your designs, believe it or not. One of our friends. In Maine, you did their vacation home, and we visited last summer. That was when Cara started really getting serious about wanting to hire you for a design. But your client list is long, and life always has a way of—"

"Getting in the way," Cella interjected, laughing under her breath. "Tell me about it. I also have a waiting list."

Gian made a face, one that managed to look both arrogant but slightly bashful at the same time. How was that even possible? "Well, I *hoped* my connection to your father and that very nice check I sent over would possibly put me at the top of said waiting list. And look, it worked."

"Seems it did, yes. Is the penthouse the job?"

"How did you know? I was thinking about an entire redesign—whatever you want to do, as long as you think it'll be tasteful and my wife will enjoy it, then you have free reign."

"It's beautiful."

"But?"

"Outdated."

Gian nodded. "It is, and Cara has mentioned that once or twice in the last few years."

"Really, only once or twice?"

"Every single time we visit, honestly."

Yeah.

Cella thought so.

"I thought maybe she would want to sell it—good and bad memories," he added quieter, but didn't bother to elaborate. "So, as far as she knows, it's going on the market. Although, I have no intention of selling it. It's been in my family for many years, and when we're not using it, one of our five sons do for one thing or another."

"*Five?*"

Gian glanced her way. "Pardon?"

"You have five sons."

"We do."

At that statement, his gaze dropped to her daughter. For the most part, Tiffany had been happy to silently listen to the conversation. Always wanting to learn, after all. No doubt, Cella would get the million and one questions about it later.

"And this is your *petite fille*, hmm?" Gian asked. "Sorry, second nature to use my French—your little girl, yes?"

"Yes, my Tiffany."

"Hello, Tiffany." He kneeled to be closer to eye-level with her daughter. "My wife would *love* that pink dress of yours."

"*Bonjour*, Mr. Guzzi. Thank you very much. Ma bought it for me."

Gian grinned widely, giving Cella a look. "Is that the only French she knows?"

Cella shrugged. "That, and how to tell someone to stop."

Tiffany beamed. "My teacher at daycare showed me."

"And how old are you?"

"Five."

"Not in school yet?"

Cella answered for that one. "She turned five in the middle of the year—I didn't want to send her to kindergarten for half the year as a four-year-old. She starts in the fall."

"Ah, and I bet you are excited, yes?"

"Can't wait," Tiffany said.

Gian stood straight, fixing the lapels of his blazer when he said, "She's free to run around, if she wants. There's not much trouble she can find here, and there's a few toys in the living room that my wife keeps here for our grandkids."

Tiffany peered up at her mom expectantly.

"Go ahead. Any mess, you pick it up. Got it?"

"Got it, Ma."

The girl didn't need to be told again before she darted off. That left Cella alone with Gian, and she took a moment to look around again.

"So, a surprise for her, huh?"

"That's what I am hoping for. I will stay removed from it as much as possible, seeing as how my wife always seems to find out when I directly try to plan things for her."

Cella smiled softly. "I think I can handle it."

"How long do you think it'll take?"

"Three months, maybe. Give or take."

"*Perfetto*. My oldest son, he'll be on hand for anything you need. He's coming over later to give you his details—how long are you staying today?"

Cella met his gaze. "A while. I like to … envision."

"Envision away, Cella. It's all in your very capable hands now."

Yes, it was.

* * *

Cella walked through the back hallway of the penthouse, stopping at each room to take in the different spaces, and what they had been used for. Several bedrooms were located further at the back, while a small office that also seemed to act as a library was set up closer to the entrance of the hall-way. Each bedroom had its own private bathroom. Another, far larger bathroom with a clawfoot tub and a walk-in shower that would make *anyone* jealous with the size, was located beyond the left side of the office between it and before the last bedroom at the very end of the hall.

The master bedroom.

The biggest room in the penthouse, really, and that was saying something considering the size of the main rooms like the kitchen and entertaining areas. Cella kept her notepad out and on hand to do what she usually did when she walked through a new space that she was meant to redesign. Some jobs were more complicated than others. They required more work, for whatever reason. And she didn't often take on ones that would need anything more than a wall or two taken out to redesign the floorplan. It wasn't that she couldn't do it, but those took longer … most of her clients were on a tight deadline, and she also liked that fast pace more often than she didn't.

Given Gian hadn't said anything about redesigning the floorplan of the penthouse, and his focus was more on updating the space to be modern to the times, she wasn't concerned about this job being anything unusual.

Well, except for the fact that his wife was a fan of her work.

That made her a little nervous.

Just a bit.

Cella wouldn't admit it out loud, though.

She roughly sketched out the master bedroom in her notepad, taking a moment to stare at the mostly bare walls in the space, and skipping over the four-poster bed dominating the middle. That would have to go, if only because it really seemed to take away from the size of the space. The large windows behind the bed would be a perfect place to set something like a platform bed with a half a dozen decorative pillows. Morning light would come in to spill across the blankets and touch whoever was sleeping in the sheets.

Before long, she had moved from the master bedroom to the other spare bedrooms. Given she didn't have much of an idea what to do with those, and Gian hadn't given her an idea to go on with what his wife might like, she simply wrote down a few notes to look back at later. Then, she moved onto the bathrooms.

Sometimes, her designs came from things she wanted to see, because that's what the client preferred. Knowing what little she did about Cara Guzzi, she thought perhaps the woman might prefer her spaces to be designed more to her personal tastes.

But that would be hard to do when apparently, this was meant to be a surprise. It wasn't as though Cella could go have dinner with the woman, sit down and chat about what she wanted to see in her penthouse. Or hell, even bring the woman here to do it.

That made the job more interesting.

And *tough*.

Cella liked a good challenge, though.

It was only as she was coming out of the main bathroom that she realized how quiet Tiffany had become during her mother's walk-through of the place. Not that she was concerned her daughter found trouble because that was the last thing her child seemed to do.

Soon enough, she found Tiffany.

In the living room.

With a man.

His back stayed turned to Cella as the unknown man kneeled in his sharp, black three-piece suit that seemed tailored-to-fit on his tall, lean form. Broad shoulders covered by expensive fabric led down a back made up by hard, firm lines that had Cella stopping in the entryway to the space instead of walking forward.

Well, that, and his laugh.

It was a lovely sound.

Deep.

Full of bass.

Every part of her heard it and felt it, she was sure.

It was then that Tiffany finally noticed her mother.

"Ma!"

The man stood and turned to find Cella standing in the entryway. At first, his face took her by surprise. If only because it felt like she was looking into a mirror of Gian Guzzi—only a younger version of the man, with just slight differences. Just enough, really.

A strong jawline. Squared chin. Dark, thick brows lifted when his smirking lips curved higher in a sensual smile. His brown eyes—flecked with gold—looked her over. His hair, a dark espresso color, had been cut into a style that allowed him a bit of length at the top but was trimmed short along the sides. Mostly, it just seemed as though he brushed the strands back to keep them from falling into those eyes of his.

Eyes that still hadn't looked away from her.

"Cella," he said. "Good to see you again."

She swore it was like stepping back in time.

They'd met before.

At a very dark time.

Back then, Cella hadn't taken the time to notice very much about Marcus.

"Marcus Guzzi."

His smile deepened. "I hear you need me."

Did she?

Cella dragged in a quick breath.

Her heart thumped hard.

What was that?

CHAPTER
3

It took Cella a moment to respond to Marcus, but he took those few seconds to take in all the changes in the woman since the last time he saw her. Of course, that had been a bad day for her, he bet. She'd been young, with a new baby, and burying her husband. There hadn't been time for conversation, not that he thought for one single second that she would have been interested in it.

It took weeks for him to get the image of her heartbroken face out of his mind after that day four and a half years ago. Of those tears that stained her face, making lines through the makeup that someone had clearly applied to try and hide the fact that the woman wasn't sleeping. Not that it helped—those dark circles had made her wide eyes appear far bigger than they really were and showcased her soul.

So fucking lost.

Broken.

Lonely.

Yeah, he remembered all of that.

And more.

The woman standing in the entryway now, however, was not the same woman he met all those years ago. Gone were the dark circles, and the pale skin that lost its gleam. She'd traded in the standard black funeral dress for a red number that hugged her curves, stopped just above her knee, with a slit in the skirt that showed off all kinds of leg in those heels of hers.

Things he probably shouldn't notice.

Like the brightness of her blue eyes. Or the way her eyelashes framed the orbs to make them seem even bigger.

It was impossible not to notice those things. Not to mention, that despite the fact she did look far better than their last encounter, and she didn't seem as sad on the outside, there was still something there. A shadow, perhaps, that clouded her eyes when she smiled.

As though she were haunted.

He bet she was.

One wouldn't soon forget burying their husband—the father of their child. He seriously doubted this woman's life had been an easy road for the last few years, but unless she offered to talk about it, he knew better than to ask.

Rude, and all.

When she smiled, it made the bow-shape of her lips even more prominent and set off her features in the best kind of way. She looked delicate—yes, that was the best word for her. From the line of her shoulders to the peek of her collarbones that her low-cut dress allowed him. Even the way her cheek-bones caught the lights up above, and …

Yeah.

He noticed way too much.

Not that it was a bad thing. He wasn't sure if the woman had moved on after her husband's death years ago, though. Had she remarried, or was she currently with someone now?

Those things weren't his business.

And he didn't intend to ask.

For now.

"I'm not sure that I need you," Cella said, laughing quietly.

Nervously, he thought.

Even her cheeks pinked, coloring that dusky olive-tone of her smooth skin a sweet color that had this throat tightening in a way he hadn't experienced in a long while. Not to mention that strange weight that had come to rest in the middle of his chest, determined to keep his breathing short and sharp.

Christ.

What was wrong with him, anyway?

"Wrong choice of words," he said, shrugging one shoulder. "I meant to say, my father tells me you're going to need me on and off for the next little while. Redesigning the penthouse, hmm?"

Cella nodded, seemingly happy to take the chance to look away from him so that she could stare around at the space they currently stood in. Tiffany had gone back to playing with the few toys that she found in a box set to the side in the living room. His parents always kept them there for the grandkids, and sometimes, the kids brought more that just seemed to ... well, stay.

So was the way of little ones, he'd learned.

"That is the plan, apparently," Cella finally said, her attention coming back to him. "And you're to be my ... what?"

"*Assistant?*"

She laughed. "Don't think so."

Yeah, him either.

"If you need anything, I am here," he said, stuffing his hands back into his pockets. "Whatever makes this job easier on you, then I am here to make that happen. I can give you my number, so when you're in town or whatever, you can easily contact me. Mostly, I think my father just wants as much distance as he can get from this project so that Ma doesn't find out. She acts like she isn't, but she's very nosy. Especially when it comes to her husband or boys. If she thinks we're up to something, she digs until she finds it, and then denies that's what she did."

That had Cella smiling.

And *shit* …

Marcus liked the sight of that.

Probably more than he should.

It'd been a long while since he found damn near an instant attraction to a woman. Usually, it took a conversation or more, a few drinks, or a need he just couldn't fucking scratch alone, and then he was gone before morning because he didn't have time to indulge his interest in someone else. So was his life, and given how busy he always seemed to be, the lifestyle suited him just fine. He didn't lead people on, and anyone who went into a one-time thing with him knew exactly what they were getting.

Right now, though?

Well, a part of Marcus found it all too interesting—and perfect—that Cella would be around to do this job for his father, not to mention he would be on her contact list as a go-between for it all. That meant she was going to be coming back, and well …

Marcus shook the thought off.

Not now.

It was not the time.

Tiffany saved Marcus from making the situation awkward when he couldn't find his words to speak when she stood from the toys and asked her mother, "Where is my water, Ma?"

"In my purse—I left it down the hall."

"Okay!"

Tiffany darted past Marcus, giving him a smile that he returned as she went. Such a sweet child, really. She had been willing to talk to him, though she was quick to explain she wasn't supposed to talk to strangers.

"I hadn't realized who she was until you came in," he said.

Cella's brow furrowed. "Pardon?"

"That she was your daughter. I didn't know who would be here to do this today. So, yeah, I only realized she was your daughter when you came in. God, she's gotten big since I saw her last, huh? And smart as hell, too."

Ten feet away, Cella seemed to quiet as she stilled on the spot. "Yeah, I mean … she was eight months or so when we met at the funeral."

Shit.

Yeah.

"Sorry," Marcus said quickly, "I didn't mean—"

"No, it's okay. I know you didn't mean anything by it. Sometimes, I get used to not having to talk about it or whatever, and then I do have to, so it takes me by surprise."

"You look like you're …. doing better. Happier."

Cella nodded, a stark honesty reflecting in her gaze when she replied, "Most of the time, I am."

"Good."

"I did go back to my maiden name, by the way."

Marcus instantly felt slightly less guilt about his not-so-innocent thoughts regarding this woman. If she used her maiden name, she hadn't remarried. He wasn't overstepping a line in his mind even if he didn't say those thoughts out loud.

"Did it help?"

Cella shook her head. "Not in the slightest—I thought I wanted to do it so that I wouldn't have to explain as much about my married name. Turns out having a kid on your hip with no father beside you makes it even more awkward to explain why that is."

He swore under his breath.

She brushed it off.

"So back to this, yes?"

With a wave at the space around them, she effectively changed the conversation. In a way, he was grateful, but at the same time … he wanted to ask her more. She said she was doing better, and that was great, but part of him just wanted to know everything.

And since he couldn't explain why, Marcus chose to shut the fuck up.

Seemed like the way to go.

"Did you have an idea you wanted to work with?" he asked.

Cella laughed. "Well, that usually depends on the client, and this is an unusual job for me considering your father intends for this to be a surprise. Makes it a little harder."

"Why's that?"

He enjoyed the sight of her admiring the space with a keen eye. He bet if he could see inside her mind that he would find it was an amazing thing to witness. It was almost as if he could see the wheels turning as she spun a circle, her sharp stare not missing one single thing in the room.

He couldn't imagine that. Looking at a space and changing it in his mind. He wasn't that good with designs. Didn't have the eye for it, really.

"I kind of got the impression from your father that this is a place your mother really likes—they hold it dear, don't they?"

"Absolutely. It's been her escape for … well, longer than I have been alive."

Truly.

His mother lived here when he was born.

A long damn time ago.

"So, he probably intends for it to stay the same in that way. A place she can sneak away to, or whatever."

"She brings the grandkids here, too. Or they stay here

with her when one of my brothers that live in the states come home for a visit. It's got a lot of purpose for her and us."

"And potential," Cella murmured, turning back to him with a grin. "See, this would be easier if I knew your mom, I guess. When I design a space for a person, and not the people, then I often incorporate them into it as much as I can."

"Oh?"

"Try, anyway."

"And you don't know my ma, huh?"

"I know of her," Cella returned, "but not who she is—not what she likes the most or loves the deepest. Those are things I can do something with, you know?"

"And what if I could do that for you?"

Cella's eyes widened. "Pardon?"

"Let you have some time with my mom. Well, you know, without her knowing about this whole thing, and whatnot."

"Sounds like you're adding more to your plate than was intended."

Marcus chuckled. "You would be surprised to know it's nothing new for me to be busier than I can usually handle. Not that I mind—I tend to like it. But would that help?"

"Depends on what you had in mind."

"Give me some time. I am sure I can figure something out."

"All right."

Before the two of them could say anything further, Tiffany came back through the entryway. In one hand, she carried her mother's purse with the water bottle sticking out of the top that she'd asked about earlier. In her other hand, she held tight to a small brown bear with a blue bow tied around the neck.

Marcus grinned. "Hey, you found him."

Tiffany beamed back. "It was in a cupboard in the hallway."

Ah.

So, that's where one of the kids hid it.

"He's very soft," she added.

"He's mine." Marcus quickly corrected that with, "Well, he was mine when I was a baby. He's never left this penthouse; my mom just kept him in her bedroom, but one of the kids must have taken him out to play with, and he went missing."

With her big, blue eyes, Tiffany looked between him and the bear. "Oh."

He heard the sadness.

She looked at that bear like she loved it.

"You could have him, if you'd like," he said.

That smile was back.

So was her happiness.

Like her mother, she was so much more beautiful when she was smiling and happy. How could Marcus possibly tell her no for anything? Hell, she hadn't even asked for the bear, and he was more than willing to just give it to her, even if its history in this penthouse was as old as the place itself. Not to mention what it meant to his mother.

He didn't think Cara would mind, though.

"Really?" Tiffany asked.

He looked to Cella. "If it's fine with your mom, of course."

Cella sighed. "She has a million stuffies already."

"But not a brown bear with a blue bow," the girl pointed out.

Quite smartly, he had to admit.

Marcus hid his grin by looking down. He'd learned with his own nieces and nephews that it was not very smart to make kids think their quick mouths were amusing because that only notched up the attitude, and the adults in the room tended not to appreciate it.

"Yeah, not a brown bear with a blue bow," Cella echoed. "I don't see why you can't take it. And thank you, Marcus."

"Yes, thank you," Tiffany whispered, hugging the bear.

Marcus only looked to Cella. "Not a problem at all. Should we exchange numbers, then?"

Cella nodded.

Her smile was back, too.

And he couldn't look away.

Neither could she, it seemed.

"Absolutely, Marcus."

* * *

"Three-hundred cases of the Quebec farm's syrup went through the border last week. According to the driver, there were dogs at the crossing and they checked the trailer. Didn't even sniff the sections of the trailer where we would use to smuggle, though."

"Mmm."

"You're not even listening to me, are you?"

Marcus glanced up from his phone but couldn't even be bothered to have the decency to seem ashamed about the fact his attention was *not* on this meeting with Chris at one of their many warehouses for the maple syrup farms. Today was mostly for updates which meant he didn't give a shit about the mundane things—only when something went wrong, so he could fix it as soon as possible before it made a bigger mess.

So far, everything was on the up.

That's what counted.

"This is kind of important."

He met his brother's stare overtop the dusty boxes in the

back of the warehouse. For the most part, many of the workers at the syrup farms didn't know about the illegal activities that happened because of the Guzzis' ownership of the businesses. So, when they did show up to go over the usual, they tended to stay away.

Hence, the boxes.

And dust.

"Someone needs to clean up in this backroom," he muttered, brushing off his blazer.

Jesus.

He hated dirt.

"That shipment, *Marcus*," his brother said shortly, "proved we can export using the maple syrup farms, too. That's good news. More money."

"Right, right, except we have our usual ways, and we'll take a far greater hit to our income—and probably freedom —if one of the shipments gets picked up on the maple syrup side of things, *oui*?"

Chris sighed, glancing down at the clipboard he held. "Probably, but—"

"Unless we can get someone at the border that we're paying, I don't want any of the maple syrup shipments to be used for that purpose. Any that get shipped out on the cargo boats—that's different. We've got our contacts. Otherwise, we need a more foolproof plan for having shit on the roads, that's all I am saying. Ever since Cross Donati had that gun shipment picked up in Maine … well, I don't want to play with fire."

"Yeah, yeah. Got it."

"And don't fuck around like that again. I don't want to find out after the fact that you've put something through the border as a *test*, Chris. Fuck."

"If you were paying attention—"

"I paid attention. I heard you. It proved we could *possibly* do it. Don't do it."

"Fine."

Chris went onto something else—the money going into the business accounts this month, by the sounds of it. More of the usual, which Marcus had little to no interest in hearing about. He knew how all that worked, and exactly how they would launder all that dirty money through the maple syrup farms to clean it before it came out the other side looking like profits on the books.

That's what mattered the most.

Profits.

And with Chris distracted by the next topic of discussion about the farms, Marcus went back to his phone and the last text that he'd been sent.

From *Cella.*

A week after their penthouse meeting, and he still tried to check in with her once a day just in case something came up that she needed help with for his father's surprise. Yes, that's what he was going to tell himself. It was all about the penthouse, and not at all because he constantly found himself wondering when the next time would come that the two of them might be able to meet up.

Right.

Her text cleared that up, though.

Next weekend, it read, *I can come into town.*

That had been in response to his question outright asking, *When are you coming into town next?*

"You're not listening again. What the fuck is so interesting on that phone of yours?"

Marcus didn't even get the chance to hide the screen before Chris leaned over the boxes like the asshole he could be and grabbed the device straight out of his hand. That was a good way for his brother to get a punch in the throat. It didn't matter that Marcus was almost thirty and Chris was a father to two kids, he'd still hurt his brother. Absolutely. But as soon as Chris saw it was a woman's name on the contact for the text messages, he handed it right back to his brother.

"My bad."

Chris put his hands up, and everything.

Marcus gave him a look. "*Merci*."

"*Cella*, huh? Like Cella Marc—"

"She's doing a thing for Dad."

"What kind of thing that requires you to ask her if she's coming into town, or—"

"I will shoot you in the face."

Chris grinned. "No, you won't."

Bastard.

"I'm her contact for Papa, that's all. She's redoing the penthouse as a gift to Ma. Interior design, and whatnot."

"Ah."

"Stop looking at me like that."

Chris's sly grin deepened as his eyes widened in fake innocence. "Like *what*, man?"

"Like you think you know something. Stop it."

"Awful defensive, no?"

"It's not a thing, Chris."

"Right, right. Well—"

The phone ringing in Marcus's hand stopped Chris from finishing his sentence. And lucky for him, too. The name on the contact said *Cella*, and he gave his brother a look as he turned his back to Chris to take the call.

"Hey," he said, putting it to his ear.

"Any reason you're asking me about my plans for next weekend?"

Her voice was still just as musical on the phone as it was in person. Not quite as effective in making him feel like he suddenly didn't know how to breathe, but still fascinating. Not that he could afford to focus on that right now.

Marcus laughed. "Well, to help *you*, I guess."

"And what does that mean?"

In the background of the call, someone shouted before a horn honked.

"You busy?" he asked.

"No, just heading to my car. How are you helping me by getting me into town?"

"My mother is having a dinner party. Pretty normal for her. She throws one or two a month. This one, though, is for a shelter she just helped to open in the city. It'll be at the mansion, which will let you see the house where she lives, and you'll get lots of time with her. I'm expected to bring someone with me, and I thought it could be you. It'll look like a date to her."

"*Like* a date?"

"Mmhmm, what's the problem?"

"Sounds exactly like a date, Marcus."

"Well—"

"Are we just *saying* it's a date?"

"Does that word make you nervous? It's for the penthouse, Cella. That's all."

"Right, but yes … a little. I haven't been on a proper date in years."

Ah.

"No pressure," he murmured.

Her light laughter had him smiling wider than ever. And of course, his brother just happened to see that smile when he turned around, too.

Dammit.

He gave Chris a look.

His brother averted his stare.

"Anyway, are you up for it?" he asked.

Cella barely hesitated before replying, "Yeah, I am definitely up for that."

Perfect.

"I'll let you know the details."

That was that. Except he wondered if it was going to end up being a hell of a lot more.

CHAPTER

4

"And why can't I come this time?"

Cella had all she could do not to laugh at how indignant and offended her daughter managed to sound as they climbed the steps to her parents' house. "I told you why—I'm not doing things that five-year-olds can also do."

Which wasn't entirely a lie, considering she didn't know very much about the dinner party at the Guzzi mansion. Nothing except for the details of what she should wear, as there apparently was a dress code, and that alone told her maybe Tiffany wouldn't have very much fun being stuffed into a pretty dress and made to sit still and behave for hours on end. Truth be told, she hadn't really thought to ask if that was the case.

"So, I think you'll have more fun with Aunt Lucia and Uncle Ren this weekend. Plus, I hear Uncle John has a movie he wants to take you to with the rest of the kids."

Tiffany at least had the decency to look as though she were actually considering her mother's words. Like which one might be more interesting to her because she didn't truly know. In a way, Cella loved that all her daughter wanted to do was *be with her mom*. All the time, no exceptions. Tiff really was her little mini-me, all things considered. But how could she not be when for most of her life, her mother was all she really had?

At the same time, Cella often wondered if that was

healthy for her girl. It was why, even when she knew Marcus wouldn't have a problem with her daughter tagging along this weekend for his plan regarding his mother, that she decided it would be better to drop Tiffany off with her parents for the day before she spent the rest of the weekend with her aunt and uncle.

Space was good.

For *both* of them.

Plus, though it made her guilty to think about it, Cella hadn't taken time away from her child in *years*. Well, never. Those first few months after her husband's death was nothing more than a blur in her memories, and that was probably the time when she accepted the most help from others with her daughter. Not that she ever spent time *away*, but there were spans of mornings where her mother woke up with her child instead of her, and even times when one of her sisters would take Tiffany out to the park or to an appointment if it was needed.

Cella just … hadn't been able to do it.

Couldn't get out of bed.

And then they would bring her daughter to her, the girl would climb into her mother's bed, and that's how they would stay. Tucked in with one another, her breathing in the familiar *baby scent* and memorizing every single part of her daughter's features that she took from her father.

The depression cleared, though.

Eventually.

Still, she never took time for her. Not even a day—she always made sure to schedule things for her *around* her daughter's needs. When Tiffany was in daycare or visiting with her grandparents.

Not this weekend, however.

That was for Cella.

Well, her and the penthouse job.

Yep.

That's what she was going to keep telling herself, anyway. It certainly had nothing to do with the fact that this *not a date* felt like a date, in a way, and the longer she had time to think about the man who would be accompanying her that weekend to the dinner … well, the more she liked it.

Nope.

Wasn't thinking about that at all.

"Ma?"

Cella glanced down at her daughter. "Yeah, baby?"

Tiffany smiled back. "Are we gonna go inside?"

Dammit.

She had been so distracted in her thoughts that they stood on the porch of her parents' home for God knows how long. Sighing, and catching the sight of her kid's snickering out of the corner of her eye, she didn't even bother to ring the bell or knock before entering the house. Not that her mother or father would care—their open-door policy for their children extended straight into their adulthood.

Yet another reason why she loved them.

"Grandmama!"

Tiffany's shout echoed through the house, and she dropped her sparkly, pink backpack full of the things she needed for the weekend to the floor without a look back. Cella smiled after her girl, knowing she should call her back and remove her shoes, but she didn't get the chance before Tiffany darted down the hallway.

She, at least, took the time to remove her coat and shoes even if she was going to have to put them right back on in a few short minutes. She couldn't stay very long given that the drive to Toronto was going to be eight hours from her parents' house, not considering the traffic, which there always was too damn much of it.

Oh, she could have flown.

Cella thought the drive might be … nice.

Time to think.

Overthink.

And that was enough of that.

Cella followed the path her daughter had taken, hearing the familiar noise of her family coming from the kitchen. Always the gathering hub in an Italian family's home, it was the first place to make her feel the safest in this house. She leaned in the entryway, surprised to see her sister and brother-in-law were already there with her parents.

Jordyn and Lucian, her mother and father, stood on one side of the island while her youngest sister, Lucia, and her husband, Renzo, stood on the other. Unsurprisingly, Tiffany sat right on the kitchen island between the four, already stuffing her face full with what looked to be cookies that her mother had probably baked just for the girl.

Her daughter at least had the nerve to look sheepish when Cella raised a brow at the sight. "What is *that*?"

"Aw, *Ma*."

Cella laughed but gave her mother a look. "Limit them, please?"

Jordyn shrugged. "I make no promises."

So was the way of grandparents.

Laughter filled the kitchen.

She soaked it in.

Needed it, really.

Yeah, Rochester was better for Cella because it allowed her time to figure out the things she really needed and wanted in her life, but at the same time … she missed being able to have moments like these with her parents and the rest of her family every day.

"So, what is this weekend away for again?" her father asked.

Cella shrugged. "The penthouse job for the Guzzis."

Lucian nodded. "All weekend, though? Never knew you to—"

"It's supposed to be a surprise for Gian Guzzi's wife—problem is, they want the space designed *for* her personally. I need to get to know her. And so, her oldest son—"

"Marcus, right?" Renzo asked suddenly.

Usually, the guy was pretty quiet. All in all, though, Cella liked him, and he treated her sister like a fucking queen. Even her own daughter adored him because he just had a way about him. Easy natured, and kind-hearted. And at the same time, Cella knew Renzo was capable of great violence, given his profession … strange how that worked.

"Yeah, Marcus."

Renzo gave Lucia a look. "Met him a couple of times. He's a good guy."

"And handsome," Jordyn added.

Cella cleared her throat. "He is, but—"

"So you noticed," Lucia noted.

Her father chuckled, but thankfully, said nothing. He was apparently the only one in the bunch who didn't want to get in on this *pile on Cella* moment they were all having. Well, excluding her daughter, but she blamed that on the fact the girl had just snuck two more cookies.

"Tiffany, enough cookies, babe."

"But—"

"Too much sugar gives you bad dreams, remember?"

Tiffany let out a huff. "*Fine*, Ma."

Cella winked.

Her daughter blew her a kiss right back.

"Back to the young man in question here, please," her father said. "I'm invested in this conversation and where it's going."

Ah, there was his add-on to this nonsense.

"How he *is* or looks, for that matter, has nothing to do

with the fact he invited me to accompany him to a dinner party his mother is throwing so that I can get to know her a little bit before I move ahead with some plans for the penthouse. Quite an evening, I guess, I even needed a new dress."

Silence saturated the kitchen.

Cella didn't miss it. "What?"

"Like a date?" her mother asked.

Great.

There was that word again.

Wasn't it bad enough that she kept thinking of it that way even if it was more for work than pleasure? She certainly didn't need other people thinking of it the same way.

"It's not a date, Ma."

"Are you sure?"

Cella sighed. "Pretty sure, yeah."

Light laughter filled the room.

Her ma was still looking at her, though. In *that* way. A way only mothers could. One that said Jordyn could read her daughter's mind and didn't believe a single thing she was saying.

Shit.

Cella didn't even believe herself.

So what if it wasn't a *real* date?

Part of her might like to think it was.

Her parents shared a look, but before anyone could say anything more about it, Cella decided to close the conversation. "I really have to get going and get on the road."

"Right, right," her ma said, "well have fun."

"And be safe," Renzo added.

She shot the man her middle finger down at her side where her daughter couldn't see it. God knew Tiffany *did not* need to be learning that gesture from her mother. Crossing the kitchen, she cupped her daughter's head full of golden curls before dropping a kiss to her crumb-scattered, smiling lips.

"Love you—be good for Auntie, okay?"

Tiffany smiled brilliantly. "I will, Ma. Say hi to Marcus, okay?"

Soft chuckles echoed around the kitchen.

Cella ignored them.

"I will, baby."

She thought no one had followed her out of the house, but Lucia quickly opened the door right after she closed it.

"What?" Cella asked, hovering by the stairs on the porch.

"Just … I know you said this weekend isn't a date, right?"

"It's really for work, yeah, but … maybe it's a little bit of both."

After all, Marcus hadn't said differently.

And he teased it like a date.

"And you're good with that?"

Cella grinned. "Lucia, I don't know what I'm good with anymore. It's been so long, and I'm not sure I would even know what to do with a guy on a date, or *after*, for that matter. So, I'm not worried about it."

Lies.

She worried about it too much.

"Well, what about him?"

"Pardon?"

"Him—*Marcus*," her sister clarified.

Cella shrugged. "He's … charming. Incredibly handsome. Probably too rich for his own good. A little confident, but I assume that comes from being who he is. Responsible, clearly. He was sweet with Tiff, and didn't seem to mind she was there. He took me by surprise, but I'm not mad about it."

Lucia lifted a brow.

"What?" she asked.

"I mean, I just meant to ask what *he* said about this weekend, but if you wanna basically tell me all the reasons you're attracted to him, go for it."

Yeah, shit.

Her sister didn't give her time to reply before she added, "Cella, have fun this weekend … don't worry about nonsense. After everything, you deserve it, okay?"

Right.

"I'll try," she whispered.

Because at this point, it was all she could hope for.

* * *

Cella tried not to be nervous as she smoothed her hands down the shimmering, golden fabric of her dress as she headed for the door of her hotel. A light knock echoed again, but she still took a second to breathe and glance in the mirror on the wall that greeted the guests to the room. She took in the way the dress fell against her body, thin straps hugging the delicate line of her shoulders and showing off more skin than she normally would what with the way the fabric dipped at her chest. It gave an ample view of her cleavage and the thin golden bar that hung from a similarly-styled chain from her throat, resting at the valley between her breasts.

Not that it bothered her.

The dress was *beautiful*.

Sparkling sequins made up the loose-fitting bodice, and the skirt with a good three layers of chiffon swished with every step she took in her gold, strappy, five-inch stilettos. The skirt fell about three inches above her knees, allowing the light to catch the shape of her calves and how great those heels made her legs look.

In the mirror, her reflection stared back. Face painted

with makeup to highlight the features of her face she loved the most—lips a stark red, eyes smoked out with kohl and lashes fanned by black mascara. Highlight on her cheekbones, and just a tint of rose on the apples of her cheeks.

Definitely not a date.

That's what she kept saying.

And yet, she dressed and looked just like it was one.

Before her guest could knock at the door again—he'd already done it twice and was probably wondering what in the hell was taking so long—she pulled the door open, hoping it would settle those beating butterfly wings in her stomach.

It didn't.

And Cella wasn't ready.

Not for the sight of Marcus behind the door.

Waiting for her.

Oh, that wouldn't have been anything special, really, but it was how he looked standing there in that three-piece suit that seemed to hug his fit, muscular lines. Gold cufflinks glittered at his sleeves, and his tie and vest matched the color of her own dress. He'd gone to the effort of slicking his hair back, which only made the strong lines of his face even more prominent, dark, and handsome what with the shadows of the hallway falling over his features the way they did.

That jaw.

His lips.

He smirked, and she dragged in a quick breath.

Marcus stared at her with dark eyes that slowly drifted over her with damning intent.

Yeah.

He didn't even hide how he drank her in.

Inch by inch.

There was nothing that could make a woman feel more beautiful than a man enjoying what he was looking at and even better if he could appreciate the sight of said woman in *clothing*. Because she could only imagine how he would stare at her if she wasn't dressed.

Finally, he spoke.

And she wasn't ready for that, either.

"Look at *you*," he murmured.

She swore his words felt like they whispered over her skin.

Cella had to remind herself to breathe again. Just like that, she needed to take one single second to step back, and figure out what exactly was happening here. With this weekend, this night, and this man.

"Marcus?"

"Hmm?"

His gaze darted up to hers from where it had been lingering on that chain at her throat, looking as though he was more interested in the way it fell between her breasts than anything else currently. She certainly liked *that*, no doubt about it, but still …

"This isn't a date, right?" she asked.

Marcus lifted a single, dark brow high. "Well—"

"No games. It's been *years* since I went out with a man, and that man was my husband. So, I get that this started out as one thing, but that it might be something different now. All I want to know is if that's the case, that's all."

His throat jumped with his swallow, an entrancing sight if there ever was one.

Yeah.

Cella was so screwed.

He smiled, then, slow and sexy.

She felt it all over.

"This qualifies as a date," he said, "but only if you want it to. I did only intend for this night to be about you getting to know my mother, but there's something you don't know about *that*, Cella."

She wet her lips, still enjoying the way he stared at her far too much. "And what is that?"

"We have rules—us Guzzi boys. Or we used to before all my other brothers got married and left me as the *hopelessly single* one of the bunch. We don't bring women home, not unless we intend to bring them back."

Ah.

She heard what he didn't say.

He was, technically, bringing her home.

"So, was it supposed to be a date? *No.* Do I care about the semantics here? Not particularly. Do I want you to have a good time, and then we can go from there? Absolutely. And that's what matters."

"Do you intend to bring me back?"

Marcus grinned, flashing perfect, white teeth in the process. "That depends on what you want here, and I don't get a say either way."

"No, I suppose not."

"But I do get to *persuade* you."

Yep.

That had her shifting on the spot, desperately trying to ignore the heat traveling through her body and how this man so easily caused it to happen.

How long had it been since she felt an attraction to a man?

Lust for him?

Too long.

And that unsettled her.

If only because a long dormant part of Cella suddenly remembered exactly what it was like to be *this* woman. The one who wanted to seduce a man—to show him she could be just as bold and alluring as him, but in her own way.

The words slipped past her painted lips before she could think better of it.

"Persuade me, then."

All at once, Marcus straightened to his full height, dropping his hands from either side of the doorway to move in closer. She felt like a deer in the headlights, a prey caught in the sights of the most dangerous but beautiful predator. She was caught by the curve of his lips, how they lifted at the edge on one side as his gaze dropped down to her mouth while he closed the distance between them.

One of those strong, large hands of his found her hip, expansive and warm as he grabbed tight before dragging her close to him. Just tight enough to make her breath catch before his lips fell down to meet hers in a kiss that had fireworks lighting up under her skin. It started slow, at first, the way his lips swept over hers, *curious and tasting*.

Soft, but still demanding.

And then she opened for him.

He blew it all out of the water.

All he seemed to need from her was that unspoken permission, and the man took what he wanted. His other hand threaded into her hair, grabbing just hard enough to wish he was doing that while she was on her knees, and his tongue licked at the seam of her lips before darting inside her mouth to slash against her own. The hot mint taste to his tongue was enough to make her want far more.

She still couldn't breathe.

Still didn't *want* to.

That kiss told her all she needed to know about Marcus Guzzi, and this night.

It was going to be a good one.

And he would be very dangerous for her.

Every single part of her.

* * *

Cara Guzzi turned on her heel with a wide smile that didn't falter in the slightest at the sight of a woman on her son's arm when Marcus said, "Ma, do you finally have a few minutes for little old me?"

The woman's gaze turned on Cella, a recognition flashing, as she took the hug Marcus offered. "Glad you could make it—sorry I've been running back and forth all night. A new company did the food; I regret telling Martina to retire, honestly."

Marcus laughed.

Cara still watched Cella, only now, with a softer smile playing at the edges of her lips. After arriving at the dinner party over an hour ago, the food had yet to even be served. Not that Cella minded all that much because it gave Marcus more than enough time to give her a quick tour and introduce her to some of his brothers that were able to attend the party. And his father, too, just to keep up the act.

His mother, on the other hand, seemed to constantly run from one thing to the next which meant this was the first time they had been able to approach her while she stayed still. God knew Cella understood, though, because her mother and the rest of the women in her family were the same way when they had an event at one of their homes.

She didn't take offense.

Respected it, really.

"And this ... the infamous Cella Marcello, yes?"

Cella let out a quiet laugh. "I'm not sure *infamous*—"

"Trust me, anyone who appreciates good home design knows *you*." Cara gave her son a conspiratorial wink before adding, "But what I would love to know even more is how my son came across you, and why he didn't think to tell me you would be his guest this evening for my dinner party. Marcus?"

Cella might have enjoyed the sight of Marcus looking sheepish at his mother's admonishment, but he just as quickly came back from it with a charming smile that had even his mother shaking her head with a happy sigh.

"I thought the surprise might be nice," he lied smoothly.

Cella had to look away at that.

"We met a while back," he explained, "she's a good friend of mine."

Cara's gaze widened. "Oh?"

"Could you not, Ma?"

"Why didn't you tell me about your *friend*, then?"

"My fault," Cella stepped in, willing to save Marcus the trouble, if only because he was trying to go to great lengths to keep his father's surprise for Cara a secret as much as possible. "It's only recently that I agreed to go out, and so far, I'm not regretting it."

The older woman laughed, the light catching her red hair that had been left down in soft waves, making it a deeper shade of maroon.

"I would hope you're not regretting it considering otherwise, I'd need to have a chat with him, hmm?"

"I will keep that in mind, Cara. And it's very nice to meet you."

Someone called Cara's name from the side, making the woman sigh under her breath with more frustration that she had shown all night. "And you, too, but it looks like *someone else* needs me again. I'm making your father call Martina, Marcus, you watch me."

"Ma—"

"I will find you later," she told Cella, "so don't you go too far."

She accepted Cara's hug, and the kiss to her cheek.

Marcus did the same, and then the woman disappeared into the crowd of people that were currently moving between the large dining room and a sitting area.

"She loves this," he said absently, his hand coming to rest at Cella's lower back.

Just that touch …

It's all it took for Cella's body to be *way up* all over again.

This man would kill her, she was sure.

"Pardon?"

"My ma," he murmured, grinning down at her with a wink, "she won't call Martina—she'll just whip the new catering company into shape, but because they're new …"

"Yeah, I get it. And she loves you, huh? I could tell that right away."

Marcus shrugged. "All of her boys. The grandkids, too. My brothers' wives. She makes time once a week for *each* of their wives, if she can. Something to do just for them. I don't know how she does it or keeps it all up, but—"

"She loves it."

She didn't need him to say it.

"Yeah, she does."

Cella's gaze dropped to his lips and the soft smile playing at his mouth. All over again, she thought about that kiss the two of them had shared, and her mind was on everything *but* this party and the penthouse job.

"Later," he said.

Her stare jumped up to meet his. "You don't know what I was think—"

"I absolutely do. And *later*. We'll get back to that later, *cara mia*."

She didn't doubt it.

CHAPTER 5

Marcus nodded in response to the Capo at his left who *truly* believed his *boss* was listening to his latest complaint about some issue his crew was having with a racket deal they'd had in the works for a year now. It wasn't something a boss could or should fix. Those were details for Capos to work out, and he planned on telling the man exactly that once he finished with his tirade.

"So, you see—"

"Did you think this dinner party was a good opportunity for this?" Marcus asked.

The Capo quieted suddenly before saying, "Well, you were here, Marcus."

"And a few weeks ago, I might have cared to help you with your situation. However, as the acting boss of this family, I no longer have the time or concern to bother with these issues. You should find someone who does. Is that clear?"

Thankfully, the man seemed to understand that he had crossed an unmarked line of some sort with Marcus. This whole party had been exactly that, frankly. One issue after another. It never ended. He just finished speaking with one man, and another would come up with something else to say. It was like they forgot Marcus was no longer the underboss acting as the go-between for them and his father anymore, and instead their *boss*.

He expected that.

Tried to deal with it.

Tonight, though, his patience was thin.

Marcus was over it.

Usually, he wouldn't be so short and quick to have a temper, but considering all these made men at the party consistently and repeatedly dragged him away from Cella's side for *business,* well … he was done with it. It seemed like Cella had found more than enough people to keep her entertained while he was taken away from her in his brothers and even his mother for a few minutes.

For that, he was grateful.

Of course.

But he was ready to get back to her side—after all, while this night had turned into something he wasn't expecting, but wouldn't complain about either, it still had a purpose for Cella with her work. And he intended to make sure she got to learn as much about his mother as she needed to get done everything.

"Talk to Chris," Marcus told the man, "or Bene, for that matter, and if they can't handle your issue, then they will bring it to me and I will see what I can do."

"Absolutely, Mar—"

He gave the Capo a sharp look, lifting his brow at the same time. A silent warning—a *reminder*. Apparently, the asshole still needed them.

"Boss," the man quickly corrected.

"There you go. Try not to fuck it up again."

His piece said, Marcus turned on his heel to leave the wet bar and find Cella wherever she had moved to within the mansion. With the majority of the dinner portion of the evening over, guests tended to move within the bottom level of the mansion freely.

He barely left the sitting room when someone else called

his name. He still sighed, his back tensing, even if this voice he recognized and shouldn't get irritated about.

"What, Chris?"

"Hey, why the attitude?" Chris asked, coming to stand beside his brother.

"For starters—"

"Listen, we have an issue, and we need to handle it."

"What issue?"

Because as far as he was concerned, unless someone died who shouldn't have died, then he didn't have a single shit to give about it. That wouldn't be his usual mood about things when an issue came up, but today it certainly was. And he didn't feel guilty about it, either.

The boss delegated tasks.

He didn't complete them.

Simple as that.

"A warehouse—"

Marcus stopped his brother, who for all purposes was acting as *his* underboss while still managing his duties as a Capo, from saying more by raising his hand. "Deal with it, Chris. I have other things to handle tonight, okay?"

"The maple syrup farms are *your* thing, man. Dad made sure of that, so no, I can't deal with it without consulting you first because the last time I did that, you didn't like it very much, huh?"

Right, right.

"What happened?"

"Just got a call—a warehouse was burned. Take a guess which one?"

Marcus chewed on his inner cheek, willing his temper to stay in check. "Please tell me it wasn't the one that we use for the new Quebec farm."

"Okay, I won't tell you that, but that's it, yeah."

Fuck.

"Dad should know the bikers are fucking with us again, you know? If they're not going to back off, then we need to handle them, Marcus."

Chris wasn't wrong.

At the same time … "I can handle it. There's no need to bring Dad into it. He stepped back for a reason, and that's what I'm here for. So tonight, you're going to do what you need to do to handle that mess, and keep Dad from finding out because he doesn't need to worry when we're dealing with the situation."

"But—"

"Chris, it'll be fine."

Eventually.

Once he handled those assholes in Quebec.

"Now," Marcus added, "I'm going to find my date for the evening unless you have something else to tell me."

Chris shook his head. "That was it."

"All right, so handle it."

He didn't even bother to look over his shoulder as he left Chris in the entryway. Soon enough, he found Cella, but she wasn't where he expected her to be. Admiring the hall of Guzzi portraits with his father at her side, the two of them seemed to be enjoying their moment with their heads tilted close together as they discussed the large painting of his mother with her boys all grown up.

"Have I been replaced?" Marcus dared to ask.

His father smiled over his shoulder.

Cella winked. "Maybe."

"Well, if that's only a *maybe* and not a definite yes, I thought you would like another tour of the place, but this time, upstairs."

Gian cleared his throat, stepping back from Cella with a nod. "Enjoy the rest of your evening; I should go find my wife." And then, as his father passed him by, he added to

Marcus, "The party is ending soon … keep it in mind, son."

Yes.

He most certainly would.

"Another tour sounds perfect," Cella told him.

Marcus grinned. "*Perfetto*. I know a couple of things you'll probably appreciate seeing, then."

* * *

"I love that she keeps a nursery set up for any new grandbabies," Cella noted beside Marcus.

His fingers flexed around hers, and he tugged her closer to his side. "Next to my dad, and us boys … the grandkids are my mother's whole world."

Undoubtedly.

She loved them all like nobody knew.

"One more thing to show you up here," he said, turning at the end of the hall to face the double oak doors that always stayed wide open unless someone was inside with his mother. "Her favorite room in this whole house."

"Really, because there's *a lot* of rooms."

Marcus laughed. "Yeah, she does everything in here that's personal to her—things she loves. My dad had it designed and built just for her. She's filled it over time."

"What?"

Not saying another word, Marcus pulled Cella forward until the two of them entered his mother's spacious library that would make any bookworm jealous. Filled from the floor to the ceiling with books, it was completed by the ladders that lined the shelves for his mother to push along and climb high if she needed to find something where she couldn't reach.

Large bay windows overlooked the property.

Sitting areas kept people comfortable.

Candy in a dish.

A wet bar to drink.

And even a desk, if she wanted to use it.

"Oh, wow," Cella murmured.

Marcus finally let go of her hand, but only so that he could admire the way she took in the space and appreciated it. Out of every space in the large mansion, this one was the most personal to his mother for many reasons.

Cella walked further into the space while Marcus lingered near the doorway. Running the tips of her fingers over a particular row of shelves that housed books that were older than even he was, she drew in a deep breath.

"Books always have a specific *smell*."

"A good one?"

"Very good, yeah."

He grinned.

Because yeah, he knew.

Cella came to stand at the main sitting area, and quieted. Two leather couches rested upon a massive, imported rug facing one another, with a bucket chair at the end and a coffee table in the middle with his mother's book still sitting atop a manila file. She glanced down, looking at the book and file but not touching it.

She did, however, say the name on it.

Marcus cleared his throat. "That would be a client of my mother's ... or a patient, depending on how you want to look at it."

Cella quieted, gaze drawn downward, and while she couldn't see anything about the patient given the file was closed and a book sat on top of it ... he could still see *something* flashing in her eyes. That haunted look again—the same one he noticed when they met again at the penthouse weeks ago.

"I forgot for a minute."

"Sorry?"

"That she's also a therapist."

Marcus stuffed his hands in his pockets and moved to lean against the wall. He figured, he might need some stability for this conversation and the wall seemed like as good of a place as any to use for it.

Cella smiled faintly, those painted-red lips of hers curving but it didn't quite reach her eyes as she glanced up at him. "They said I should come see her, you know?"

"When?"

Her throat jumped. "After William died."

He was sure that was the first time she'd said her dead husband's name in his presence. And just like that, while the mention of the man didn't make Marcus feel bad or guilty for what had happened between him and Cella that evening —so far—he did wonder if perhaps this had moved too fast for her.

Had he crossed a line?

Did he think before he acted?

Was he selfish?

"Can I just … say what I need to say? What I'm really avoiding and hiding from with you?" she asked softly.

Did she really need to ask that at all?

"Please, do. It's what I want."

How else would he know?

How else could he fix it?

"I never wanted to be involved with a made man," she explained, shrugging those pretty shoulders of hers and making the light reflect on the sequins of her dress, "because I saw all around me what happened when women lost those men … when their whole lives became entangled with those men, and they had to pay for it. *Sacrifice* for it. So, I didn't— I married a lawyer, he wasn't even Italian. But it didn't matter because I was who I was, and you can't change who you are."

Marcus said nothing.

He didn't think he should.

"So, it didn't matter that he wasn't made … it didn't matter that I married a man I thought the mafia couldn't take from me because they did it anyway. I made a promise that I wasn't going to do it again; I wasn't going to be in that position again."

Her gaze met his again.

He stared back, waiting.

"I want to tell you this can't *be* something," she said, her words clear but still full of uncertainty all the same time. "That we can't *be* something, Marcus. Like that's fair, right? I keep my promise, I don't break my one rule for myself, and nothing else has to matter."

"But?"

"Should I?"

Marcus chuckled, seriously considering her words because he didn't think she meant for him to make a joke out of it. Nor did he want to, honestly. "It's okay to break the rules occasionally … my whole life is about control, Cella. From the way I look, to how I present myself to the rest of the world. It's all I know. So when people aren't looking, I break those rules I made for myself. Otherwise, it would all just suffocate me."

"And you think that's the same thing?"

"What you feel would ruin you and what would ruin me don't have to be the same thing. It's the end result that looks a lot alike if you know what I mean."

She blew out a slow breath.

He still waited her out.

"Do they know about that?" she asked, nodding toward the floor as though she meant the people downstairs. "Do any of them know you're like a live-wire wrapped up in a well-fitting suit, but you're just ready to snap?"

A smile split his lips. "No, just you."

And he felt it was … appropriate.

"I have one more thing to show you, that is, if you're interested in seeing it."

Cella stepped his way.

No hesitation at all.

He *adored* that.

"Show me."

* * *

"Watch your step."

Cella didn't even get the chance to look down before he was there to grab her around the waist and help guide her over a particularly rough part of the trail. Her laughter colored up the darkness overhead, and he grinned back at her when she gave him a wink over her shoulder.

"Where are we going?"

"You'll see."

"What if I told you that I hate surprises?"

"Then, I would tell you exactly where we're going. Do you really hate surprises?"

Cella pressed her lips together, eyeing him as she now walked backward. A feat in and of itself considering the height of her heels and these precarious trails that weaved throughout his parents' property.

"No," she finally said.

"Then stop asking questions, *donna*."

"You know, I don't think you've used your French nearly as often as you use your Italian with me. And that's kind of a shame, isn't it?"

Behind her, he could see a familiar clearing starting to

take shape there. She couldn't see it with her attention on him, but that was just fine.

"Does that offend your sensibilities?"

He didn't mind playing along with her game.

"Well—"

"*Ma chérie, tu es plus belle que le ciel et les étoiles, et je ne te mérite pas.*"

Cella's walk came to a stop, but Marcus continued his until the two of them stood toe to toe, and she was staring up at him. He didn't touch her, but he didn't really need to in that moment. He found all that he needed in her eyes—in the parting of her lips and the way her hands trembled down at her sides.

"Will you tell me what you said?"

Marcus wet the line of his lips. "Do you need me to?"

"I think you should."

"Close your eyes first."

Cella raised a brow. "Why?"

"Trust me, Cella, and close your eyes."

She did, making those long lashes of hers fan upon her skin as her head tilted down. He took a second, but no longer, to admire her soft, pretty features, and then he guided her after turning her around to the clearing just fifteen feet ahead. A little further, into the middle, they entered a building made of stained glass and coated on the outside with vines that grew all over the windows that acted as walls.

In the summer, it would be filled with roses.

Right now, it was only just coming back to life.

"Tilt your head up," he said behind her, whispering the words into her ear. She did, and he rounded to her front, watching her face when he told her, "Now open your eyes."

Cella stared up at the sky through the glass ceiling of a rose solarium that he remembered his mother spending a good portion of her time in during the summer months.

Another favorite place of hers.

Yeah, Cella stared at the sky.

But he watched her.

"My darling," he repeated in English, "you are more beautiful than the sky and the stars, and I am not worthy of it."

The column of her throat jumped as her gaze dropped to him, and he had the greatest urge to find out exactly what that soft-looking skin of hers would feel like under his palm while he kissed her, so he did just that. The palm of his hand found her throat under her jaw, curving tight and soaking in all her silky warmth as he closed the distance between them in a breath.

He'd been lucky enough earlier to find out there was nothing sexier in the world than this woman's kiss. And the way she gasped against his mouth when he dragged the plump flesh of her lower lip between his teeth just to see if she might *like* that.

God, did she ever.

Her fingers fisted into the soft fabric of the vest under his suit jacket, and she yanked him close enough that her soft curves molded perfectly to his hard lines. Given how hesitant Cella had seemed to be about the prospect of a date or even the possibility of *more* with this night and him, there was no shame in the way the woman yanked at his pants, determined to open his belt and fly.

Brazen.

Bold.

Determined.

She knew what she wanted, and she was going to take it. That alone had his cock pressing against the line of his pants when her fingers drifted down to work at his zipper once she'd finally gotten his belt off.

"You have something, right?" she asked.

Her words whispered against his mouth, as he still refused to break that kiss until all he could think about and breathe in was everything that made up *her*.

From that spiced vanilla perfume that she wore, to the way her skin tasted just like sugar with a hint of salt. The sounds she made when his fingers flexed at her throat, and how her body ground against his without a care but had his cock harder than ever.

"Do you?"

Her hot demand had him putting just enough space between them that his lips hovered over hers as he asked, "What—"

A pink tint heated her cheeks. "A condom?"

Ah.

And there, even in her need and shamelessness that he found so sexy, there was still that part of Cella, he realized, that hadn't done this type of thing in a while. She'd basically told him that, hadn't she?

His first thought was to slow this down. Give her a moment. Let her think about whether or not this was really what she wanted to do with him tonight. In this situation and place, no less. But he knew better. She'd been sure of what she wanted a minute ago … Without even needing to hear what this woman wanted, Marcus already knew it.

And still, he had to ask, "Yes, I have a condom, but is that what you want—for me to fuck you out here where someone might see you backed up against a wall with your dress yanked up to your ass? Allow me that, *bella donna*, and let me make you scream into my tie when I stuff it into your mouth. Tell me yes, and trust that the rest of this night is going to be all about what you need."

She didn't even hesitate when she replied, "And what if I said no?"

"Then it's no."

"And what if that turns me on because no one's ever asked to fuck me quite like that before, Marcus?"

A dark noise fell from his lips. "Then, I'd say that's a shame, and you should let me make sure you never have to worry about not knowing what that experience is like again. Tell me *yes*, Cella."

She did. Clearly, though the word came out softened by the heat in her tone. And still, he loved the way she said that, "Yes, please yes."

Marcus didn't need to be told again. His lips found hers against for another hard, burning kiss. The force alone was enough to have her taking several steps backward with him walking right with her until her back met the glass wall. On the other side of it, the vines grew thickly along the wall of windows, but they had yet to reach the top where the majority of the light spilled in during the day.

Though there were still patches where the vines had yet to cover, allowing him a peek at the trail where they'd come from outside. But he wasn't very focused on watching that when the woman under him was a far more interesting sight.

Especially when he dropped to his knees and bunched her skirt up around her hips in his fist. Her head fell back to the glass as he leaned in to kiss her inner thighs, enjoying the way her skin shuddered under his lips.

Need shot down to his cock.

Fuck.

His balls ached.

"I want to fuck you more than anything," he told her, looking up to meet her gaze as he spoke, "but I want just a taste of you first. How fast do you think you can come with just my mouth on your pussy, Cella?"

A low whine escaped her.

That wasn't quite good enough for him, though.

"If you're going to let me do this to you, then I at least want to hear you use your *words*."

"I don't know how fast, but I want to find out."

Marcus gave her one of his grins. "That's what I wanted to hear."

He kept the skirt of her dress high with one hand, and used the other to drag the black, lace thong she wore underneath it down her legs, his cock still biting against the only half-opened zipper from the sight of that *piece of scrap*. It'd looked so good covering the apex of her thighs, but now he had an even better view.

She was bare.

Waxed.

With her thighs already open for him, he had the perfect view of her pussy, and the wetness already starting to gather there for him to taste. Pink, and soft, and *so fucking hot* under his tongue when he leaned in for that first tease with the flick of his tongue against her silt.

She trembled.

Ragged breaths all the way.

And he just wanted more.

To see more.

Hear more.

Taste more of her.

Her fingers threaded into his hair, manicured nails dragging along his scalp as he stopped teasing her all at once. He had neither the patience nor the control to do that with this beautiful woman tonight.

Another night, certainly.

Tonight, he just had to have her.

His tongue flattened against her slit, and then dragged up to her clit to slash back and forth across the taut nub while two of his fingers slipped into her slick pussy. Her sex tightened around his fingers with every twist of the tips against her G-spot.

And her sounds got *louder*.

So did those, "*Please, please, please, oh my God.*"

She was so fucking close.

In no time at all.

It kind of made his nerves chaotic at how responsive this woman was to his touch. That made him hotter than ever.

And when she did finally fall over that edge by his mouth and fingers, what a sight she was to see. With her chest and shoulders thrust out away from the wall, her head tipped back to the glass, and her still stained-red lips parted with his name falling to the sky.

Yeah.

All his control was gone.

Although she didn't seem to mind a bit when he raised from the floor of the solarium, already yanking open what was left of his fly while he dug in his back pocket for the spare item he kept on hand—always—as a just in case. She helped to shove his pants down, taking his kiss one more time while he ripped open that package.

He broke away from letting her taste herself on his mouth just long enough to slip the condom down his length before her hand replaced his to stroke him. Tight and fast. From the base to the tip. *God*. The groan that came out of him ached all the way out.

And then she was lifting her leg, tall enough in her five-inch heels to be able to accommodate his six-foot-three height, to wrap around him while her knee hooked around his hip. She guided him where she wanted to be, and he took her in one thrust.

"*Fuck*," he breathed, settled deep in her clenching pussy while her fingernails dragged lines over the material of his suit jacket. Her moan, louder than even how it had been when he was between her thighs, reminded him that he still needed to keep her quiet, and she only grinned at him with hazy lust in her eyes when he yanked off his tie before using it to gag her quiet. But to see her like *that* … "God, look at you."

She was quite a sight.

Pushed against the wall.

Bare ass to the glass.

Spread for him.

Filled with him.

And all she could do was mumble into the tie, "*Fuck me, Marcus.*"

He used one hand to keep her leg tight to his hip, but his other found her throat again. Pushing the back of her head to the glass so that she had to look up at him, he got the best view of the pleasure rippling over her features as he fucked her with a fast, deep pace.

"You take me so well, babe," he murmured, "pussy's so goddamn wet, huh? You like that, Cella, letting me use you like this—fuck you like this?"

Her nod answered him back, before a broken cry accompanied it with a muffled yell into the tie. One of her hands slipped down his lower back, and under his boxer-briefs to grab tight to his ass when he fucked her a little harder.

With the tie in her mouth, she couldn't speak.

Not that he was in any better position than her because with each drive and pull of his hips, Marcus came that much closer to his own orgasm. He could feel it in the tightening of his back, and the heat in his balls. Never had he busted a nut so fast with a woman, and yet, Cella seemed to be the one who was going to humble the *fuck* out of him.

Still, he refused to let himself lose that control until she came one more time. Leaning in, his lips melded against hers when he ripped that tie from her mouth and he demanded,

"Come on, give it to me ... show me how good you can come for me again, *tesoro*."

She did.

Panting into his kiss.

He swallowed all her cries.

It took all of four more thrusts before he followed right after her, too. Releasing into latex, tight to her and deep inside her shuddering pussy ... *best way I spent a night in a long while.*

Best fuck he'd ever had, if he were being honest.

They took a moment to breathe, or rather ... catch the air they both needed. With him still inside her, and her leg trembling against his hip, she let out a soft laugh.

He did, too.

Because *damn*.

"What now?" Cella asked.

Marcus chuckled deeply.

"What?"

He shook his head and dipped down to press a fast kiss against her still trembling lips. "Now you fix your dress, and I'll help, if you need me to. We're going to smooth down your hair, make sure we didn't smudge any makeup, and we'll walk back to the mansion to say goodbye to my parents before you let me take you back to your hotel, so we can do this *again*."

Cella dragged in a shaky breath under his weight still pressing her to the window of the solarium. "Oh, we're just going to go right back in there then, after *this*?"

"Believe it or not, but that drives me crazy thinking about knowing I'll have just fucked you, and I'm thirty minutes away from getting another taste of you, all the while no one gets to know that except me ... and you're treated like a queen whether or not I'm making you scream with my cock or saying goodbye to my parents. And you *definitely* want to find out what happens after that."

"Pretty sure that would be against *some* rule somewhere. It has to be."

He lifted his brow once suggestively. "What'd I say about having to break them sometimes, huh?"

"You're going to kill me, Marcus Guzzi."

He flashed a grin. "I'll go down with you."

CHAPTER
6

It wasn't the hint of sunlight dancing into the hotel room that woke Cella from her sleep, but rather, the quiet conversation coming from somewhere to her right. She did her best to stay still, and not let her companion know she had woken up during his little chat because …

Well, how could she not?

"Ma said I won't have to ride the bus when I start school," Tiffany explained, her young voice taking on that *no-nonsense* tone she liked to use when she wanted to sound older than her five years. "Someone will drive me."

"You don't want to take the bus even once?" Marcus asked.

"It's *yellow*."

She said that as though that should just explain all of her feelings on the matter. Cella had all she could do not to laugh, but she did smile against the soft pillow under her head. Marcus, on the other hand, laughed hard and loud, but quickly quieted.

Maybe because he thought she was still sleeping.

Who knew?

"Well, they're yellow so people can easily see them," he said.

"Yeah, *well* …"

"No school bus, I get it."

Tiffany sighed, the phone call she talked on with Marcus

only distorting her voice slightly. The girl had learned to use the phone when she was three, and now whenever she stayed a night away from her mother with her aunts or grandparents, she used the phone to call and check in. A lot, although Cella never told her to stop.

Whatever her kid needed to feel safe.

"Do you want me to get your mom to call you back when—"

"We can keep talking," Tiffany said brightly.

Because *of course*.

That was her kid in a nutshell.

Never stopped moving those lips.

"Do you work with my mom?" Tiffany asked.

Marcus cleared his throat. "Do you mean with the penthouse?"

"Yeah, making people's houses *pretty*."

Cella dared to crack her eyes open, then, if only because she wanted to see where Marcus was and watch him while he talked to her kid. She wasn't sure why he picked up her ringing phone, but she could deal with that later.

A quick scan of the space and she found him sitting on the chaise near the window of her Four Seasons' room. He'd not bothered to get dressed beyond pulling on a pair of boxer briefs. His hair hung down around his dark eyes, the strands damp from a shower he must have taken. How long had he been up? He stared out the window with the phone in his hand, silent.

And what a sight he was.

All those hard, defined lines of his lean form available for her to admire. The way his jawline looked carved from steel and softened only the slightest when he smiled in response to whatever her daughter just said to him. A muscular torso and firm abs that led down to a narrow waist where the waistband of his boxer-briefs rested upon the cut V of his hips.

The man truly was beautiful.

In a suit, and without one.

Damn.

It wasn't as though she got very much time to enjoy him in his naked glory the night before. In the solarium, he hadn't even bothered to take off his clothes when he fucked her except to shove his pants down just low enough to get the job done. Not that she minded, and in fact, she'd had *very* good dreams because of that.

And then, once they'd arrived back to her hotel … well, *because* of the solarium, all she could think about was getting that man in her bed. Nothing else mattered, and she didn't waste time getting what she wanted. Not that Marcus complained because he certainly didn't.

Now, though, she was enjoying what she missed.

Nothing wrong with that, right?

Yeah.

"I'm helping your mom," he replied, "but that's not what I do for work."

"Well, what do you do, then?"

Cella smirked at the way Marcus cocked a brow and smiled a bit at that question. Her girl was smart as hell, and quick as a whip. She would keep asking those *whys* or *whats* until she got what she wanted from the conversation. But considering Marcus had yet to realize she was awake, she said nothing and simply took in the show.

"I do a lot of different things," he said carefully, "but right now I work the most with a bunch of maple syrup farms my family owns."

"*Really?*"

Little Tiffany's screech might have broken glass. There was one detail about her daughter that Marcus couldn't possibly know, but he soon would.

"I *love* maple syrup!"

And she truly did.

Not that fake shit that was only flavored like maple syrup, no. *Real* maple syrup, and she swore her daughter could tell the difference just by smelling it. Cella kept a jar on hand of her daughter's favorite kind, but it was getting terribly low.

"It's *real*, right?" Tiffany demanded on the call. "Because my Uncle Ren tried to tell my ma it was real, but it *wasn't*."

In the background of the call, someone, it sounded like Renzo, said loudly, "Listen, not *everyone* knows there's a difference, Tiffany."

"Everyone should know it!"

Cella couldn't help it, she laughed, finally making Marcus aware that yes, she was awake and watching him. His grin turned on her, that intense gaze of his softened more than usual. Maybe it was because he was currently talking to her daughter, but whatever it was, she liked it.

A lot.

Tossing her a wink, he went back to the conversation with, "Very real—I promise."

"Can I see the farms?"

"Not the one I'm currently working on because we only recently bought it. *But* … I think I could make something work for another farm, so you could come in and see how everything is done. Would you like that?"

"Um, *yes*."

Marcus laughed in that sexy way again.

Or maybe because it seemed as though he liked her kid that she found attractive.

Who knew what it was?

"Then, we'll make a date," he promised. "Now, would you like to talk to your mom?"

"Yes, please. Thank you, Marcus. It was very nice to talk to you again."

Cella pressed her lips together to hide her smile as she sat up in the bed, dragging the sheets with her to hide some of her nudity as he crossed the room. He shrugged one bare shoulder when she took the phone, but Cella was quick to cover the speaker to ask him, "She kept calling?"

"I thought it might have been an emergency after the fourth call, so I picked it up. Sorry, if I crossed a—"

"It's okay."

"She's a sweet kid."

Yeah.

She really was.

Cella took the kiss he dropped to her lips—one that didn't linger, but damn, she still felt it all over—before taking her hand off the speaker and microphone. "Good morning, baby."

"I miss you, Ma."

"I'll be home soon."

"I know. Hey, guess what Marcus said I could do?"

Cella shook her head, but couldn't help but eye the man across the room who looked a little too smug with himself. For what, she couldn't quite say, but she wondered if it might have anything to do with the fact he just basically made sure she would be coming back to Toronto, and not for the penthouse, but likely *with* her daughter to spend more time with him.

After all, no parent liked to break their kid's heart.

Or a promise.

"Yeah, a maple syrup farm, huh?"

"It's gonna be *awesome*," Tiffany breathed, her excitement clear.

"No doubt, baby."

Cella finished her conversation with Tiffany, promising to call her daughter as soon as she got on the road, so the kid could watch the clock. Because *she would*. Once the phone was forgotten to the sheets, she turned to Marcus who was now sitting on that chaise again, still in nothing but his boxer-briefs, and looking like absolute sin.

And temptation.

Yes.

Her greatest temptation.

"She doesn't do that, you know?"

He arched a brow. "Pardon?"

"Tiffany. She doesn't talk to men outside of the family often, if at all. I can count on one hand how many she will talk to. I think it's partly because she's never really had a male figure in the house what with her father dying when she was still a baby. It's another reason why I'm nervous about her starting school when I suspect there'll be male teachers, and—"

"She talks fine with me."

Right.

Then, Marcus asked quieter, "Did I cross a line? I didn't mean—"

"No, of course not."

All Cella's feelings were *hers*. Just hers alone to handle, not his. It wasn't his fault that she didn't know if this felt like betraying her dead husband's memory, or not, and she certainly wouldn't make him think otherwise. Or hell, maybe it was the fact that she *didn't* feel badly about this that had her in a strange headspace. Whatever nonsense her heart wanted to produce about this wasn't something she would put on his shoulders. And once she had time, she might sit down and try to figure it out.

What else could she do?

"So, you made a date with my daughter, huh?"

He stood from the chaise, all lean and tall but so fit and looking *damn good*. She would be a liar if she said every step he took toward her on the bed didn't have her entirely entranced. Once he came to the edge of the bed, he put his hands on either side of the mattress beside her, and leaned in close so that their lips barely grazed.

An almost kiss, but not quite enough.

"And you, too, I hope," he murmured. "Because it won't be as fun if you don't join, too."

Instead of agreeing, she pulled him into bed with her.

Wasn't that a good enough answer?

* * *

Cella admired the stained-glass windows of her family's church, finding herself far more interested in *that,* than in whatever the priest was saying from his pulpit. Her lack of attention in church wasn't normal. Growing up, she came here once a week, every single Sunday, never failed. She took confession here … sat in these pews with the rest of her family.

She loved the church.

Its smell.

The parish.

All of it.

And yet today, all she seemed to want to do was stare out the window that faced the graveyard to the east of the church. Because for the last week, since she'd left Marcus in Toronto and returned home, her mind had been on only one thing.

Her dead husband.

And if she was doing the right thing.

Or if it even *mattered.*

These were things she didn't know, and since she also wasn't sure how to broach the topic with someone else, Cella decided it was just better for her to stew in her feelings alone. At least that way, she wouldn't have anyone else's judgments about her life choices. And at the same time, she also didn't have anyone to vent to.

What a wonderful mess this was.

"Cella, sweetheart?"

"Hmm?"

Looking to the side, she found her mother and father were already standing from the pew where they had been sitting beside her. She tried at least once a month to make the six-hour drive to her parents' to attend church with them. Usually, she attended a parish that she found in Rochester with Tiffany, but she still found herself coming back to this place often.

More often than she cared to admit.

Sometimes, for William.

Just to say hello.

Sometimes, to be with her parents.

Of course, the Sunday dinners *after* church didn't hurt, either. She was never one to say no to food, but especially not when her mother or aunts cooked it.

Still, at the sight of her parents standing, it made Cella realize she had dazed out even more than she previously thought. A quick look around the church confirmed that, in fact, Sunday mass was over, and the church had just begun to empty of parishioners.

Damn.

"Distracted?" her father asked, grabbing his sunglasses from the pew.

Cella cleared her throat, quick to stand up and grab her purse as she did it. "No, of course not. I'm just—"

"For the last fifteen minutes of service," her mother interjected with a kind tone, "you didn't even sit or stand when you were supposed to, Cella."

Yeah.

Shit.

She tried to brush it off. "Things on my mind, that's all."

"Lucian, give us a minute, would you?"

Her father raised his brows at her mother's request, but just as quickly nodded and dropped a kiss to Jordyn's forehead before heading out into the aisle where he met up with his brothers. It was only once her father and his brothers were far enough away that they couldn't hear the conversation between Cella and Jordyn that her mother turned to her with that soft, gentle smile still firmly in place.

"Would this have anything to do with the man Tiffany keeps talking about every chance she gets?"

Would it?

Because yeah, it was pretty damn hard for Cella to pretend like there wasn't a lot more going on with Marcus Guzzi than her family knew when he was the first and last thing her daughter seemed to want to talk about every chance she got.

Not that Cella complained.

She adored that.

Her daughter *liked* someone she had an interest in. Shouldn't that be a good thing? Shouldn't that mean this could be something amazing if she was just willing to see it through?

"Cella," Jordyn urged softly.

Her gaze turned to the stained glass window again, and the graveyard she knew was hidden by a high, stone wall and an wrought iron fence.

"It's been months since I visited William," Cella said, glancing back to her mother. "Almost a year, actually."

"You're busy—you have your career, a business to run, and a child to take care of."

"Yeah, but—"

"Your love for him isn't determined by how many times you make a six-hour drive to sit at his grave, Cella."

Of course.

She knew that.

And still … "When is it okay for me to move on?"

Jordyn dragged in a quick breath. "When you feel ready."

"When is *that*?"

"I don't think it's supposed to be something you just *know*, baby. At least, not for everyone. We're all different people. Maybe it's something you just do. It is about him, isn't it? Marcus?"

Cella held tighter to her purse, hoping it hid the trembling in her hands. "I don't know if it is that, or if that's what I want it to be. But he's made me think about these things, or at least consider them, when I haven't done that before. He's *there* … no one's ever been there for me in that way since William died, and I don't know how to move forward."

"But you want to."

It wasn't even a question.

Her mother didn't need to ask it.

Cella didn't need to have an answer.

It felt like, in a way, that the answer was already there staring her in the face. She just chose to ignore that nothing was ever going to be black or white for her here because her situation was not the norm. No young woman should be forced to bury her husband before it was his time with a baby on her hip.

"I don't want to feel guilty for being happy," Cella muttered.

Jordyn's bright smile widened. "The only person you need to worry about making you feel guilty for that is yourself. The rest of us? We only want what you want. And William? He wouldn't want you to pine the rest of your life away—he'd never ask you for that, Cella. The only thing he ever tried to do for you was to make you happy. So *be happy*."

It was such an easy answer.

A complication simplified like nothing at all.

Well, to someone else looking in.

But to Cella?

Not so simple.

Marcus Guzzi was anything but simple, and the way he just swept into her life when she was least expecting it was the perfect example of why.

He was the kind of man who wore three-piece suits with diamond studs in his cufflinks, who opened doors or pulled out chairs for her, and exuded control and charm with every conversation. Always the gentleman. Forever the most enigmatic man in the room. Respected and revered. He was also the kind of man who could make her forget her own name, strip her of shame with a heated word, and could make her beg with nothing more than his stare.

In another life, a man like Marcus would have been everything perfect for Cella.

In her life, though?

A man like him was terrifying.

"Would you watch Tiffany for me? Her booster seat is in the back of my car—just switch it over and take her to dinner. I'll meet up with you after."

She watched the windows again.

In her mind, she saw that graveyard.

"You don't even have to ask," her mother assured. "And say hello to William for me, okay?"

Her gaze darted back to her mother.

Jordyn only shrugged, though.

She just knew …

"It's strange, you know?"

"What is?"

"To miss two different men for reasons that have nothing to do with each other."

Jordyn's smile faltered for the first time. "Only one is *here*, though."

Right.

As for the other?

She just wanted to keep his memory alive. Not hide it. Or pretend like it hadn't been once upon a time.

Was that too much to ask?

CHAPTER 7

"Hmm, okay, did you get that last email?"

"I did," Marcus replied to Cella, clicking to download the attachments so that he could preview a few of the sketches and blueprints she had drawn up for three of the rooms in his parents' penthouse. "Give me a second to get it all up."

"How big is your computer screen?"

"It's a laptop."

"Not big enough, then."

Marcus barked out a laugh. "You don't know that—it could be plenty big enough."

"Not for the *small* details. They get lost on a screen less than twenty-two inches. I know, it's why I make sure all my clients that demand to approve every single last detail know they're going to miss notes and certain things if they don't view it on an appropriately sized screen."

"You take this too seriously, woman."

He swore he could feel her smile through the phone when she replied, "Or you just don't take it serious enough, hmm?"

"Well—"

"I mean, what would you say if I was like, *Marcus, drop your Capos and replace them with whoever I demand because I said so, and I clearly think I know more about your business than you do.* What, huh?"

Marcus sucked air through his teeth, still waiting for the preview of Cella's attachments to come up on the email as he replied, "You know, not *all* my work revolves around the mafia, no?"

"Mmhmm, but I assume you'd be even less likely to accept someone else's direction for that side of your business than you would the legal."

"Wrong. "

His word came out in a murmur.

"Pardon?"

Marcus chuckled. "It wouldn't matter *what* business it is, I would still tell someone to stay out of my work. So, before you get all proud and say *I told you so, Marcus*, I will just say this … later, when I am at home and have my larger computer screen, I will go over these emails again. Just to make sure I see all your little details for the rooms."

She quieted for a moment.

He let her have it.

"Thank you. I appreciate that."

Finally, the previews came up for the attachments. He was seriously regretting spending this working day in the office of one of his restaurants because the internet connection here was the shittiest he had ever seen, and there wasn't one goddamn excuse for it.

Next thing on my list.

His ever-growing list.

It still hadn't stopped.

"I am not such a prideful man that I can't admit when I am wrong about something," Marcus replied, moving his cursor over the screen to move it back and forth. Several pictures laid out ideas *similar* to what Cella had planned for two of the bedrooms in the penthouse, not to mention the main bathroom guests would be using. "And what do I do with the blueprint type stuff?"

"Mostly dimensions and where things would go based on the size of whatever is going into the rooms. I need to measure the other spaces as well, but I tend to work on two or three rooms at a time, and while those begin to have work done, I move onto the other spaces."

"Ah."

Well …

"I think my mother is going to like this." He smiled at the one spare bedroom that looked as though roses and stained glass would be a prominent decorative feature. "Where on earth are you going to get stained glass to frame, anyway? I like the roses in that room, also."

She laughed nervously.

Still, he heard what she tried to hide.

That heat.

Because fuck yeah, he bet she was remembering their moment in the solarium just as well as he currently did. Quite frankly, the memory of that and the night that followed in her hotel room was the only damn thing that got him through the last two weeks of not seeing her.

Cella had quickly become *something* to Marcus.

Something he didn't understand.

An addiction, maybe.

An obsession, almost certainly.

She filled his thoughts when he should be focusing on literally anything and everything else but her. He struggled to keep his questions to himself while the two of them had a moment away from their very busy lives. All he wanted to ask was *when are you coming back to me?*

The woman wasn't even *his.*

And fuck, he felt like maybe she could be.

Maybe he wanted her to be.

Those were very dangerous feelings for a man like him.

Beyond that, it was quite the precarious situation he found himself in day after day. Never had something—or someone, for that matter—swept into his mind and life the way Cella Marcello did.

Nothing took away his focus.

And yet, she did it without trying at all.

La famiglia had been Marcus's first love from the time he was old enough to understand what it meant to be a Guzzi son and appreciate his family's legacy. To be made … that was the only thing he ever wanted and worked for. Once he was a made man, taking care of the family took over his every waking moment.

Rarely did he do something for him. *Never* did something take away his attention. Except this woman, it seemed. And he couldn't find it in himself to hate it.

"Marcus?"

"Hmm?"

He exited out of the previews of her plans, not at all concerned with the direction she had chosen to go with it. Frankly, he didn't need to give his final okay, anyway. If anyone should be doing that, it was his father, but Gian wanted to be distanced from all this lest Cara stumble on something and ruin her great surprise.

Thing was, his father put all his faith and trust in Cella and her talent. He fully believed the woman would turn the penthouse into a modern space that Cara would adore and appreciate simply because it *was* Cella's designs.

Marcus believed the same.

He didn't need to give approval, either.

"What is it?" he asked when Cella stayed quiet on the other end.

"You're … uh, interested in me, right?"

His brow furrowed, and he almost turned to look at the

phone he was holding as though it would allow him to look directly at the woman on the other end. "I'm sorry?"

"Me—you're interested in me."

"Wasn't that obvious enough, or did I not make that clear for you? I can fix that if you'd like. *Yes*, I am absolutely interested in you. How could I not be?"

"Right," she said, laughing dryly, "how could I think otherwise? No man just looks for only sex from a widow with a kid, I suppose."

"Cella—"

"I don't know, maybe a part of me wondered if that's what it was. *Just* that for you, I mean. Or if I was reading too much—"

"*Donna*, you didn't read nearly enough into it. If all I wanted was to fuck you, I wouldn't still be on the phone with you right now. I am too busy of a man to make that much of an effort just to get a good lay."

She made a soft noise.

He laughed.

"Listen," he said, sighing, "I know you haven't dated since … well, in a while, and we didn't exactly go over the fine details here, but just know no matter what, it's all on you. Slow down, speed up … tell me to fuck off; that's all on you, I promise."

"William told me something similar when we first started dating, although that was mostly because I was young, having fun, and didn't know if I wanted to be serious with someone. Entirely different reasons, I guess, but basically the same sentiment."

"Smart man, then."

"That's how you reply to me bringing him up?"

"Why not? How did you two meet, anyway?"

Cella dragged in a quick breath, and then laughed lightly.

"He uh, was helping to work on my brother's case after John got arrested and was looking at ten or more years in prison. I still felt some kind of way about my brother at that time— long story, let's not bother, I'm over it—and I said something to the effect of *should leave him there*. William had come to my parents' house for a dinner, so he was being the polite, respectful man he needed to be. But that must have just rubbed him the wrong way because he looked at me, cocked a brow, and replied *except that's not my job*."

Marcus hummed under his breath, leaning back in the office chair as he asked, "And what happened after that?"

"I thought I would hate him."

"But you didn't."

"He was a hard man to hate."

Silence stretched on between the two, but Marcus didn't mind. He took in all she had told him, and felt like ... well, what a privilege it was for him to be told something that personal about her life and a man she had fallen in love with.

"Thank you," he finally said.

"For what?"

"Telling me a little about him. He's someone you love. Not *loved*, you see ... I understand that, and so of course, he's going to be on your mind. I wouldn't expect anything different, and I want to know about all the things you love, Cella. The important things, and the stuff you think is nothing at all."

"Are you sure?"

"Why not?"

"Does it make you feel like you barely know me?"

"No," he answered honestly, "it makes me feel like there's so much more to learn. And *that* ... well, I look forward to that, *tesoro*."

* * *

Considering the fact that Marcus's earlier conversation with Cella ended on a good note, and he had managed to stay on top of *all* his tasks despite how they seemed to snowball on him at the worst of times, he felt pretty fucking good about his day.

Maybe that was why he went into yet another meeting with the biker gang feeling on top of the world when he should have been laser-focused on getting those assholes to back the hell off any and all Guzzi business. Although this time he was lucky enough to get a sit down with the actual *president* of the club and not just the man's right hand.

It was very possible, because of his good mood and all, that Marcus was willing to offer yet another peaceful solution to the bikers instead of just finishing the job. Besides, he knew for certain it wouldn't look good on him to go into taking over the family as the official boss when it was the time to do so while being in an active war with another organization, but especially one that was as close to them as the Quebec Riders.

As the *acting* boss … he needed to show he could handle issues like these without first defaulting to the worst possible scenario before trying everything and anything else. He didn't need more judgment and opinions chasing his status in his *famiglia* than what he already had.

A boss that sat in his seat during chaos was doomed to have that same chaos follow him throughout his reign. Or, that's what he'd always been told.

Marcus worried it was the truth.

"Listen, Guzzi—"

"This disrespect again," Marcus murmured from his position across the table from the biker gang's president. "I expected it from your vice president the last time I had the unfortunate displeasure of discussing these problems with him, but I assure you I won't sit here and let you do the same shit, Junior. You don't *demand* things from me—you discuss them respectfully, or I will see myself out with the rest of my men. Is that clear?"

"Just who do you think you—"

Marcus turned his head to the side, catching his brother's gaze as he smiled tightly at Chris. "Who asked for this meeting?"

"The Riders," his brother replied easily.

"Yes, they did."

Chris nodded, but otherwise, said nothing more from his position against the far wall. One of *six* men Marcus brought along to attend this meeting with the gang to handle the little problem of them *burning* a fucking warehouse. Thing was, Chris, like the rest of the Guzzi men in attendance here, didn't need to be told how to *act*. He just fucking knew.

Marcus went as far as having this meeting in a place the *bikers* chose, although his men arrived first to the rundown strip club, did a walk-through, and checked for any possible issues that might have been planted by the assholes from Quebec.

Like a trap.

There were none.

So, what did these assholes really want from him?

"I've made myself perfectly clear," Marcus said, turning his attention back to the man sitting at the table with him. "We're not doing business with your people or organization. That's not how the Guzzis work, and we're not going to change our practices simply because you demand it."

He crossed his arms over his chest, continuing on with, "It doesn't matter where our farm is located, or what business we're doing with the farm, you're not *owed* anything because of territory. And if you want to really get into those semantics, it will take all of a week for the Guzzis to take over what remains of your very small territory, anyway. Would you like to continue this discussion as we are, or take the way out I've given you? At least that way, you go back to doing your business, and we leave you alone. Otherwise … it won't end the same, I assure you."

"You talk about *respect*, Guzzi, but you forget that's a two-way street in this life. You expect respect, but you're not willing to *give it back*. See, I know how fuckers like you work. You … *Italians*. If someone were to go onto your territory and make themselves a nice little spot to work, you'd be the first asshole in line to make them pay what was due to you. Are you telling me I'm wrong?"

No.

He wasn't.

That changed nothing.

"Do you know when people like me are willing to sit down and allow people like you a *say* about business or money?" Marcus asked.

"No, but I'm sure you plan to tell me."

"Well, *oui*, otherwise, how will you learn your place?"

"My *pla*—"

"Yes, your place. Because you see, the Guzzis didn't just become who we are overnight. We didn't turn around and suddenly *be* this massive organization with a reach that crosses not only *this* country, but other countries as well. And you think, with your thirty club members, your little dealings in pills, and whatever else you make your *paltry* money in that somehow allows you a seat at our table. And you could not be more wrong. You are not nearly big enough to cause me real concern, and so I won't allow you to think you do, either. That's not how this works between us."

Like his vice president, this man kept his head shaved which only made his double chin and large size all the more apparent. He hadn't bothered to throw anything on except for a pair of jeans, combat boots he laced haphazardly, and the leather vest with his obvious patches sewn on with more care than he even took to manage his overgrowing beard.

Oh, they *wanted* a name in the criminal world, to be sure.

Marcus would not be giving them one, however.

"You burned our warehouse," Marcus continued, not even bothering to allow the man the chance to speak. "And this is the last warning you are going to get from me—we don't intend, today or tomorrow or *ever*, to do business with you or your people. There is nothing you could do that will allow you a seat at my table. Every step you make after this one, however, will put another nail in your coffin. Do what you will with that, Junior. We're done here. Consider yourself lucky I even allowed you this second meeting, and the only reason I did that was so that boss to boss, we could have a conversation. But now it's finished."

And he was over it.

Marcus stood from the table, not the least bit interested in the strippers working the poles or the scantily clad women walking around the club to serve the patrons. He came here for business, and his pleasure wouldn't be found in a place like this. Turning away from the table, he hoped everything would be crystal clear between the Guzzis and the Quebec chapter of the Riders, but he couldn't be sure.

"That's what it is, then?" the man still sitting at the table asked. "You think you're *better* than us?"

Marcus scoffed, turning around just enough to look at the man. "There's no *thinking* in this equation. It's a matter of facts and standing here."

"I find that ... *offensive*, Marcus."

"So, be offended. That's not my problem. As long as you

and your hurt feelings stay the fuck away from the Guzzi business, then I don't care what you feel about it."

"Or maybe you just need a lesson in humility, hmm?"

Marcus felt the presence of his men closing in around him. After all, their boss had moved from the table, and so they had to act accordingly. Still, he stared down the man at the table, unwilling to move.

"Is that a threat?" he asked the president of the gang. "Because if we're going to start throwing around threats, I promise mine will be something worth listening to."

Junior smiled back, cold and tight. "Have a nice day, Marcus."

The asshole would pay for that one.

Marcus didn't say another word or give away a single emotion about Junior's parting words, the meeting itself, or otherwise as he left the club. That wasn't how a boss should behave, and every lesson he'd ever learned from watching his father while he grew up came down to moments like these. Not only when you were on display for your enemy, but to your own men, as well. It never ended well for a boss who showed weakness, even if that weakness meant something emotional like *anger*.

His men rushed to leave the club before him, and then gathered fast around him, making a protective wall from not only any fool with a gun who might be waiting outside, but also from the unlikely event their meeting had been recorded by police officials seeing as how the mafia was *always* on their radar.

Marcus still said nothing until he slipped into the passenger side of the car that quickly pulled up, his other brother who had come to this meeting, Bene, in the driver's seat. Chris slipped into the back, the windows tinted so darkly and the exchange so fast that it would *appear* like Marcus might be sitting in the rear.

They took no chances.

They couldn't being who they were.

And it never failed to amaze him how his own *brothers* would protect him above even their selves, but so was their life. It was who they were raised to *be*.

"Send him a message," Marcus said as the car pulled away, and he allowed his first show of emotions in private with his brothers. The *only* men in his life, next to his two other brothers that lived in another country now, and his father, whom he trusted enough to show that *weakness*. "I want a fucking message sent to him. Otherwise, we'll look weak to our men for not at least making sure they understood their disrespect. And to those Quebec *fucks*," he uttered, teeth clenching like his jaw, "if we don't answer back with something, they will still see us as a target. So, send them the fucking message they all want so badly, but then we're done with them."

Chris opened his mouth when he leaned between the front seats of the Mercedes SUV as though he were going to say something, but Marcus held up a hand and added, "Make sure it fucking hurts them where it will count. Cut the head off the fucking snake, for all I give a damn, but don't forget I want them to really learn from this."

Verbal confirmation came from his brothers.

Marcus turned to watch the buildings pass them by as they headed further east. His reflection on the glass caught the glimmering lights overhead on the street, the dark sky painted a bright black with scattered splashes from the stars.

"You're doing fine," Bene said beside him, "you know that, don't you? You're doing exactly what Dad taught you to do, Marcus."

"Did I *ask*?"

"No, but—"

"Then, don't *talk*."

Chris made a grunt behind them. "They really pissed you off, yeah?"

Marcus sighed, shaking his head. "Yeah … the fucking disrespect of them, you know?"

"Yeah, man."

"We know," Bene echoed.

CHAPTER

8

"Do, do, do, do, do, dodo! *Dance*!"

"How many times are you gonna sing that song, kid?"

"Fifty more times!"

"*Perfect.*"

Cella smiled from her spot behind the desk in her Rochester office at the conversation happening outside in the hallway. Sometimes, for whatever reason, but usually work, when she was unable to pick her daughter from pre-K or daycare—when she attended—then one of the trusted Marcello drivers made the trip to Rochester to do just that.

Today, it had been one of her brother's men because apparently, John hadn't minded allowing Cella to call on one of his enforcer's for the day, and it was just her luck that he was available to pick Tiffany up from pre-K. The guy was one of the only people that Tiffany preferred over others when it couldn't be her mother there to pick her up. She'd made friends with the man—who looked better suited on the defense line of a football team—during her movie night sleepovers at her uncle's place.

Soon, her daughter darted through the doorway of Cella's opened office wearing the sky-blue leggings that didn't match the green shirt and pink shoes she'd picked out that morning. Five was a cute age for kids—or maybe it was just girls. Tiffany was determined every single morning to pick out her own clothes, and sit next to the mirror to do her hair and *pretend* like she was putting on makeup the same way her mother did.

Yeah, Cella could have put her foot down and made her kid wear clothes that matched, or even straightened her messy pony, but where was the fun in that? How would Tiffany ever learn to be independent and happy with herself when someone else was always trying to change something to make it better?

So, she let her kid pick out her outfits.

Unmatched colors and all.

"Hey, Ma!"

Tiffany's bright smile and twinkling eyes greeted her as the enforcer came to stand in the doorway, too. Pushing her chair away from the desk slightly, it allowed her daughter the chance to slip in behind to give her mother a hug.

That wasn't good enough for Cella.

She missed her kid so much.

All the time, really.

Once she had little Tiffany pulled into her lap, Cella wrapped her daughter in a tight hug and breathed in the familiar scent of her child. No matter the stresses of the day or what was going on in her life, all she needed to do was hug this girl to make it a million times better. Maybe that was the most beautiful thing about unconditional love.

"How was your day?" Cella asked.

Tiffany leaned back, still beaming while she stared at her mother. Thankfully, the French braid she'd allowed her mother to put her hair in that day managed to stay put through all her playtime and whatever else she'd taken part in at pre-K. "Pretty good—I missed you, though."

Cella pressed her lips together, smiling just a little bit. "Yeah, me too, but you know it's good to go to school, right? That's how you get smarter, and—"

"I know, Ma."

And yet …

"Still missed you," Tiffany said.

Cella sighed.

Because where was the lie?

This was just yet another reason why she found herself constantly worrying about what would happen when Tiffany started kindergarten in the fall. Right now, she spent only a couple of hours here or there in daycare and two days a week at pre-K. Cella's job allowed her the privilege of having her child with her throughout the week a lot of the time.

Once school started, though?

That would all change.

How Tiffany might react to that was still up in the air, and a major source of worry for Cella the closer the time came for her girl to start the school year. Then again, this girl was constantly surprising her mother with the level of maturity she showed at just five years old, so anything was possible.

Hell, maybe it would be Cella who cried that first day. Not that she would tell anyone she did so. Those little moments were her secrets to keep.

"If that's all …"

Cella forgot all about the waiting enforcer in her office doorway. Meeting the gaze of the man, she smiled and nodded. "That is all. Thanks again, Alex, for looking after my girl."

"Anything for family of the boss. Have a good day, Cella."

"You, too."

She quieted as the man left her office, and she was left with only her daughter. Tiffany pushed off her lap, talking about something she wanted to show her mother in the small backpack she toted back and forth to daycare or pre-K. Cella, on the other hand, wondered if her daughter had managed to realize just how different they were from the other people around them. Or even, if Tiffany understood that her little life was not like the other kids' lives.

How many kids had a driver?

A *bodyguard*?

It was a conversation she knew was going to happen someday with her daughter, the same way she'd had it with her father when she was about eight years old, but thankfully … today didn't seem like that day. Tiffany was more interested in what was in her backpack, and Cella was entirely willing to push those thoughts of the mafia and this life they lived to the side.

It hadn't touched her daughter yet.

Not in a way Tiffany understood.

Sure, the mafia took her father, but Tiffany didn't *know* that. She didn't know that the death of the man who helped to give her life came from the connections of people she loved more than anything. Cella had a long time to settle her mind and heart with those things, and she still wasn't sure that she dealt with it.

At least, not well.

And here in Rochester?

She felt like it wasn't in her face all the time.

Or maybe that was just her running.

Who knew?

"Here it is," Tiffany said, pulling a craft from her backpack that was slightly crumpled but it didn't detract from the finger-painted tree. "S'a maple tree, Ma."

Cella took the picture from her girl, sighing under her breath at the reminder staring her in the face. "Still on the maple thing, huh?"

"Marcus said—"

"Oh, don't worry, I remember everything *Marcus* says."

Far better than her daughter knew …

That man filled her thoughts constantly. For reasons she very much liked, and for others that kept her up at night worrying and wondering and … *everything*.

"You know it's not maple season where he lives, right?" Cella asked, lowering the picture to meet Tiffany's expectant gaze. "You can't go out and tap a tree until like February, or something."

"But he said I can see how they *make* stuff."

"Yes, but—"

"When are we going to see Marcus again?"

Cella pursed her lips.

This kid pulled no punches.

"I was thinking next weekend, I would probably go to Toronto to *work*, and—"

"I can come, too!"

Cella's immediate reaction was to explain to her child that it might be better if she stayed. After all, no one said she could just tote her kid with her while she worked. Even if this weekend wasn't about work. The rational side of her brain was louder, however, and those first thoughts weren't what slipped out of her mouth.

"How about we call Marcus, and you can ask him if he'd like for you to come next weekend with me to Toronto?" she asked.

Tiffany's whole face lit up all over again as she nodded fast. "Okay, you call, I'll talk."

Her laughter colored up the office as she reached for the phone. Even as she dialed Marcus's number, she had no doubt about what his answer would be for Tiffany. The man had no qualms about showing his obvious affection for the girl. As sweet as it was, and as much as it melted Cella's heart into a puddle of emotion she couldn't understand, it also scared her a little bit.

Surely, that was normal.

After she'd dialed the number, she put the phone on speaker for Tiffany to talk when Marcus picked up the call. The last time Cella talked to him had been a few days ago when she sent those sketches and other emails which then led into their conversation about her husband. She hadn't called again because nothing work-related was needed between them, but she found herself struggling not to pick up the phone just to chat because she *wanted* to.

And that had nothing to do with work.

"*Ciao*, Marcus here," came the familiar dark voice on the phone when the call was picked up.

"Hi, Marcus!"

He didn't even need to ask who it was.

The man just knew. "Tiffany—your mom knows you have the phone, right?"

"I know," Cella said quietly.

Faintly.

Her heart was doing that *thing* again.

Beating too hard.

Making her confused.

"Ma said I could ask you if I could come with her to Toronto next weekend," Tiffany said, smiling at her mother when Cella nodded.

"Well," Marcus drawled, "I should hope your mom brings you along. I miss you."

Somehow, Tiffany brightened even more.

Cella knew Marcus didn't intend to do it—he was just a *good* guy with an honorable heart and far too many things about him made the man *very* attractive to her—but he was drawing her in like a fish on a line. Every word he spoke; each thing he did … it all reeled her closer.

And she was helpless to stop it.

What was going to happen when he finally caught her?

That's what terrified her.

* * *

"Cella, what are you up to, *dolcezza*?"

"Hi, Grandpapa Lucian!"

Her father's chuckles echoed throughout the car at Tiffany's greeting. She'd shouted it from the backseat like she was sure her grandfather wouldn't hear it otherwise, and Cella was positive that hurt her father's ears. Not that he said a word one way or another.

"Hi, sweetheart. I thought you were with Grandmama today?"

"She was," Cella said, coming back into the conversation, "but I grabbed her a little earlier than I thought I would."

"Ah, yes, because you're heading to *Toronto* for the weekend, right?"

"Yep."

Her father cleared his throat, and Cella tried to focus her attention on the road ahead of her. It was a little difficult when Lucian said, "You know, I would believe this was only for work if you went alone, but when you bring Tiff along, too, my opinion begins to change, Cella."

Right.

And that was enough of that conversation happening while her daughter could hear. Cella was quick to hand the headphones for the tablet her daughter used on long trips to play her educational games. Without even needing to be told, Tiffany put the headphones atop her head, the large muffs covering her ears entirely before she turned them on. Only then did Cella return to the conversation with her father, feeling slightly safer that little ears weren't still listening in.

"Do you mind?" she asked her dad.

Lucian laughed, clearly unashamed. "Sorry, did I touch a nerve there?"

"No, but—"

"Cella, you know I don't have a problem with this … thing you have going on with Marcus Guzzi, don't you?"

"Even if you did," she muttered, "not sure it would make a difference to what I wanted or did, Daddy, let's just be honest here."

She swore she could feel her father's smile when he replied, "And I would expect nothing different, I promise. *But* … my bigger concern here is just making sure you're happy. You keep saying *work* like it's supposed to distract from the fact a lot of this is clearly not about work, sweetheart, and that worries me."

"I don't see why it should."

"Because I'm not sure if you're trying to deflect the rest of us from whatever is happening, or yourself."

Yeah, her father pulled no punches.

"I'm not trying to distract from anything," she said, although she couldn't say it was entirely *true*. That was another thing for a different day that wasn't today. "I'm just … letting things happen, you know?"

"You understand who he is, right?"

"Of course."

"No, Cella," Lucian said, his tone softening a bit, "I mean, who he *really* is. He is the oldest son of the only Cosa Nostra boss to have survived his reign in Canada. His five brothers? Two of them remained in the family—another went to the Chicago family, and another works for an outside organization. *Marcus*, though? He's followed right after his father. And knowing what I do about your feelings regarding this life and the mafia, I have to wonder if you really understand what you're doing or if you're just sticking your head in the sand."

"Daddy—"

"I only care that you're happy. And the rest of that all

goes back to being *happy* at the end of the day with the choices you have made."

"I am happy. I'm trying to stay that way. The rest isn't really important right now, is it?"

Or maybe it was just like her father had said, and she was purposely choosing to ignore it. Cella wasn't sure, and right now didn't seem like the time to sit down and figure it all out. Not when she was on her way to Toronto to see Marcus, spend the weekend with him, and if the truth was told, very little of it would be spent doing *work*.

"I know why you're worried," she said before her father could say anything more, "but right now I'm just trying to figure out what I even want here."

"He is not immune because he's a made man, Cella."

"What?"

"From being hurt—getting his heart broken. Just because he's a made man doesn't mean he doesn't have *feelings* here. So, while you figure out what you want, please remember that there are more people than just you in the equation. If you're being selfish for the first time in your life, then that's okay … but self-seeking doesn't always have to mean harmful to those around you."

Cella let out a slow breath. "Okay."

"Just okay?"

"I'll keep it in mind, Daddy."

"And look out for your heart, too. It's taken enough of a beating … it's time to take care of it, now."

* * *

The most relaxed Cella had ever remembered seeing Marcus was when he pulled open the door of a three-level home tucked away in a gated suburb just outside of Toronto's city limits. In a pair of gray sweatpants and a white T-shirt that he'd rolled up the sleeves a bit on his shoulders, it was like meeting a whole other man.

Gone was the three-piece suit. His hair had been mussed into a sexy disarray. Everything about him screamed laid-back and *easy*.

"Working out?" she asked him.

Marcus winked her way before dropping down to his knees to greet her daughter standing in front of her on the porch. "Hey, you."

Tiffany managed a tired smile. "That was a *very* long drive."

"I bet. Heard your ma picked you up at your grandparents and then drove here, right?"

"Mmhmm. Like *six hours longer*."

Cella laughed.

"Should really start flying instead of driving," Marcus told her girl.

As though *Tiffany* made the choice.

"Should tell my ma that," the girl returned.

Marcus nodded, running his tongue along his teeth and sucking in air at the same time like he was considering that statement. "You know what, maybe I'll just buy the tickets and send them over, huh?"

"That won't be needed," Cella spoke up.

The damn man—looking entirely too sexy and tempting where he kneeled—glanced up at her with a grin that told her tonight would be very fun for the two of them. Or maybe it was that glint in his eye when his gaze took her in, slowly drifting down her body and lingering in all the right spots before his attention went back to Tiffany.

Yep.

Definitely missed him.

"Well," Marcus said to Tiffany, "how does some popcorn and a movie sound? I think it'll help you fall asleep, and then tomorrow you'll be ready for all the stuff we're gonna do this weekend, *oui*?"

"What movie?"

"It's on the TV, you just have to press play on the remote to get it started. The Princess and the—"

"*Yes*." Tiffany didn't even wait for Marcus to finish before she pushed past him to go inside the house. He laughed as he stood. Cella had a good mind to correct her daughter, but the girl was already shouting, "Thanks for remembering, Marcus!"

Cella's confused expression wasn't lost on Marcus because he turned to her with a shrug, explaining, "That first time I talked with her on the phone—"

"At the hotel?"

"Yeah … she told me all her favorite things. The movie was one of those."

And he remembered.

Just because, apparently.

She decided to go for a change in topic. "I thought you stayed at a place in the city?"

"Most of the time," he replied, "but this is my *private* residence that a lot of people don't know about except family, and I'm trying to lay low for a bit."

Cella wasn't sure if she liked the sound of that. "Why?"

"Just let me worry about those details."

What did that mean?

Marcus flashed her with a confident smile as he stuffed his hands into the pockets of those loose-fitting sweatpants, and stepped to the side a bit as if to let her into his house. "So, you coming in, too, or are you going to keep standing there like you're not sure if I might bite you?"

Cella gave him a look. "You don't *bite*."

He winked. "Not unless you ask nicely, anyway."

Hell.

There went her panties. Just like the rest of her was gone, too. All because of this wickedly attractive man, and the draw he seemed to have on her.

"You're dangerous for my heart," she told him before stepping past him into the house.

Marcus followed behind, and when she peeked over her shoulder, she found him watching her with an intensity that had her fine hair standing on end for all the right reasons. "*And?*"

He said that as though it wasn't a problem.

Damn.

Maybe it wasn't.

* * *

"Did you mean what you said earlier?"

Cella dragged in a quick breath, because the second she'd closed her *now sleeping* child's bedroom door, Marcus murmured those words against the back of her neck as he stepped in behind her. Her fingers tightened around the knob, a thrill running through her because oh, yes, every single part of her body hadn't forgotten what this gorgeous man could do to it.

"How do you know she's asleep in there?"

"Because you don't seem like the type of mother who would leave her child to fall asleep in a new place when she seemed nervous about it not an hour ago after you told her it was time for bed."

Jesus.

He'd noticed that?

Tiffany tried to hide it, clearly not wanting to make Marcus think she didn't like his house or even *him*, but Cella knew her child better than anyone. So, without saying a thing to him about it, she promised her girl that he wouldn't feel badly, but they didn't have to mention it, and she would stay with her until Tiff fell asleep.

Kids were all about compromise.

It worked.

As quickly as those thoughts of her daughter drifted through her mind, they were just as fast about flying away with his next touch.

Marcus pressed a soft, hot kiss to the back of her neck, just below her hairline where she'd pulled the strands up into a messy chignon. The comfortable dress blouse and *thin* leggings she'd worn to drive in leaving nothing but the thick line of his erection pushing into her backside while his fingers flexed at her waist.

Cella had been tired.

Eight hours *plus* of driving?

Yeah, she was done for the day.

But not now.

Now she was wide awake.

"Okay, so she *is* sleeping in there," Cella said quietly, "but we should move before you do something that wakes her back up. Nothing like a kid to cock block—"

"*Mmm.* Good point."

As fast as he said that, Marcus snagged Cella's wrist in this strong hand, and dragged her away from the door. The hallway became a blur of colors as the two of them flew down to the last door on the left. His bedroom, she would guess, for the quick moment she was able to admire the cherry oak furniture making up a four-poster bed and matching dressers. The only other thing she was able to get a peek at was the large chandelier hanging over the bed before her back hit the wall, and Marcus clouded her vision.

So fucking tall.

She loved that she had to look up at him.

"Now, will you answer me?" he asked.

Cella blinked, the strength of her desire for this man surprising even her when she tried to clear the haze in her mind. "Answer *what*?"

"What I asked—did you mean what you said earlier?"

"What did I say?"

"When you got here. That I'm dangerous."

Cella licked her lips, saying, "For my heart."

"Yeah, *that*."

"I don't say things I don't mean, Marcus."

His gaze dropped to her mouth as he said, "Good. But you should know there's no reason to worry about your heart here, Cella."

A breath caught in her chest.

Why, she almost asked, *because you're not here for my heart*?

His next words came too fast for her to say anything at all. "I couldn't hurt your heart—wouldn't even try. Besides, I might like to keep it."

Why would he say that?

Words like those made it hard for her to protect the heart in her chest. She wasn't sure if she was ready to give it over to him quite yet. He saved her from having to make a choice right then and there by kissing her instead of saying anything else.

He fucked like he kissed, she had come to learn. With no restraint, and totally willing to take every single bit of her that she was willing to give him. Wild or not, soft or so rough … any of it, he would take. Their lips moved in a familiar dance, tongues slashing together for just another taste while the two of them began shedding clothes.

One piece at a time.

Lips only parting when necessary.

Before Cella had met Marcus again, whenever she thought about *dating* … these moments that she shared with this man had been the kind of thoughts that would freeze her with fear. Her body had changed after her child, and while she was proud to get it back to the trim state it had been before, that didn't mean everything was the same. Silly and vain, maybe, but with dating and relationships came *sex*.

Truth be told, she never worried with Marcus.

Never even thought about it.

It made her realize that it wasn't the faded, few white lines on her tummy that scared her, or even the fact that her hips were slightly wider from carrying a child, but rather … the fact she just hadn't been ready to be intimate again with someone.

Except now she was …

Didn't even have to think about it.

That's what this man did for her.

She adored him more because of it.

Marcus's hands slid up over her hips, over her waist, atop her breasts, and then came to a stop at her throat. Those deft fingers of his circled the column, making her heart thrum harder against his palms. She didn't have to wonder if he liked the feeling of making her heart race. She could see it in his eyes that he did.

All that was between them now was a bit of air, and she closed that distance easily enough when she circled his cock with her palm. The first stroke of her hand along his pulsing length had him jerking closer to her. The second brought him close enough that he flattened her back against the door again while his hard lines molded against her feminine curves.

One of his hands slipped higher on her throat, coming to rest on her jaw as his thumb dragged over the pad of her lower lip. The urge to suck on the tip of his thumb came on swift, and his approving groan echoed in the bedroom when she dragged the digit between her teeth to get a taste of his skin.

"There's something about the look of you like this," he told her.

Hungry.

Rough.

That's what his tone sounded like.

He spoke even while she continued tugging on his cock, and rubbing him against her body while she tried, and failed, to help with her own need. Nothing would help with that until he was between her thighs and making her pray in a whole new way.

"Oh?" she whispered.

"Mmhmm, when you let me put these hands on that pretty throat, and you look so fucking close to begging when I haven't done barely anything at all. It's … perfect."

"Would you like me to beg?"

Marcus's lips titled upward in one corner, that wicked smirk of his making her ache between her legs in a way she would never be able to soothe. "I would—yes."

Cella didn't even have to think about it.

Not really.

The words slipped out so easily.

"I want you to fuck me, Marcus. *Please*, fuck me."

She dragged in a lungful of his unique scent, her mouth watering from what she was sure would come next, but he always had a way of surprising her. This time wasn't any different, but a thrill shot through her all the same when he replied, "Once you get on your knees and *show me* how badly you want me to fuck you, then we'll see what I can do for you, *mia tesoro*."

Her hand stilled on his cock. He pressed a fleeting kiss to her lips. His grip on her finally loosened when she lowered to her knees in front of the closed bedroom door, but only so that he could press his palms to the wood as she took the tip of his cock into her mouth. The taste of salt and man hit her tongue, the soft skin on the underside of his length throbbing from the pulsing vein there when she took him deeper into her throat.

"Fucking *hell*," he uttered.

Cella would have smiled.

Her mouth was a bit *busy*.

He let her toy with him just long enough to get his hands shaking when he let go of the door to thread his fingers through her hair. She stilled, feeling the way he struggled to keep still when she took him right down to the very root of his cock.

"*God*, Cella … that mouth of yours, woman. I'd start wars for that mouth."

She could see when he lost his sense of decorum—all that control he prided himself on left in a flurry of his clenched teeth, and the harsh curse that left his lips. It took nothing more than her dragging her mouth up his cock again, only this time she used her teeth to tease, too.

A man who lost control was the best kind, though. She found with him, it's what she liked the very most. It was why when he dragged her away from his cock, and up from the hardwood floor, all she could think about were those hands of his pulling and grabbing and *wanting*. So rough, and unforgiving in the way he pulled her to the bed.

Shit.

She didn't even make it entirely *to* the bed.

Marcus bent her over the side of the bed with no gentleness to his movements. That only made Cella want him even more. There was something about the fact he didn't treat her like precious china when he fucked her that made her so damn wet and crazy.

Speaking of wet …

"Fuck," Marcus said, his approval coming out in a rumbling moan when his hand slipped between her thighs to find her pussy that she'd already spread open for him to be slick. "So needy, this pussy—you feel that, Cella?"

"*Yes.*"

Each drag of his fingertips against the slit of her pussy had her clenching for him.

"You have no fucking idea how much I thought about this pussy of yours. How often I wanted to be fucking it or eating it. All the goddamn time. I woke up hard because of you for *weeks*. All I could think about was the way your pussy looked when my cock was stretching it out, and all those pretty sounds you make when you're coming for me. Is that what you want again?"

She was shameless, now.

Rubbing her pussy back against him.

"More than you know."

Marcus chuckled. "Oh, I know."

He leaned sideways, but she didn't notice it as much because he slipped two fingers into her pussy at the same time a drawer creaked. Just as fast, he hovered over her back again, those lips of his ghosting over her trembling shoulder when foil pressed into the curve of her ass.

"Get your fingers inside your pussy and fuck yourself while I put this on, yeah?"

She did, surprised at how hot and wet she was, the sounds of her arousal turning her on even more as her fingers slipped in to take the place of his before he withdrew his own digits. That brief second of being filled with her own fingers and his had Cella moaning for more.

He didn't waste time giving her exactly that.

Just long enough to get that condom on.

"Rub one out while you sit on me, and then I'll fuck

another one out of you before you can ride me until you can't breathe. How does that sound?"

Cella let out a shaky breath, her fingers already pulled out of her slit to pull all that wetness up to her clit, so she could rub fast circles into the bud. "Like you're going to make me too tired to even dream."

The head of his cock filled her.

It wasn't nearly enough.

It still took her breath away.

"Yeah, that's the plan."

He thrust all the way in, then.

His cock filled her full.

Stretched her open.

Her fingers stilled at her clit as he worked in and out of her for just long enough to have her shaking all over while she shuddered against the bed. He was so—each stroke he made deliberate and not nearly enough to get her off.

Which she was sure was the point.

Then he yanked her brutally onto his length, stilling all at once while his fingertips flexed hard enough along her ass that he stretched her open and made her whine. She was sure there would be bruises there in the morning, and yet the thought only made her hotter.

"Now, you can get yourself off," she heard him say.

That permission …

She hadn't realized that's what she'd been waiting for. Although as soon as she had it, there was no going back, and she couldn't even have stopped if she wanted to try.

Cella did exactly what he told her, drowning in the sound of his dark promises while he rubbed at her clit. He did nothing but hold her body tight to his cock. Entirely filled with him, she trembled through the first orgasm of the night.

"There's my girl, huh?" He met her gaze when she threw

a desperate look over her shoulder, but then his hands landed to her body even tighter than before. A hand to her shoulder, and one to her hip. With no warning, and deep enough to surely leave her sore though she loved it, he started fucking her with earnest. She hadn't even finished panting through that orgasm. "Now you're going to do it for me again—and all you have to say is, *please, Marcus.*"

She couldn't breathe.

It didn't even matter.

"*Please, Marcus.*"

He fucked her to a harder, *longer* second orgasm. He didn't even have to tell her to beg for a third. She was all too willing.

CHAPTER 9

"Is it going to be a long drive?" Tiffany asked.

Marcus didn't miss the roll of her eyes and the smile Cella shot his way. No doubt, Tiffany was worried the drive they were taking from the suburbs to the city would be like the over eight-hour drive she'd taken the day before with her mother.

"Not very long—an hour, depending on the traffic."

"An hour is sixty minutes, right, Ma?"

Cella nodded. "That's right."

And given it was the weekend, most of the work rush happened during the week, not to mention it was only seven-thirty in the morning, he doubted traffic would be horrible. They'd make it to the city in no time, and he suspected the drive would be a lot better for Tiffany than yesterday had been. Also, he was serious on just *buying* Cella plane tickets.

That was next in his plans.

Added to *the list*.

Cella stared up at the bright, early June sun as she slid a pair of large sunglasses over her face. "You know, there's a portion of Americans who believe Canada is cold all year round."

"No, they don't."

"Yes, they do."

Marcus's brow knotted. "Really?"

"Yes—but this heat is about to kill me."

He laughed and put a hand to the small of her back before slipping his other in with Tiffany's to walk them both down the stairs of his front porch. As always, his gaze scanned the street as he directed the girls toward the waiting SUV in front of the two-door garage that was currently closed, just in case. Habit, really, and while only his family knew he used the house in the suburbs when he needed to get away for a time, that didn't mean word couldn't get out.

Considering the biker gang was still reeling over the hit Marcus had gotten his men to put out on their president— he figured what better lesson than *that*—he still needed to be extra cautious. Nothing said the club knew about his house in the suburbs, so that was why he decided this would be the best place for Cella and Tiffany to be while they were here, and the nonsense with the gang worked itself out.

As for the hit?

That lesson?

It went through successfully.

Marcus's hope was that would be the last message he needed to make where the bikers were concerned. They could now focus their efforts on picking a new president to run their chapter, stay the fuck out of Guzzi business, and hope-fully come to an understanding that they were never going to be invited to sit at the table with him in business.

But what did he know?

The fuckers had surprised him before.

So, he wasn't taking risks.

At least, not while Cella was in town with her daughter. He didn't want his business touching them. Not if he could help it.

The enforcer that kept an eye on his house had taken the SUV out of the garage that morning at Marcus's direction, but the man was nowhere in sight as he helped Cella to transfer Tiffany's booster seat from her vehicle to his. Once the girl was buckled into her seat in the back behind Marcus's driver seat, he and Cella rounded the back of the SUV to put the bag in the rear hatch.

He took his chance to kiss her, then. To push her against the back of the closed hatch after they'd tossed the bag in and wrap his hands around her trim waist while he got a taste of whatever lip balm she'd smoothed over those plump lips of hers that morning. Her soft gasp was swallowed by his lips working against hers, and when she opened that sweet mouth of hers, he didn't waste time deepening the kiss.

Cella's fingers twisted into the dress shirt stretching across his chest, and he slowed them down just enough to press two fast kisses to her lips before he pulled away with a ragged breath. The very last thing he wanted to do was stop touching this woman—she had quickly become an addiction of his that he was more than happy to feed—but someone else was waiting in the car, and he couldn't forget that, either.

"Okay, now we gotta get in the car," he muttered.

"After that, huh?"

Marcus grinned. "I've been waiting all morning to kiss you like that."

Her expression softened. "Thanks for thinking about her … you know?"

"Of course."

Did she expect anything different from him?

Marcus understood something *big* was happening here with Cella, but he also knew she had to think about her child. And the decisions she made for that girl weren't choices he had any say in, or could even share his opinion about, really. She did, however, allow him to be around her daughter, to bring her here, and that meant she trusted him.

He wasn't going to abuse that.

He certainly wasn't going to confuse the kid about what was happening between her mother and him. Those were things for Cella to explain how and when she wanted to. He wouldn't speed it up by the kid seeing things she was too young to understand.

Simple as that.

"Care to tell me what these plans of yours are for us this weekend?"

Marcus smirked, and pulled Cella away from the SUV's hatch. Walking them around the side of the vehicle, he took the time to peek in the rear passenger window to find Tiffany was still fully engrossed in the movie her mother had put on her tablet to watch. "Well, we're going to start with breakfast at a *very* kid-friendly business my mother loves to take the kids to, and then we're going to go from there."

"Yes, but *where* are we going?"

"Let me have a little fun, Cella."

She passed him a look as they came up to the passenger side of the front, and he pulled open the door with a wink that had her shaking her head. She looked damn good standing in his driveway in a summer dress that was just loose enough to let the breeze flow through the fabric, but still fitted enough for him to admire all her curves. Those curves he'd spent the night *adoring*. As she deserved. Her scant makeup gave her cheeks a bit of color, and the sunglasses hid her blue eyes though he could tell by the way her lips turned upward that she was more than enjoying his staring.

Good.

He loved to stare at her.

And so much more, too.

But he'd get back to those thoughts later.

Today was about them, and fun.

"Just trust me," he said.

Cella sighed. "I guess I don't have a choice, hmm?"

"Tiffany will have a blast."

"Is it going to tire her out?"

"Oh, absolutely."

Her laughter soothed the ache in his chest. A new thing he noticed whenever Cella was near, but he wasn't touching her. Something else for him to obsess over, even though he was sure that was anything but healthy.

Oh, well.

This was much more fun.

"Was that purposeful on your part?"

Marcus cocked a brow. "Pardon me?"

"Make sure my kid was good and tired so you could have me all to yourself for the evenings?"

"Not particularly, but if things work out in my favor that way, are you really going to complain?"

The prettiest red flush heated her cheeks, but Cella didn't act the least bit ashamed when she replied, "Definitely not going to complain, Marcus."

"Get in the car," he told her. "Because I'm trying very hard to remain a gentleman, Cella, but you make it hard, *cara mia*."

"You have a way with words, but I'm sure you know that."

"*Get in the car, woman.*"

She did, laughing the whole way. Marcus certainly tested his limits and enjoyed teasing Cella when he could, but the woman knew how to give it back to him just as strong. He liked that a little too much for his own good, really.

Just before he rounded his side of the vehicle, the phone in his pocket buzzed.

Again.

The tenth time, at least, this morning.

Marcus had cleared his schedule for the weekend, and made sure everybody that needed to know *did*. He didn't want anybody calling unless there was no other choice because the boss had to be involved in whatever emergency came up. Still, it annoyed him like nothing else to pull the cell phone out, and see his brother's number on the screen.

Chris, that was.

There was no way, on Saturday of all days, the first day of his weekend, something had already gone wrong. Marcus ignored the call. He had better things to do and other people to take care of for the moment.

Like the woman staring at him from the passenger seat, waiting.

And the little girl in the backseat.

Chris would understand.

If not, well then, he'd get over it.

*　*　*

"Christopher, if someone isn't dead to explain why you're calling my phone every ten minutes when you *know* I have other things to handle this weekend—"

"Thanks for finally picking up," his brother replied cheerfully, although still managing to sound sour at the same time.

Marcus scowled, pinching the bridge of his nose but remembering where he was at the same time. He had just enough sense to turn his back to the indoor playground where he'd brought Tiffany to burn off all her energy once their breakfast crawled closer to noon. The place sported entire climbing gyms, trampolines, rock walls, ball pools, and far more. It was even big enough for the adults to get in and play with the kids, if they wanted.

Exactly what a high energy child like Tiffany needed to burn off energy. All his other plans for her and Cella would happen tomorrow, but he figured this would be enough for the girl to have lots of fun today, anyway.

"You're really testing my patience lately," Marcus warned.

His brother chuckled dryly. "Same, man."

"You know, I'm almost positive Papa never had as much trouble with his intended underboss or consigliere that I have with you sometimes."

"Nah, you're just in a mood and I'm not here for your shit, Marcus, that's all."

Jesus Christ.

Yes, that's what he needed.

Jesus.

To save him from killing his brother.

"Don't you think," Chris started to say, annoying Marcus even more with just his tone alone, "that if I was calling all morning, it might mean there was something going on that I wanted to bring to your attention?"

"What did I say about this weekend?"

"Marcus—"

"No, my bit is important, Chris."

"So is mine!"

"I am sure whatever it is, it could have waited for Monday."

"Oh, you think? Because I'm not so sure. And pretty soon, I suspect word is going to get back to Papa about all this shit going on, and then neither one of us will be very happy. Hmm?"

Fuck.

He had a point.

"I just want the weekend," he told his brother. "That's it. Why can't I have it?"

"Because the boss never gets a day off, man. Welcome to *la famiglia*—you're in, and there isn't any way out."

Yeah.

Didn't Marcus know it?

"Whatever it is, it's that important that you want to bring it to my attention?" he asked quietly.

"I wouldn't have called otherwise, okay? I know you're … doing your thing with the chick from New York, and all."

"She has a name."

"I know her name, Marcus," Chris replied, "and I also know that whenever someone brings her up to you, you get defensive as fuck like you need to protect her. You know where she comes from, right? Her father was the underboss to—"

"I know who her father is, thank you."

"Just saying."

"Tell me what the issue is, Chris."

Before I get annoyed again.

Marcus was dangerously close to just hanging up the phone, but as annoyed as Chris made him sometimes—and he swore he loved his brother to fucking death—the man also wasn't stupid. Just like him, his brother had been raised in this life, too. He knew how to act, and what was expected of him when it came to his boss, brother or not.

"I have it on good sources that the vice president took over after the whole … death of their president thing," Chris replied.

"Please tell me that's not your breaking news I just *had* to know."

Because frankly, Marcus expected that outcome. He'd simply hoped that the lesson of the Guzzi boss ordering the hit on the president of the motorcycle club would be enough to teach the vice president that they were no longer playing games here. The Guzzis were done entertaining their bullshit, and they needed to move on.

"No, that's not all."

"Keep going then, keep my interest."

"Could you cut the attitude?"

Marcus thought about it.

For all of two seconds.

"No, not particularly."

"You're fucking insufferable."

"And you're wasting my time."

"The sources say the VP has been making calls—all across Canada, apparently."

"I don't follow."

"To other chapters around the country, Marcus. Calling in for help, basically. From what I understand, he's been saying you ordered the hit on their chapter's president without provocation."

"That's bullshit," Marcus snapped, "and anyone here involved with the business would know it, too."

Hell, the entire reason he ordered that hit was because the bikers kept coming back for more. Their provocations against the Guzzis became progressively more and more violent and problematic until they gave him no other choice *but* to act against them. No boss in this position, but especially one who was only the *acting* boss, wanted to find themselves in a war with a rival in a nearby city.

And yet, they forced his hand.

He wouldn't pay more for that.

Absolutely not.

Now his patience was running thin for an entirely different reason. Either the bikers were just incredibly stupid, or far too confident for their own good. A hit from the mob on one of their people should have been more than enough to end this little problem. And yet, it only made the assholes look for yet *another* way to use it to go against the Guzzi family.

"They're trying to get others to ride in, I guess," Chris said, "a bigger threat in numbers, and all that. There's a very good chance that it'll work, too, considering the way the chapters tend to band together with one another when business is threatened. The chapter in Quebec isn't that big of a threat to us, Marcus, but the club as a whole … that's a different story."

"Or we'll put word through for a warning against anyone coming into Ontario or Quebec with the intention to go against the Guzzis means they have signed their death warrants. Dad has had good relations with the clubs across Canada for years. That's not going to change just because the fucks in Quebec have a problem."

"Already planned to do that, but—"

"I'm not entertaining these people anymore, Chris. Do you know what their plan is for sure?"

"Not particularly."

"Okay, well let me know when you do, then."

"Marcus, this is important."

"No, it's inevitable, and you know what my plan B is for them. We went with plan A, and so if it didn't work, we wait until they force me into plan B. Otherwise, there's nothing else I care to do or say here with them. They're *playing games*, and bosses don't do that. I don't sit down at the table to play games with someone else, not when I have better things to do."

Marcus sighed, his brother waiting for him to finish whatever he planned to say, but otherwise staying quiet. For once in their whole conversation. He appreciated that. Turning a bit to stare over his shoulder, he just caught sight of Tiffany running across a netted, wobbly bridge while her mother chased after her.

He would much rather be *there* … with them.

That was the whole point of this day.

Still, he went back to his conversation, hoping Cella hadn't noticed his distraction with his phone because she was too busy attending to her daughter. "Listen," he told his brother, "I'm a young, *new* boss—they're just seeing how far they can push, and that's all. I bet it'll be the same shit with anyone that rolls into town thinking they're going to go on a row with us. Everyone has to see how far they can get with a new boss before he pushes back. If they continue with the plan to bring people into town, and they step over the lines we've drawn, then we go to plan B, Chris. My stance isn't changing on that."

"Plan B is a mess, Marcus."

"Yeah, well …"

What could they do?

"How do you plan to get away with wiping out an entire *chapter*, huh?"

"Well, we're not there yet, so let's worry about it if we have to cross that bridge."

"If, or *when*?" Chris asked quietly.

Yeah, that was a good question.

And not one he had an answer to, either.

"Marcus, come play!"

Glancing over his shoulder, he found Tiffany waving to him from the tallest tower of the indoor play gym. Behind her in the small window, Cella winked his way and smiled. To his brother, Marcus replied, "*If*, Chris, not when. It is always *if* because, despite who we are and the things we do in this business that make us bad, we are still honorable where it counts. And so that means we give people the chance to correct their wrongs before we act against them for what we assume they might do to us."

"You sound just like Dad."

Well, he'd learned from the best, hadn't he?

"Call me back if you learn more," Marcus said.

"Will do. Enjoy your weekend—although I'll see you tomorrow at the mansion, hmm?"

"We'll be there."

"Her, too?"

Marcus smiled. "Yes, her too."

Once the two said goodbye, he hung up the phone and pocketed the device even though he didn't turn it off. He wouldn't be ignoring anymore of his brother's calls, but he suspected Chris wouldn't call back unless he had no other choice, either.

Coming to stand next to the large piece of play equipment, Marcus glanced upward and smiled at the two ladies looking down at him. "Now, how exactly am I supposed to get up there?"

Cella looked all too pleased with herself when she replied, "The same way we did—climb, jump, and *crawl* your way up."

"You think I won't?"

"In that silk shirt and those pressed pants, Marcus? I don't know."

She made a disbelieving noise to go along with her statement.

"How little faith you have in me, *mon amour.*"

A little play didn't scare him, and his godson—along with the rest of his nieces and nephews—had taught him when it came to kids and fun, fuck all else mattered. You were going to get dirty, you would be tired, and it would still be fun.

Marcus glanced up, and gave Cella a wink before he headed into the domed entrance of the play gym. He heard Tiffany's accompanying happy shout—her celebration that he agreed to join them. He also hadn't missed that softness in Cella's stare, either.

It almost haunted him.

Even though he liked it.

That look on her face?

It spoke of falling in love; of being *ready* to fall. But with the fall came a crash. *And God,* he knew that feeling all too well now because of her.

He still wondered … would there be a crash?

She liked this man she saw *now*, but would she like the same man if she knew he had just been on the phone planning the slaughter of a rival organization?

Because those two men? This one she liked, and the one she didn't know? They were the same.

Marcus wasn't sure if she understood that, though.

And he was too much of a coward to ask.

CHAPTER 10

"I know this wasn't part of the plan for this weekend, but—"

Marcus laughed, using the arm that wasn't busy holding a tired Tiffany over his shoulder to pull Cella closer to his side as they rode the elevator higher to his mother and father's penthouse. She peered up at him, her lips tilting upward in her happiness before he dropped a kiss to the crown of her head. Those lashes of hers fluttered shut while he lingered there, not even pulling back from the kiss as he murmured, "No worries, it's fine. I'm happy to do whatever you want while you're here. Even if what you want to do is work."

Her eyes popped open again. "I just want to … *envision*."

"I have no idea what you're *envisioning*."

His teasing wasn't missed. She smacked his stomach with the back of her hand, giving him a look at the same time. All he gave her in response to that was a shrug and a grin. What more could he do?

He found that teasing this woman was a form of foreplay in and of itself. She might not realize it, but he certainly did and he didn't plan to give it up anytime soon.

Or her …

He wasn't sure he wanted to give her up, either.

"What's that for?" she asked softly.

Marcus's brow lifted. "What's what for?"

"That look."

"What look?"

He knew exactly what she meant, but fuck it if he wasn't still a man at the end of the day with more pride than brains sometimes. There was also that whole fear of being vulnerable to someone else, he supposed. It was hard for him to let down that wall, even if everything about Cella screamed it was safe for him to do exactly that.

"When you just … stare at me," she said, reaching up to cup the side of his cheek with her palm. The warmth of her skin soaked into his, and he was more caught up in that feeling than anything else at the moment. "Your eyes soften, you just smile, and I wonder what's going on in your head when you do it."

"You see all that when I'm staring at you, hmm?"

"Yes."

Marcus nodded. "When I stare at *you* …"

Cella's gaze stayed locked on his, and Marcus winked the longer she stayed quiet. Because frankly, she had answered her own question, and he didn't think she really needed for him to add his own explanation. Not when it was obvious.

He looked that way when he stared at her because it was her.

And she was amazing.

Cella let loose a quiet sigh, her gaze breaking away from his as her throat flexed with a swallow. Her attention went to the girl that was still snoring lightly away on Marcus's shoulder, and her smile grew a bit wider. "She must be getting heavy."

"Not really."

"She doesn't usually sleep so hard—I think today really tired her out."

"Good. And she had fun, so that's what matters."

"Too much fun, maybe," Cella replied, snorting under her breath.

"No such thing as too much fun, Cella."

"Have you never seen a toddler that's had just *too much*? Too much sugar, or stimulation … whatever? They're like—"

"Little monsters on steroids, yes I know. I have nieces and nephews, one of which is my godson who I take on the weekends pretty regularly to give his mother and father a break. He was named after me, but we mostly just call him Marc."

"Right, I met them at the dinner party."

Marcus grinned. "Mmhmm, so I do know. I just think they're only kids once. And they're little, so they don't understand. Is it really their fault if the adults around them indulge them too much? Can they be blamed, then?"

"The kids must love you, huh?"

"*Well …*"

Basically, yeah.

Cella's gaze drifted back to her daughter as she said, "You know, she's not forgotten at all that you promised to take her to a maple syrup farm. In fact, she mentions it at least once a day."

"I'll take her. We have a farm in Eastern Ontario that is actually open to the public, so people can do tours and whatnot. We're not in the season right now, won't be for a while, but they have a small staff that keeps certain things open for tourism in the summer. She can still see the basics, even if she won't be able to tap a tree and see it all from start to finish. I'm working on it. And then when we are in the maple season, I'll take her out again, so she can do everything that she wants."

Cella cleared her throat, quieting.

Marcus didn't miss it. "Did I say something wrong?"

"When is the season?"

"Beginning of the year."

"It's summer now."

"And?" he asked.

Cella looked his way. "I just … you expect we're going to be around then?"

Oh.

Yeah.

He knew what he said, now.

"I certainly hope so, Cella."

There.

It was out there.

No taking it back.

Cella wet her lips and glanced up at the lights above the elevator illuminating floor levels that said they were almost to the penthouse. "Me too, Marcus."

Shifting the girl on his shoulder so that her little head tucked into his neck better for cushion, Marcus added, "And tomorrow, Ma is having all the grandkids over. She's planned this for two months, making sure everybody and their brood could come and have a summer party. It's not often she gets all of them together like that. I thought Tiffany would have a lot of fun, and you, too, with the rest of us."

"Was that the second surprise?"

"I mean, I couldn't tell my mother no because you were coming, and I wasn't willing to tell you not to come this weekend because she had something planned. Tiffany will have fun with all the kids, and I know my mother will be *very* happy to see you there with me. My brothers will certainly drive me up the wall because at least one of them has a big mouth, and he knows something is happening here with you and me—Chris, that is. My father will be there to keep everyone in line, as he usually does. A pretty typical Guzzi gathering. I figured it just worked."

Cella laughed. "It definitely works, Marcus."

The elevator jerked before finally coming to a stop at the top floor. Doors slid open to welcome them into the penthouse, which already looked far different from how it used to. Even the entry hallway with its high, vaulted ceiling was bare of furniture, photographs, and the other artwork that had given it life, even if it was an *old* life.

A lot of the items that had filled the penthouse before were already removed. He'd been here when the team of movers Cella had hired were first granted access to the place to begin the process of taking out the old to get it ready for the new. A lot of it went into storage for his parents to decide what to do with after the surprise was finally revealed. Some of it, like cabinetry and appliances, had already been given the okay from his father to be sold or donated as they wouldn't need it for anything.

"You go do what you're going to do," he told her as they stepped into the penthouse, "envision, or whatever else, and I'll find a place for this one to lay down."

Cella nodded, standing up on her tiptoes in her ballet flats to press a kiss to the back of her daughter's head. Just as fast, she gave Marcus a quick kiss, too.

"Some of the furniture for the living room was already delivered, right?"

"All under plastic until your team comes in to do their thing."

"Perfect," she said, "then just put her there."

"That was the plan. Now, go work."

She did.

Marcus watched her go.

* * *

Marcus carefully pulled the plastic wrap away from the cream-colored leather piece of the sectional that would undoubtedly take up a good portion of the living room area in the penthouse once it was all put together properly. The damn thing was huge. It came in *six* pieces. How Cella managed to find something that big, he didn't know.

It was a good choice, though.

It would comfortably sit fifteen or more people, and considering how big his family was when they all got together and they all used this penthouse frequently when one of his brothers from out of the country came to visit, it would work well for their needs. The leather, which as far as he knew was going to be treated once the couch was ready to be set up, would take a beating from the kids and many people that would use it. Stains wouldn't be a worry when any liquids would roll right off it, and the light color scheme matched the white walls Cella decided to keep in the space to go along with the large floor-to-ceiling windows that allowed in all the light.

And right now, the piece of the couch served his purpose of finding somewhere comfortable and safe for Tiffany to sleep. Once the plastic was discarded to the floor, he slowly laid the still-snoring girl to the couch, cautious about not making too much movement or noise lest he wake her up. It *had* been a long day for her going from one thing to another in the city, never complaining but always wide-eyed and ready to have more fun with whatever Marcus had planned for her.

Shrugging off the blazer he'd brought along for the day just in case, he used it to cover Tiffany while she shifted on the couch to find a better sleeping position she liked. Which apparently just happened to be on her stomach, face turned into the back of the couch, with her hands under her head to act as a pillow. He wasn't sure if that was entirely comfortable, but another thing he'd learned from all the kids in his family was that children could sleep literally anywhere if they were tired enough, and not be any worse for wear because of it.

Once he was sure Tiffany would stay sleeping, he set his phone down on the floor, turning the playlist on with the volume down to low to play through the songs she had seemed to like in the car earlier. At least then, with the place so empty, the echoes of her mother working or their conversations wouldn't wake her up, either.

Marcus went in search of Cella.

He found her in what used to be the master bedroom.

Leaning in the doorway, he admired the new hardwood floors that were far deeper brown with a tone of golden honey throughout the grain. He hadn't seen it since the workers came in to install it, but he liked it.

"The floor turned out good, huh?"

Cella, who was currently standing in the middle of the room with her hands on her hips, turned to face him with a nod. "Yeah, it really did. I'm wondering if it was the right choice now, though, or if I am just thinking crazy things about this space."

He had no idea what she just said.

None at all.

"I'm pretty sure anything you decide to do with this place is something my mother will love for no other reason than *you* designed it, Cella."

Cella laughed. "Right, you mean even if I take her old master bedroom, because it's literally the largest space in this penthouse, and turn it into a playroom with everything and anything a kid could want to go crazy … she would love that?"

Marcus thought about it for all of a second. "Yeah, absolutely."

"Convince me of why, then."

"For a couple of reasons—one, she loves her grandkids, and there's gonna be more in this family, so it'll be put to use for a long time. And two, because we almost died in this room. Me and her, I mean. She's never been able to sleep in it since then, or that's what my father always told me. I know she wanted to change it, but she just got used to using another bedroom whenever she was here. Something like this would really help with replacing those bad memories with something to make new ones."

Cella just stared at him.

Marcus wasn't sure why.

"You almost died in this room?"

Oh.

Yeah, *that*.

CHAPTER
11

"Don't think I'm being blasé about this," Marcus said, "but it happened when I was a very young—still basically brand new, so I don't remember anything about it, and I only know what happened through my father's story. My mother has *never* told me the events through her perspective, and it's an unspoken rule between my father and me that I will never ask her because it was traumatic. It's not something she wants to keep revisiting, and I'm more than good with keeping my mother happy."

Cella swallowed hard, the lump in her throat growing painfully. It nearly kept her quiet, but still, she managed to say, "Sure, okay. I'll keep it in mind."

"My father was married before my mother came along to a woman who had manipulated him into the marriage with lies and a false pregnancy that she later said she miscarried. She had her reasons, apparently, for needing a marriage. Basically, to get away from her situation at home, and she thought using my father would work for that. After they married, she left … for all purposes, my father was separated from his wife for quite a while before my mother came along."

"Except, there's no such thing as divorce in Cosa Nostra, Marcus."

"My mother didn't know he was married."

Cella dragged in a heavy breath. "*Ouch.*"

"Anyway," he said thickly, standing straighter in the doorway and shoving his hands loosely into the pockets of his slacks, "that's their story … but the *wife* came back into the picture because my father took over the family, and circumstances brought her back into the fold. His wife became involved with someone in the family—sexually and otherwise—while my mother was pregnant with me. She then committed suicide but not before making this man believe it was entirely my mother and father's fault. Oh, she was pregnant with the man's child, too, when she did this."

God.

He was wrong.

Marcus thought he would sound indifferent or unbothered but he came off as the exact opposite. Clearly hurt by a past that he didn't even remember and had only heard through other parties involved, it was obvious that it affected him. Or maybe it was the fact that it was something that hurt his parents, and that was why he showed emotion talking about it.

Either way, it killed her.

Cella stayed quiet and let him keep talking.

"The man attacked my mother in this room—I was in a thing that she used for me to sleep on the bed as he beat her and tried to strangle her. He intended to kill me, too. Clearly, he didn't succeed because we're all still here, but that's the story."

The only thing she felt was okay to say?

"I'm sorry."

Marcus shook his head, lifting those broad shoulders of his even as he offered her a thin smile that didn't quite reach his eyes like it usually would. "We've all got a story—our family's is just a little darker sometimes."

Didn't she understand that?

"We're all like that," she assured, "we just keep it to ourselves."

"You think?"

Cella knew it.

Her sister?

Beaten in the back of a limo by an ex who tried to murder her years later.

Her mother?

Practically a slave to a biker gang before her father found her.

All her cousins?

They had stories, too.

Her aunts … uncles. They had theirs to tell as well when they felt like it. It was a big piece of what made their family such a strong unit. They all knew what it was like to need support and love surrounding them in their darkest moments.

"Yeah," she told him, "we all have a story. A past, Marcus, it's part of what makes us who and what we are, and I'm only just starting to learn that, you know? I was never bitter about being born into this life they made for me, but I was never quite sure that it was what I wanted, either. I'm just coming to learn that perhaps I should be grateful about the parts of my life they gave me that I love, and focus less on the pieces that have taken from me when I wasn't willing to give those things."

"People forget, Cella."

Their stares met.

Her still standing in the middle of the room.

Him in the doorway.

"Forget what, Marcus?"

"That everyone sacrifices in this life of ours. *Oh*, we call it the good life, right? And it is when it's good, because then it's so fucking great, but those times make us forget that if we haven't already sacrificed to be these people, then we soon will."

Cella sucked in another lungful of air, her eyes burning from tears she refused to let fall. "I think I've sacrificed enough."

Marcus nodded, and in five long strides, he'd crossed the room to come stand in front of her. His hand found the side of her cheek while his thumb stroked the line of her cheekbone before he pulled her in for a kiss that almost felt like the parts of her heart that were still a little broken had begun to mend again.

Because of him?

This thing they were doing?

Most likely.

She'd deal with it later.

Marcus kissed her one more time, softer although it didn't linger because he held her stare as he said, "I agree, *bella*. You have absolutely sacrificed enough—let yourself be happy now."

* * *

"Ah, Marcus brought you along again, did he?" The dark-haired, blue-eyed man winked at Cella as he leaned over the table on the back terrace of the Guzzi mansion to grab a piece of cut watermelon which he gave to the baby hanging off his hip. "He must really want to keep you if he brought you back for another round with this family, huh?"

"*Alessio*," Cara chided.

Well, *tried*.

The man in question only laughed and shrugged.

"Little bites," he quickly told the baby on his hip with brown eyes that looked nothing like his. They matched the eye color of the man standing next to Ginevra across the back lawn with their toddler daughter dancing in a waterfall of bubbles her uncle, Beni, was currently making for her. Still, Alessio interacted with the child the same way he did the little girl who *did* have blue eyes. "Careful, Lev. Jesus, gonna give Dad a heart attack here."

The baby boy—who recently turned one, according to Cara when the woman filled her in on all her sons' wives and their large brood of children—smiled back at his father with a toothless grin that was filled with chewed up watermelon.

"Gross," Alessio muttered.

"*Gwoss*," the baby repeated.

"Anyway." The man's attention came back to Cara and Cella who were currently working to chop up more fruit for the kids while they waited for the pizza to be delivered to the mansion. "I was kidding, Cara, you know that. And Cella," he added, giving her a smile, "it really is great to see you around again. If Marcus knows what's good for him, we'll see you more often, yes?"

"Okay, you go help with the rest of the kids now," Cara ordered with a laugh.

Alessio did as he was told, chuckling the whole time.

Cella shook her head. "Is he always like that?"

Cara made a noise under her breath. "Depends on the day with Les, really. He's like Corrado, which is maybe why they're such a good fit together, when he has his days. *Moods*, as Gian likes to say. They come and go."

Huh.

Interesting.

Cella stared out across the grass where Ginevra stood up on her tiptoes to press a kiss to the underside of Corrado's cheek. She always figured … someone else's bedroom and life were theirs to do with as they wanted so long as everyone was adults and consenting to what would happen. That didn't mean she wasn't curious about a lot of things.

She didn't want to be ignorant about it, however.

"And how does … is she their wife … or, I guess they both couldn't marry her, right? Is she married to one of them?"

"Ginevra?" Cara asked.

"Yeah."

"Oh, no, uh, Corrado and Les married last year, actually, for legal reasons regarding the children. Mostly because they were concerned if something happened to one of them when only one man's name could be on the birth certificate then it kind of allowed them a loophole for custody reasons. I mean, those are circumstances no one wants to think about but …"

"Necessary in their situation, right?"

Cara nodded. "Exactly. Anyway, the boys married but it wasn't an affair, they didn't want a celebration, and it was Ginevra that suggested it. It happened at the courthouse in New York, Christopher flew in to be a witness for Corrado, and I believe Les asked one of his adoptive fathers to witness for his side."

"They don't wear rings or anything, I noticed."

"Little tattoos. Venn diagrams on each of their index fingers. All three, not just the boys."

Oh.

Well, she hadn't noticed that, either.

Cara glanced her way, asking, "What was the question about Ginevra that you were going to ask me?"

"Just … how does she fit in there, I suppose."

"Perfectly," Cara replied without even thinking about it, "she fits with them perfectly. A good balance to the boys, and I don't think they would be the same today had she not come along."

"Hmm."

Cara grinned a bit. "A little unconventional, I know."

"If it works, and they like it, I love it."

"That's a good way to look at it."

Cella laughed under her breath. "I think a lot of things in this world would be better if people adopted that perspective, but that's just me."

"Well, I don't disagree."

They went back to chopping the fruit, Cara focused on the task, and Cella enjoying the view of the family with all their kids playing together. It was a lot of people to keep up with, but she did her best to try. No one seemed offended if she mixed up one of the kids' names, or something silly like that. Tiffany didn't have any problem at all fitting right in with the rest of them.

Currently, she found her daughter in the middle of the French gravel pathway jumping up and down beside Marcus as he finished tacking up the horse that had been attached to a small carriage. The only animal on the property, Cara had told her, because otherwise, they didn't have enough time in the day to take care of it all and animals deserved love and attention, too.

"He loves taking the kids out for rides," Cara said, noticing her staring at the horse. "Chris had him shipped in from Mexico for Val … Butter, that's his name. He was hers there, and after a bit of negotiating on his part with her sister-in-law, she allowed him to bring the horse to Canada."

"He's beautiful."

"Isn't he?"

"Ma! Come on!"

Cella's attention flew back to her daughter, who was now being lifted into the carriage by Marcus. He turned her way, too, and with a wave of his hand, she knew what they both wanted. So did Cara, it seemed.

"Go ahead," the woman told her, grinning like she didn't mind being left alone to finish slicing the fruit. "Enjoy your day—have fun. That's all we want while you're here with us."

"I don't mind helping."

"I know, but *he* would like to spend time with you, and that matters more to me. Besides, I'm sure you don't want to spend your last day here working to feed all these people, hmm?"

Actually, she didn't mind that at all.

"One ride," she told Cara, "and then I will be back to help you serve the pizza when it gets here."

"You're a very sweet woman, Cella."

So was Marcus's mother.

"Besides," Cara added, "I won't complain about the extra help, *and* it gives me the chance to work on this waiting list of yours that I hear you have for your design clients. How might I get myself to the top of that?"

Cella pointed at the woman, taking a step away from the table. "Ah, now I see what's happening here."

"Go on your ride—you know I'm kidding with you."

She did.

And hopefully, Cara would love what Cella was doing for the penthouse. They were going to have to just wait and see on that one, though.

Cella headed across the grass where Marcus waited next to the carriage, his grin making her own grow the closer she came. Cara had been right about something else, too.

She was leaving tomorrow.

Thing was … she no longer wanted to go.

Life couldn't be easy, though.

It never was.

CHAPTER
12

While the flat screen on the opposite wall to his desk in the office of his home played through the highlight reels of the weekend news for Central Toronto, Marcus sipped on two fingers of cognac on ice and half paid attention. The news was always a good indication about just how much of Guzzi business went under the radar when there were issues. Especially if those issues originated *outside* the organization. Like right now with the bikers.

Of course, with the chapter of the Riders in Quebec being small, the death of the president of said chapter hadn't been a *big* news story when it happened, although it had made the highlight reel.

Now, it wasn't mentioned at all.

And the Guzzis name had never been brought up.

Marcus took all that as a win for him.

Sighing because it had a been a long, busy day but still happy with how it turned out for Cella and Tiffany, Marcus finished that last bit of cognac in the glass. Setting it down to the desk, he picked up the remote for the television and turned the news off. With the screen blank and his home mostly quiet with Cella getting her daughter ready for bed, he tried to decompress a bit.

To put the mafia business aside.

Enjoy his last night with Cella before she went back.

You should just ask her to stay—that's what you want, idiot.

His mind was a special brand of hell tonight.

Turning, Marcus stared out the windows. The first thing that greeted someone when they walked into his office was the large windows that dominated one entire wall of the space. An inky sky overhead twinkled with stars that he couldn't see nearly as well in the city, which was yet another reason why he preferred staying in the suburbs more than he did elsewhere. He waited for Cella to finish up with her child's nighttime routine before she would come to find him.

Then, regardless of what his crazy mind—or was that his heart?—wanted to do, he was going to enjoy his last night with her in Toronto *without* making any demands of her. He wouldn't even speak his wants when frankly, even those could come off as him not thinking about what she might want from all of this.

Surprisingly, it wasn't Cella who found him.

Well, no one really *found* him.

He heard the soft footsteps coming down the upstairs hallway first, and then the tired sniffles echoed the closer the noise came to his office. Turning on his heel, he found the source of the sadness just starting to walk past his open office door.

"Tiff?"

The little girl in her pajamas decorated in pink hearts held a pillow tight to her chest that practically swallowed her in size. It wasn't that she was a tiny child—she was small, yes, but normal for her age and stature. The pillow was just big enough that it seemed she needed both arms to hug it in order to keep a good hold on it.

She sniffled again, tipped her head down to wipe her few tears on the top of her pillow. For a split second, he wondered if maybe she was having another one of those nights where she was afraid because it wasn't her home and bed she had to sleep in.

"Where's your ma?" he asked, taking a couple of steps toward her.

She still didn't come into his office. Shrugging one shoulder, Tiffany said, "Aunt Lucia called, so she went downstairs to talk. I was supposed to be sleeping, but she forgot to get my pillow for me. I didn't mean to rip it, Marcus."

"Rip what, *dolcezza*?"

Tiffany turned the pillow around to show him whatever had her so upset. It looked like any decorative pillow with a cotton case and a design in the middle. Or rather, a logo.

There, in the middle of the pillow overtop a faded band logo that he recognized had been popular a good fifteen years ago or so, was a three-inch long rip.

"Oh," he said, kneeling down. "Come here, let me see it. I'm sure it can be fixed."

Tiffany held even tighter to the pillow, as though she was not going to give it up not even for the world, and didn't move an inch. "I tried to pull it out of Ma's suitcase, and it caught on the zipper. I'm sorry. I wasn't careful like I promised to be."

He didn't understand what the big deal was.

It was just a pillow.

Right?

"Your Ma won't be mad about that, it was just a mistake."

Tiffany dragged in a shaky breath, hugging that pillow as hard as she could to her chest and making the tear open a little more. "Yeah?"

"Of course. Now, if you let me have the pillow, I can fix it for you."

In fact …

He stood up, remembering the small sewing kit he kept in the top drawer of his desk just in case. One never really knew when a thread was going to let go in something, and it had been a useful skill his mother passed onto him. He could easily fix something wrong with an item of clothing, at least to a point where it wouldn't get ruined further before he took it into his tailor.

Soon enough, he found the kit he needed exactly where he'd left it. Coming around the side of the desk again, he waved it for Tiffany to see as he explained, "It'll be good as new for you tomorrow, I promise."

"But …"

"Hmm?"

She squeezed the pillow, new tears starting to form. And *God* … that more than anything else killed him a little bit. He didn't want to see those tears. This sweet little girl who was always so happy, and loved to make everyone else smile, should never be *sad*.

"Don't cry, *bambina*," he murmured, coming to kneel in front of her in the office doorway. "It's not a big deal, just a little rip. I'll fix it, okay?"

"I sleep *with* it."

Oh.

Well, some kids did that, he knew. They found something that they really got attached to, and that was that. For some, it could be a pillow or a bear. Maybe a dolly, or whatever.

"I can bring it into you after, if you want?" he offered.

Tiffany managed a small smile. "Yeah?"

"Absolutely. It'll just take me a bit to get the pillow apart, so I can sew it from the inside where you won't see the seam of the tear. That's all, so you might have to fall asleep without it, but I give you my word you'll wake up with it. How does that sound?"

It took the girl a minute, but eventually, she nodded. Then, with shaking hands, she handed the pillow over to him. The soft cotton of the covering felt warm to the touch, a true testament to how close and tight she'd been holding it.

Marcus looked over the pillow, and the band logo on the front. "Where did you get this from, anyway?"

"My Uncle John." Tiffany brightened when he met her gaze, waiting for her to explain more. "He gave it to Ma when I was a baby—it's my daddy's shirt. Ma put pictures in my room, but I like his pillow shirt the best. I get to hug him and say goodnight. He comes with me everywhere I go."

Well …

That explained so much.

Jesus Christ.

He couldn't imagine the man he might have become without the influence of his father. He couldn't stand to think about the pain that would have caused his mother to lose her husband with a young child in her arms.

"I'm sorry you lost your daddy," Marcus murmured.

"Me, too." She glanced up from the pillow in his hands, meeting his gaze with wide eyes that spoke of knowing and truth when she said, "My daddy would like you, Marcus."

"You think?"

Tiffany nodded. "You make Ma smile. She said he loved to make her smile."

"Huh."

How did one respond to that?

"Take good care of my pillow, please."

He'd not seen the pillow before now. It must have been something Cella kept just between her and her daughter, so he didn't take offense. However, it's significance wasn't exactly lost on him, and all he wanted to do was make it better.

Marcus cleared his throat, refusing to acknowledge the thickness building there when he said, "I will be extra careful with it since it's so important to you. Thank you for trusting me with it."

Tiffany smiled again.

And it made everything better.

* * *

"What are you doing?"

Marcus didn't bother to look up from his current task at Cella's question. He'd known the very second she came to stand in the doorway. It wasn't as though she tried to be quiet, but he suspected she hadn't expected to see him sitting there fixing the item in his hands. And considering the significance of the pillow covering, well, he didn't blame her for needing a moment before she spoke.

Sitting comfortably on the leather chair that faced his desk, he pulled the needle through the delicate cotton fabric. "Fixing Tiffany's pillow—said it caught on the zipper of your luggage when she tried to pull it out. She was quite upset, and I offered to fix it for her."

Cella cleared her throat. "Oh, uh … do you know what that is?"

"A shirt of your husband's that your brother had made into a pillow after he passed, yes. Tiffany explained to me. That's why I am handling it with care, and making sure it gets fixed so that she can wake up with it like I suspect she's always done since you gave it to her. When was that, by the way?"

He glanced up to look at her.

In the doorway, Cella kept eyeing that pillow covering he held, shifting from foot to foot while her throat flexed with every swallow. Clearly chewing on her words, he gave her the moment or two that she needed to gather her thoughts and speak.

"It was very recent after his passing when I got it," Cella managed to say. "But she was older when I gave it to her."

He hated that her voice was so faint.

The memory of pain, he bet, never quite went away.

"Is she sleeping?" Marcus asked. "I heard you go check on her before you came in to see me. I worried she might not fall asleep without the pillow."

"She is sleeping, but she'll appreciate waking up to it."

"Good."

Once more, Cella went quiet as Marcus continued to work. It hadn't been as simple as just sewing the rip together when the shirt had been sewed closed around the pillow as a covering. He'd needed to rip the seam open at the top, pull the covering off before turning it inside out, and then sew the tear. After he finished closing the rip, he'd need to sew the seam he'd ripped open almost entirely closed, but for a couple of inches, stuff the pillow back in, and then finish the seam.

Eventually, Cella joined him, coming into the office to sit on the stool in front of the leather chair. She held the pillow while he worked to close the seam after finishing with the tear. All the while, she said nothing but didn't look away from the item in his hands either as he worked.

He thought … well, he just decided to ask, "It's important to you, too, hmm? The pillow, I mean."

"For different reasons, yes. William only wore suits—part of the job, you know? So on the weekends, he'd wear anything *but* suits. This shirt was one of his favorites. God, it was old. I almost threw it out a few times, but I couldn't. My mom saved it when they cleaned out his things from the house because I couldn't do it. It was in the dirty laundry, so she washed it and my brother took it to have it made into a pillow."

"You said *reasons*, meaning more than one."

Cella sighed. "My brother, I guess. We didn't have a great relationship, and it just felt like when he gave me that, it started to fix something that had been broken for a long time with me and him. I never explicitly said it, and neither did he but it happened. Anyway, Tiff was about two when she started sneaking it off my bed and taking it to her own. I never stopped her. I thought she probably needed it more."

"Cella?"

"Hmm?"

Her gaze lifted to meet his, and while he *hated* when this woman had tears in her eyes, the wetness he found staring back at him let him know every little last thing running through her mind. Both for the things she'd lost, and everything that she was finding *now*.

Was it hard to come second—to be a man who came into a woman's life when she'd already had love taken from her by no choice of her own, leaving her afraid and hurting always?

Yes.

It made this situation between them much more delicate, but he wasn't a fool. He knew these things, and so every step he took with Cella, he kept that in mind. He kept the man who had been here before him in mind because he knew that man was constantly on hers.

"I hope you know," he said quietly, "that I have no intention of trying to replace your husband, or her father. That was never my purpose here, Cella, and it won't be regardless of what happens after today. I don't want to be a replacement for someone who isn't me—what I do hope for, though, is that you'll make space for me here with you. If you can make space for me with you and her, I would be forever grateful."

The shaky exhale that left Cella's trembling lips made her words all the more faint when she asked, "Where did you even come from—I wasn't looking for someone like *you*."

"Sometimes, that's the point. You shouldn't look for the good things, Cella. They should just find you when you need it the most."

"Forever, you said?"

Marcus grinned. "Is that all you heard?"

"It's quite a statement to make."

"Could I have that?" He pointed to the pillow in her hand. "I just have to finish the seam once I put it back in the cover, and you can take it back to Tiffany."

She handed it over, asking, "Who taught you to do something as menial as sewing?"

"My mother."

"I'm not at all surprised."

Marcus laughed. "Yeah, she's quite the woman."

It took him no time at all to finish the pillow. Packing the items from the sewing kit away into its box, he then picked the pillow up from his lap and flipped it over once to show Cella the front with the logo all fixed, and the new seam where he'd fixed the rip was barely visible at all. Someone would *really* need to be looking for it what with the trick he used to repair it.

"Almost perfect," he said.

Cella took the item and shook her head. "No, I think you made it better, Marcus."

"I don't see how—"

"Because you just seem to do that. You've made a lot of things better for me. I don't think I've ever told you that, and I'm sorry because you should know what you've done to and *for* me."

Those words had barely left her mouth before she closed the bit of distance between where she sat on the stool, and him in the chair. Her lips melded to his with a sweet, and yet still hungry intent. Her kiss reminded him that it, better than anything else about her, reflected who Cella truly was. A woman with a heart of gold, sweet as sugar, and yet on the flip side of that same coin she became a woman with determination surrounded by an aura of passion that couldn't quite be tamed but for the one lucky man she would purr for—*him*.

A woman made for him, really.

Who he was.

Who he *needed* to be.

Who he could be with just her alone.

Marcus was not sure how he found that woman.

One like *her*.

He never intended to let her go now that he found her, though.

Her one hand coming up to cup his jaw as her tongue slashed against his the second she allowed him to deepen the kiss had him biting her bottom lip the first chance he could. Just to feel the tremble of her fingers against his skin when she gasped.

"I have to—"

He kissed her again before she could finish, although he knew what she was going to say.

"*God*, you make me crazy," she whispered when he pressed his lips to hers yet again. "Let me take this, so she'll have it if she wakes up, but—"

"You'll be *right back*."

His stare nailed to hers.

Her tongue peeked out to lick along the seam of her lips.

Cella swallowed audibly, a sexy smile coloring her features. "I promise."

"Make sure it's somewhere that it'll be the first thing she sees when she wakes up."

For a brief second, she shifted from the woman ready to climb into his lap into the sweet single mother doing her best to keep a father's soul alive in her daughter's heart. Right before his eyes. And then just as fast, Cella winked and blew him a kiss. It reminded him all at once that she was such a multifaceted woman.

"Be right back."

He nodded.

She stood straight, leaning down to give him a quick kiss and one more whispered *thank you for this* before she left his office. Marcus took that chance to put his mini-sewing kit back inside his desk drawer and pour himself another two fingers of cognac—no ice this time—to sit back down in the chair and sip on until Cella came back.

He'd just taken his second sip of the drink when she slipped back into the office. She closed the door behind her, already reaching to pull the spaghetti straps of the silk nightdress she'd pulled on earlier down over her shoulders before she had even reached his spot. Marcus had enough time to set his glass to the small decorative table beside the chair and then Cella climbed into his lap.

Her thighs straddled his hips as she leaned in for a kiss. Marcus gave it to her, letting her taste the flavor of the cognac he'd only just swallowed still fresh on his tongue while her hands pulled at the buttons of his dress shirt. He was already yanking the fabric of her nightdress up around her stomach before he shoved a hand right down her panties to get his palm cupping her sex. His fingers drifted through her slit, already finding her slick and hot to the touch.

"Fuck, do you feel that, Cella? So wet for me already."

Her airless laughter wrapped all around him, tightening against his chest and making him feel more insane than he already was with her near.

"See what you make me want to do?" she breathed against his mouth. "Look how you make me *act*, Marcus."

"Fucking *perfect*. That's what you are."

And she was.

Cella might never believe it, but he would give away every last dollar in his bank account, if it meant he was allowed the pleasure of telling her that for the rest of his life.

Because that's what she did to him. *That's* how she made him want to act.

So yes, he understood.

All too well.

She finally got his shirt pulled apart, her impatience earning her at least one popped button from his shirt. Not that he gave a single damn. She could ruin the fucking shirt, and he would thank her for it, quite frankly.

His mind fell to something else when she grabbed for the button on his slacks. "We need to go to the bedroom. My condoms—"

Cella's hands hesitated, her head tipping up just enough for her gaze to catch his. He found the same desperation he felt that currently thrummed through his blood with every beat of his heart was reflected in her stare. He wanted nothing more to be inside her, fucking her crazy while she moaned his name loud enough that he'd hear it for days in his mind. That look in her eye said she wanted the same.

"It's just you and me, right?" she asked. "That's how it is for *me*."

His hand that was still stroking her pussy just enough to tease and toying with her clit to keep her thighs trembling came to a stop. Just for that brief moment when he needed her to hear him the most more than he wanted to touch her.

"*Just* you and me," he promised. "Unless you ever tell me otherwise."

"I'm on the shot."

"I don't mind. It's just down the hall, Cella."

"*No*. I want you to have me like this, too"

That was all he needed to hear. Two of his fingers thrust into her pussy, twisting into her G-spot when she pulled apart the button on his slacks. He didn't even care about the bite of the zipper against the length of his cock when she pulled him free from his boxer-briefs without waiting for him to lift a bit to give her more room to work with.

All he thought about was her.

How she looked on him.

How it would feel to slide into her so slowly that she would whine.

When she *came* that first time ...

Those were the things he wanted, and he didn't care about a little discomfort if it meant getting those things from her. His fingers withdrew from her sex, and still wet with her arousal, he fisted the gusset of her panties and shoved them to the side as she raised higher.

His other hand flattened to her ass with a crack from a slap, and then his fingers flexed into the pert roundness to get her really feeling him while she lined his cock up to her slit. She rubbed the head of him against her, wetting him with her and teasing herself.

But then she slid down him.

He held her tight, listening to the air rush from her parted lips as he made her slow down.

"*Fuck*, yeah, just like that," he told her.

Cella took him slow.

Inch by inch.

His heart thundered so hard in his chest, each beat urging him to *just fucking take her*; a rhythm demanding he fuck her until neither of them could see straight, and his sleep would be a blissful and dreamless from being spent with her.

He didn't, though.

Couldn't.

Not when he enjoyed the sight of her like this, too.

Cella let out a hard breath, those blue eyes of hers wide and locked on his as she seated down on him entirely. "Oh, my God ..."

He kept holding her in place on him, even when her hips shifted like she was trying to get friction between them. "How bad do you want it, Cella?"

"Marcus, *please* ... just *move*, or—"

"Do you feel that sweet pussy of yours trying to flex around me. But you're *so full*, my sweet girl. Don't you feel that?"

Her hips grinding against him faster, but he let her have that. Not much more, though.

"You're going to ride me until you come," he told her, "while I stuff your ass full of my fingers, and then you're going to fuck me dry. What do you think about that?"

Her lips parted, pink and swollen from his kiss. "I want that."

Marcus loosened his hold enough to let her move more; to fuck him wild until she saw stars and whispered his name like a prayer. "Fuck me, then."

Her lips crashed down on his as she did what he demanded of her. The rhythm of her hips rising and falling against his had her panting into his kiss within seconds. She knew exactly what she wanted and needed to get off on him, and her determination in getting that only made him hotter.

Marcus's hand on her ass slid down between her thighs as his other grabbed tightly to her hip. He gathered the wetness she left at the base of his cock to slide up to her ass while their tongues lashed together. He teased the tip of his fingers against the tight ring of muscles as her movements came faster on top of him. He worked at her ass until his fingers slipped in easily, and he could match the pace of her rhythm with his own. When she'd fill her pussy with his cock, he'd pull his fingers out of her ass. And as she came off of him, he'd shove those fingers in deep until she was moaning hard into his mouth.

"Right there, oh my, God, Marcus, right there, please ..."

"Give it to me, come on, *amour*, look at me."

She did.

Still wide-eyed.

Wildness in the baring of her teeth.

Truth on her lips.

"I love you," she breathed.

The air came out of his chest hard.

"Say it again," he whispered.

"I love you, Marcus."

He kissed her hard, promising those words right back to her as her movements came to a stilted halt and a low, broken cry accompanied the quaking of her orgasm.

"Love you," he murmured, his own control gone from the clenching of her inner muscles. Not that he intended to follow her so fast, but nothing felt better in that second than emptying his balls while he held this woman deep on his cock with those *words* on his tongue. "I love you, Cella."

His air wouldn't come.

Didn't move through his chest no matter how hard he tried.

Cella licked her lips, her gaze a little hazy before he kissed her again. "I felt you *come*."

"Give me a few minutes, and you're going to feel it again."

"I better."

Oh, she certainly would.

Cella wasn't quite done with him, though. She lifted from him as he asked, "And you love me, hmm?"

"Apparently I'm not alone in that."

"Definitely *not*."

Cool air drifted around his cock when he left the warm silkiness of her sex. She hovered above him, his cock still hard and jutting high toward her body as her fingers drifted down between her thighs. She leaned back just a little bit on the chair. It was enough to give him a view of his semen coating her fingertips and they drifted through the lips of her sex.

"That's the hottest thing I've ever seen."

His words *ached*.

He still couldn't breathe.

Cella's light laughter only had him spinning higher. She looked so damned good; his wettest dream come to life.

And good God, he loved her more for it.

CHAPTER

13

The knock on Cella's office door in Rochester had her leaving the conversation she was currently having with Marcus on the phone to see her assistant standing in the doorway. Not that her assistant was stepping in on something she shouldn't hear, but that didn't matter to Cella.

"Hey, what's up, Kinsley?"

"Just got confirmation back that the company for the play equipment will be able to make your deadline as long as they get access to the penthouse within a week to do all the measurements."

Cella rolled her eyes. "What, they don't trust my measurements, or …?"

Kinsley shrugged. "That's what I was told, boss."

"Did you hear that, Marcus?"

On the speaker, the man who had kept quiet during her interaction with her assistant finally spoke up, replying, "I did, and I can make whatever you need to happen. Just let me know when."

Lucky for her.

And that company who would bring in the play equipment to outfit the entire space of what used to be the master bedroom into the ultimate playroom.

Marcus had really been a life saver when it came to this penthouse project. Probably more than he knew, honestly. Cella had a team that she worked with, sure, and any one of them could have handled staying in Toronto during the entire term of the project but that would have costed more money which in the end, meant less profit. Not that this job was all about the profit to her, but it didn't hurt and she *liked* making money. Having a contact in Toronto to be a go-between for contractors or whatever else that she didn't actually have to pay was a card in her pocket that she appreciated.

She made a mental note to *thank* Marcus for that in her own special way the next time she saw him. She was sure he'd appreciate it, too.

"Get a date from them when they want to go in," Cella told Kinsley.

"Will do."

"And close my door on your way out."

All she saw was the swish of the girl's corkscrew curls before she headed out of Cella's office. The door closed behind her, and Cella put her attention back on the phone call that, before this moment, hadn't actually been about work at all.

She just liked talking to Marcus.

"Now, before she came in," Cella said, "you were about to tell me what you're up to today, weren't you?"

Marcus laughed. "Nothing very important. Handling business, a meeting with an associate or two, a very boring lunch as I have no one to keep me company, and missing you. That's my long day in a nutshell."

Cella grinned, picking up the item she'd placed on the edge of her desk that morning after emptying out the pockets of her blazer. Her thumb pressed along the edge of the key to Marcus's house in the suburb. The key he'd given her to use *at any time*. If what he said could be trusted, then she was welcome to use the key whenever she pleased.

"I just left yesterday," she said, "and you miss me already?"

"How can I *not*?"

Cella bit her lower lip, murmuring, "Same."

"Is Tiffany—"

"At her pre-K classes. I'm going to pick her up for lunch. I promised her those awful burgers she likes so much. Which means I'll have to grab a second lunch for me, but whatever makes her happy."

"Now *that* is unconditional love."

Her laughter colored up the quiet office. "Something like that. So, over the next couple of weeks, I'm going to work on finalizing the details for the remaining rooms in the penthouse. The other rooms that need their flooring and painting will be finished next week—I'll send over the details for the contractors so you can go in and check up, if you want to."

"Sounds good to me. What kind of timeline are we looking at for *everything* to be finished?"

"Depends on these last couple of rooms; the playroom will be the one that's going to take the longest, probably."

"She's going to love that, though," he said.

Cella nodded. "I think so, and the kids, too."

"Of course. Can't forget those little monsters."

"And I'll make the trip to see the rooms that will be ready to finish in two weeks, just to give the okay. They could send pictures, but—"

"You *want* to come," he interjected.

What was the point in lying?

"You do seem to make that trip worth it every time I make it, Marcus."

His dark, husky laughter had a heat warming her cheeks, and while he didn't know it, the sound alone was enough to make her shift in her seat to soothe the sudden ache between her thighs. Not that it helped.

Nothing but that man *between* her thighs helped with

that. It was both a blessing and a curse, but not one Cella would complain about, honestly.

"I can't convince you to come back sooner?" he asked. "Because I am *sure* you could get the same work done here that you do there."

"You know I have other clients, right?"

"I do know this. You're very much wanted everywhere you go, Cella. And while I might want you for other reasons than your clients do, that doesn't change the fact I still want you."

God.

This man.

"So," he added, tone lowering to that sexy drawl she loved so much, "if there is literally *anyway* at all that I could possibly convince you to come sooner—say this weekend—then please let me know because I will happily make it happen."

She wanted to say yes.

So badly.

Cella had every reason to agree, and without a doubt, Tiffany wouldn't mind at all. In fact, for the entire drive home the day before, her daughter continued to ask when they would be going back to see Marcus again all the while holding her father's pillow because she was so happy that he had managed to fix it for her.

Thing was, Cella felt like she had been neglecting the people she cared about *here* as well. The job in Toronto had taken a lot of time away from her other clients that she had already been working with before she agreed to take the penthouse contract on. So, she worked on her other contracts during the weekends and weeks when she wasn't traveling.

When did that leave her time with her family?

Basically never.

Or that's what it felt like.

Of course, her family knew she was busy and all the things she had going on. Some of them even knew a few details about her relationship with Marcus, although she didn't give them much more than hints and vague statements to go on. Not that it mattered, as they all gossiped amongst one another, anyway, and basically put all their information together to draw their own conclusions.

Sure, her parents never said anything about the fact she was coming around even less than she used to. And her siblings, at least the ones who lived in New York, didn't mind the sporadic phone calls and lack of visits.

She cared, though.

"I promised my parents I would do dinner with them this coming weekend," she said, knowing that wasn't the answer Marcus wanted to hear. He was enough of a gentleman, however, that he wouldn't tell her to cancel those plans with her family for him. She decided, along with all the other reasons he had given her so far, she loved that about him. "And next week, Tiffany has her pre-K graduation, so …"

"Speaking of your parents. Well, *her* grandparents, I guess."

"What about them?"

Marcus cleared his throat. "I just realized I hadn't asked about Tiffany's father's parents, or his family. Does she have anyone from his side?"

"An uncle that lives in the UK. He comes to visit once a year. William wasn't on great terms with his parents while we were together—they flew in for the funeral and didn't even speak to me. I didn't know them to begin with, they didn't attend our wedding, and he made it clear that was for the better."

"You can tell me to mind my own business, but why?"

Cella laughed under her breath. "He just said they didn't know how to love their own kids; he wasn't going to let them try to learn again on his. Given they didn't seem to care about Tiffany at the funeral, I never bothered. Her uncle checks in occasionally on her when he's not here for a visit."

"Ah, I see. Sorry."

"She has my family."

"Quite a large family, too."

"Yeah, but that's also why I want to keep my promise about this upcoming dinner. I feel like it's just her and I a lot of the time. She needs them, too. My family, I mean."

"I agree. But *next weekend*," he hinted.

She smiled to herself. "I am all yours, and I was coming to finalize those rooms, anyway."

"I think I can work my plans around that, then."

Cella's brow knotted. "What plans?"

"I promised Tiffany something. I have been waiting to make it happen for her."

"You're too good to us, Marcus."

His chuckles rocked through the phone. "Not nearly good enough, actually. Getting there, though."

Well, they'd see, wouldn't they?

Cella couldn't wait.

* * *

Noise greeted Cella as she pushed open the front door of the familiar home. She'd barely even taken a step inside when voices filtered down the hall.

"Lucky, you better be sharing with your sister!"

"I *am*!"

Tiffany had already dropped her bag to the floor as soon as they walked into her parents' home. The long drive had her ready to play with her cousins, and the flyby of Lucky— the closest of Tiffany's cousins to her own age—running from the sitting room to the kitchen across the hall sent her daughter running after him.

"*Lucky!*"

Lucky, or *Luciano*, as he'd been named at birth was her brother's oldest son. The kid was all about having a good time, making as much noise as he could while he did it, and making a mess to boot. Cella swore the kid also got away with literally everything because he was his father's little mini-me, but she knew better than to say that to anyone.

"Lucky, that is your sister's toy!"

A very tired-looking Siena came out of the sitting room right after the kids, but at the sight of Cella at the end of the hallway taking off her shoes, the woman smiled. The two shared a look that said *kids, huh?*

Because yeah, these kids never stopped.

"Good to see you around," Siena said.

Cella laughed and hung her purse on a waiting hook. "I know, I've been kind of MIA for the last while, I guess."

"Work, right?"

"That, and other things."

Siena raised her brow, leaning against the hallway wall as Cella came closer. Her brother's wife had always been probably the easiest person they welcomed into their family folds. There was just something about Siena that seemed warm and wonderful.

Plus, she loved John.

Like *crazy*.

Cella considered all of that a win and counted Siena as one of her friends. But like everyone else in her life that was important, Siena was yet another person who she felt like she had left to the wayside as she worked on this Toronto project and handled this *thing* between her and Marcus.

"What other things are those?" Siena grinned. "Because I heard from a little bird that there might be a man in Toronto that caught your eye, huh? I was waiting to hear it from *you*, but I mean … if the bird's info is correct, I might listen to him a little more."

Lord.

They were all nosy.

She kind of loved it, though.

Before she could answer her sister-in-law's question, the kids came flying back through the hallway. This time, it was Tiffany leading the pack with the skirt of her pink dress swishing wildly with every step she took. John wasn't far behind the kids, his laughter making the house even noisier than it already was, but he loved this, she knew.

All his kids.

His wife.

These years were some of the *best* for her brother after the hell of the previous ones. He seemed content to live in the present more than he ever did his past, which was yet another reason why Cella attempted to mend those bridges between the two of them.

John let the kids continue into the sitting room where all the toys were set up without him, and stood next to his wife to sling an arm around her shoulder. Pulling Siena in close, John dropped a kiss to her head before turning his attention on his sister.

"What was this I heard about some bird telling you things?"

"Shut up, you know that was *you*, John."

He laughed. "Yeah, well—"

"If you all could not talk about my private life when even *I'm* not talking about it," Cella interjected before anyone else could say anything more, "then that would be great."

"I didn't mean any harm," John said, "you know that, Cella."

Yeah, she did.

Still …

"I didn't even know what I was doing with a certain someone until just recently, so there wasn't very much to tell."

Siena grinned. "But that sounds like now there might be something. Am I right?"

"Well …"

"You finally made it, did you?" Jordyn poked her head out of the kitchen with a beaming smile. "I wondered if you would."

"Of course, I came, Ma. I said I would."

"You're very busy lately."

"Is that Cella?"

Her father's call from within the kitchen had her shaking her head.

"Yes, Lucian," Jordyn replied, "stop yelling, my God."

"Tell her to come help with these cross buns," another voice yelled.

Her sister.

Lucia.

Which undoubtedly meant Lucia's husband, Renzo, was there, too. The house really was full, which explained all the noise. Not that it bothered her. In fact, the effect was quite the opposite, and Cella smiled from the warmth spreading in her chest.

The sight of her mother had Cella happy all over again. Just like the voices of her family. Even if she was *sure* this dinner would be full of questions just like the ones Siena had been asking her, it didn't even matter. Her family was only curious *because* they wanted her to be happy. She understood that; it was the opening up part that she struggled with.

Cella would work on that.

She had to.

"Okay, guys, you *have* to share," Siena said when the kids

started shouting in the other room. She pointed a finger at Cella, winking as she told her, "And you, we're going to chat later about what I know, yes?"

"We'll see."

"What does she know?" Jordyn asked while Siena headed into the other room.

"Marcus," John said under his breath.

Jordyn grinned. "Oh, yes. That. I'm very curious about that as well."

"Me, too!"

That time, it was her father.

"Could you guys *not*? Or at least, one at a time and not everyone all at once, okay?"

Jordyn put her hands up. "Sorry, won't say another word. *But* you should definitely invite your friend in Toronto, to dinner with us some weekend if he'd like to come. We would be happy to have him."

"Ma."

Her mother winked. "Just saying. And when you're ready, we could use your help in the kitchen."

Her brother chuckled as Cella grabbed her cell phone from her bag after her mother disappeared into the kitchen. "You know she's just happy, right? Like the rest of us. And a little nosy."

"Don't worry, I know."

"And you're happy, too, yeah? Because of … him?"

She hesitated as she came up beside her brother in the hallway. John looked to her expectantly, waiting for her to answer him.

"If it is because of him," Cella said, "would that be surprising?"

"No."

"But?"

John shook his head. "No buts, Cella, I just hope you understand who Marcus Guzzi is."

"He's a lot like you, isn't he? Or Daddy."

"There was a time when *like us* was something you didn't want."

He wasn't wrong.

"He's what I want now, John."

Her brother nodded. "All right."

"Don't worry about me, okay? I know what I'm doing."

"I don't doubt that," he replied, "as long as you're happy."

"I am."

She continued walking toward the kitchen ready to get a start on spending quality time with her family before she made the long drive home. Because once she was home, a long phone call with Marcus would be waiting while she enjoyed a glass of white wine in the bathtub. That was, by far, the next best thing to being there *with* him.

Behind her, John added, "But if anything changes, we're all going to be here for you then, too. No matter what, Cella."

Yeah.

She knew that, too.

* * *

"Ma?"

"Mmhmm."

Cella kept her focus on the freeway while she waited for her daughter to ask whatever question she had on her mind. Thankfully, traffic wasn't too bad, but she attributed that to the fact it was summer, the weekend, and late in the evening. Another day, and they would have been bumper to bumper all the way back to Rochester after the dinner at her parents'.

"Do you like Marcus?"

Cella's gaze darted from the windshield to the rearview mirror where she was able to stare at Tiffany who was currently sitting in her booster seat. With a book in her hands, the girl wasn't even paying attention to her mother while she awaited her answer.

"Well, yes," Cella eventually said, "I do like him."

"Well, *yeah*." Tiffany glanced up, but quickly went back to her book to flip to the next page. Cella put her attention on the road again. "But I mean, do you *like* him? You know, the way Grandpapa Lucian likes Grandmama. Or how Uncle John—"

"Tiff—"

"Why was everyone asking so many questions at dinner about him?"

God.

Yep.

This was the conversation Cella had been waiting for with her daughter. She expected it to happen, but strangely, she never considered it would be like this. Perhaps a part of her thought her daughter would ask for other reasons, but instead it seemed like the curiosity of others had her child thinking about her own questions.

"Not *everyone* asked questions," Cella muttered under her breath.

Not low enough, apparently.

Kids heard *everything*.

"Yep, everyone. Even Lucky asked who Marcus was. I told him he was your friend, remember?"

Jesus Christ.

Cella had hoped that the round of twenty rapid-fire questions she faced at her parents' dinner table would be all that she had to answer for a while. She couldn't be so lucky.

"He is my friend," she settled on saying, "and you're

right, I do like him the same way your grandparents like each other, or your aunts and uncles."

"Oh."

The silence from the backseat stretched on for at least another two miles. Cella wasn't sure if that was because Tiffany was too busy reading her book, or if she was thinking about the next questions she wanted to ask her mother. It really could go either way.

Cella checked the rearview again.

Tiffany looked up at the same time, brow furrowed. "Was that how you liked Daddy, too?"

An ache hit Cella right in the fucking heart.

Sharp and oh, so *deep*.

Because something like *that* couldn't be simplified down to a yes or no in her mind. It wasn't that easy. Although, if she were being honest, everything about falling in love with Marcus while she still grieved a man who had given her one of her greatest gifts—her child—had seemed easy almost. He was not who she expected him to be. He came when she wasn't looking for him.

And yes, she made room in her heart just for him.

But how did she explain those things to her child?

How did she tell her daughter all of that?

"Ma?" Tiffany asked.

"Yes," Cella said, "it's very much the same way I liked your daddy, but no, it's also entirely different because they're not the same people. I liked your daddy because of who he was, and I like Marcus for who he is to you and to me."

"To me, too?"

Cella smiled. "Of course—you're everything I love the most."

So, he'd have to love her, too.

"Okay." Then, quieter, Tiffany added, "I like Marcus."

"I know you do, baby."

"Do you think that would make Daddy mad?"

"Absolutely not. If anything, that would make him so happy because someone else makes you happy."

"Oh."

The silence came back, but this time, Cella didn't feel like she had to wonder what her daughter was thinking about or if she had more questions that needed to be answered. She could tell just by glancing in the rearview mirror that Tiffany was lost in her thoughts and sometimes, that's all a person needed to do.

Absorb what they knew.

Consider what it meant.

Even if that person was a five-year-old girl.

"Ma?"

"Hmm?"

"Could I call Marcus? I'd like to say goodnight."

Cella nodded and pulled her phone from the cupholder to pass it back. "There you go—you know where to find his name to call. I think he'd like that very much."

In fact, she was positive he would. Something else for her to love about him. Like the man hadn't already given her more than enough.

CHAPTER
14

Tribute was, *normally*, one of Marcus's favorite times of the month. It was something he looked forward to.

He mostly blamed it on the fact he was a Guzzi, and all Guzzis loved money like it was a second God they worshipped on every other day but Sunday. What appeared to be modesty in his wealth what with his Toronto penthouse, the three-level home in the suburbs, and a couple of flashy cars he liked to keep on hand, was really just smoke and mirrors. His closets were lined with custom Armani and whatever designer name he felt like buying. He had enough leather loafers—his favorite—to provide a small army with shoes. Oh, and his investment portfolio toted over two hundred businesses spread across Ontario and Quebec which he constantly added to.

Yeah, he fucking *loved* money. Because the more he owned, the less people might be able to take from him at the end of the day. With the control of things came power he could extend when or if he needed.

Usually, that would be enough to get him to give a fuck at tribute, and put up with the theatrics of the mafia that could literally take *all day*, but today was one where his patience had run particularly thin. Or perhaps that was just his impatience making an appearance because frankly, he just wanted this day to be done with already. He had much better things waiting for him tomorrow.

Like *her* arrival back in town.

Cella, that was.

With every week that passed without him seeing Cella, he became more and more anxious. A little fucking edgy. All things that weren't particularly good for Marcus's circumstance considering his life and position, but here he was doing it all anyway.

A true testament to his feelings, really.

Since tomorrow would accompany Cella's arrival with Tiffany in tow, and today was tribute, well he was just ready for it to be done. Then, he could focus on his weekend with Cella since this was literally all he could have with her right now. Random weekends when she could make the trip, phone calls throughout the week, and text messages during the day.

It wasn't nearly enough.

It's all they had.

Marcus would take that over nothing.

"What's your opinion on that, boss?"

Marcus raised his attention from the cup of coffee he was currently dazing out on to find all eyes in the restaurant had turned on him. Not surprising, considering every person inside the business currently was a made man that answered to him, and they were all there to hand over a portion of their monthly earnings to the boss.

That's what tribute was all about.

The boss.

Another reason why he enjoyed this day was because of the memories it carried for him. From the time he was a young boy, he followed his father to every single tribute. It didn't matter that he hadn't been made at the time because he didn't need to be when he was *the* son. The oldest Guzzi boy —the firstborn.

A clear message, if there ever was one from his father.

Gian intended for him to sit here.

Marcus didn't think his father meant for him to be this distracted however because he had not one fucking clue what the Capo across the room meant by his question. "My opinion on what, exactly?"

Beside him at his own table, Chris cleared his throat as looks passed around the room. So, maybe his distraction wasn't going unnoticed—that could certainly pose a problem, if he allowed it, and he wouldn't—by everyone else.

Marcus put his head back into the game. "I asked a question, did I not? I would appreciate an answer."

"The rackets on the road construction downtown," the Capo was fast to say, clearly hearing the warning in Marcus's tone and knowing better than to play games, "I was discussing whether or not it would continue to be a profitable venture after this year seeing as how someone else won the bids for the next few years. We'll have to rework a new deal with those companies, that is if they even will take a—"

"We have an entire year to figure the details out for that, *oui*?"

The man nodded. "Yes, but—"

"It would, undoubtedly, be easier to give up the rackets but the second we do that, someone else will certainly step in to take it over for their own business. And then that money we're out will have to be made somewhere else by the Capos who should have had that cash coming in from the rackets. So, by all means, rid yourselves of the rackets if you want, but do let me know where you're going to make up that cash elsewhere while you're at it."

There.

Let them make of that what they wanted.

Because at the end of the day regardless of Marcus's lack of attention at times, he was still the fucking man sitting in the boss's seat. He knew how to behave like it, too. All the boss cared about was his bottom line because otherwise, what was the point of this thing of theirs?

Money.

Loyalty.

It's what kept *Cosa Nostra* going.

"Continue with your payments," Marcus said, lifting his coffee cup from the table to ready for a sip as he waved his other hand at the room. "One man at a time—as normal."

The tribute continued without the fanfare from before, and for that blessing, Marcus was grateful. Of course, even as one Capo at a time sent his most trusted man up, if not himself, to pay his dues to the boss, Marcus could feel his brother beside him shifting in his seat with the occasional clearing of his throat.

"What is it, Chris?" Marcus asked, picking up the stack of cash an enforcer for one of his Quebec Capos. "Just spit it out; stop overthinking whatever you want to say, brother."

Chris sighed, his gaze drifting to the enforcer who was currently waiting as the boss slipped the stack of bills into a money counter. At the same time, he kept his gaze averted from Christopher and Marcus sitting at the table, as though he didn't hear their conversation at all. Which was entirely impossible considering he was right there in front of them.

"Maybe now is not the best time," Chris replied.

"No better time, honestly."

If they couldn't trust their people to speak in front of them, then who could they trust?

It was also a good way to weed out the problems.

Loose lips, and all that.

"Fine," Chris said, "you wanted it, so don't blame me."

The machine in front of Marcus beeped with a number on the screen that made him quite pleased. He picked the cash out of the slot and put it back in to count a second time

—at its core, this business was still all about the nickels and dimes, so double counting was a must.

"Just *talk*," Marcus muttered.

"Your distraction wouldn't have anything to do with Cella coming this weekend, would it?"

Yep.

Chris had to go there.

"And?" Marcus asked.

His brother shrugged. "I get it—I'm more concerned about your plans for the weekend."

"Why is that?"

The machine beeped again. Same number as before.

"Do you really think it's smart to be out in the middle of nowhere, with very little protection, at the eastern Ontario farm when you know the bikers are rallying? At least two other chapters have come into town, and—"

"They have no idea where I'll be," Marcus said, plucking the cash out of the machine. He nodded at the enforcer, saying, "You may return to your Capo."

Christopher called for the next man to pay his boss.

Marcus gave his brother a look from the side. "The chances of the bikers attacking this weekend are less than nil —the chances of them attacking *me* is … even less. Don't be another person riding my ass. I have enough."

His brother frowned. "I worry."

"Don't."

* * *

Marcus arrived at his father's mansion a day later more frustrated than he should have been. He might be the acting boss of the family, but his father still had all the say behind the scenes. His mood wouldn't be welcomed when he was intended to deliver the tribute he collected to his boss—who *never* behaved as his father when business was in play—but he couldn't shake the irritation thickening his blood.

He blamed everything for it.

Everything but himself.

It didn't help that Marcus *should* have delivered this tribute the night before to his father, so he wouldn't have to do it today. Then, he could have been at home when Cella arrived with Tiffany after driving from Rochester. Those plans quickly had to change when his father decided he didn't want guests the night before.

Not even his son with money.

Instead, he'd called *way too fucking early* to say Marcus could come and deliver the tribute while his father took breakfast on the back terrace. Did it matter that Cella would be arriving that morning? Apparently not.

"You look sour for it being a beautiful Friday morning," Marcus's mother said, greeting him at the front door. Despite wishing he could just drop off the money and go, he knew better than that. He offered his mother a smile and kissed her cheek. "That's a little better. Things on your mind?"

Marcus lifted the envelope with the cash inside. Quite a bit of cash, frankly, because it weighed his hand down. "Business for Papa, that's all."

"I hear you have a guest coming today, too."

He couldn't help but genuinely smile at that. "I do."

His mother gave him a look that screamed *I know what you haven't told me, I can see it written all over your face.* She always had known her boys better than anyone. He wasn't sure if that was because they came from their mother—she helped to make them, carried them for nine months before giving them life, after all—or if it was her penchant for being able to shrink heads. Either way, he didn't mind.

It was just his ma.

"I'm very happy," he told her.

Cara grinned knowingly. "I can tell. See, I told you that little issue you were having would work out somehow."

"I'm sorry?"

"Months ago, all you wanted to focus on were the stupid socialite rags that wouldn't leave you alone. You haven't mentioned those once since, Marcus. And why should you? Nothing they have to say holds any importance to what *matters* in your private life. Have you even noticed them recently?"

He had to think about that.

Really think about it.

"No," he said, "I haven't."

Partly because he had better things to focus on, and also he'd been too busy to even stop at the grocery store near his penthouse in the city where the rags usually mocked him at the register while he paid. Instead, he had his assistant, someone his brother hired to handle different things for him who usually deferred to Chris and not even Marcus, when he needed something done.

"In case you're curious," his mother said as she stepped away to grant him access to the grand entry of the mansion, "they have yet to pick up wind of *her*."

Well, then …

"That's good to know."

"Your father is in the back. Find me before you leave. I might like to find out if there's a time I can sneak those two away from you this weekend."

"Well, *that* is gonna cost you, Ma."

Cara's laughter followed him through the grand entry as he headed for the back of the mansion. The shitty mood bringing him down seemed to disappear with nothing more than a conversation from his mother. Not that it shocked him seeing as how his mother always knew how to bring her sons out of a mood.

Of course, that all had to change when he stepped out onto the rear terrace to find his father waiting for him. Not that the sight of Gian did it, but rather, the fact that his father stared at him as though he were less than impressed with the sight in front of him, *and* like he'd been waiting for his son.

"Boss," Marcus greeted.

Gian smiled tightly.

Another bad sign.

"Sit," his father said, pointing at the chair across from him at the small, glass table outfitted with wicker chairs on either side. "And we'll have a chat."

"I was hoping to drop this off, and just go. I have somewhere—"

"Marcus, you will sit, and we *will* chat."

All right, then.

The fact that his father was already dressed in a three-piece suit when it wasn't even eight in the morning should have been a clue that something was up, honestly. Gian preferred to stay in his sleep clothes until he was ready to leave his home.

Taking a seat at the table, Marcus handed the large envelope over and waited silently while his father opened it up and began pulling the stacks of cash out. Gian didn't intend to make his son wait for long before he explained exactly why he was acting strange.

"When were you planning to tell me about the problems you've had with the bikers over the maple farms?"

Ah.

That explained a lot.

"Did you need to know?" Marcus asked back. "I've handled it again and *again*. And without much issues, seeing as how you're only finding out now, right?"

Gian glanced up from a wad of bills in his hand, giving

Marcus a look that practically screamed for him to check his fucking attitude. Everybody liked to talk about their mother having *that* look—a single glance that all kids recognized meant they were about to be in trouble. Well, here Marcus was as a grown man, and his *father* had one of those looks.

Came with the territory, he suspected.

"Explain to me," Gian said quietly, his tone suggesting Marcus walk a very careful line the next time he opened his mouth to speak, "why you thought an issue that could very well hurt our business and bring us much *unwanted* and unneeded attention wasn't important enough for you to … at the very least, Marcus, discuss with me. By all means, I apparently have time today to teach my son who should already know how this business works about what he needs to do, so go ahead. I will wait."

With the understanding Marcus needed to give his father the respect he was due for being both who he was, and having the status he did, that didn't stop him from getting irritated all over again.

"The issue is being handled," Marcus said, "the very same way *you* would handle it, because I kept you in mind while dealing with it. It's *still* being handled, and as the media has not yet gotten wind that the Guzzis have anything to do with the recent death of the gang's president, or that we were even in talks with them, I think that proves everything was fine, no?"

"I'm concerned that you assumed you didn't *need* to tell me, son. And what else you might not be telling me regarding business."

Oh, was that it?

"Or is it something else?" Marcus asked.

Gian raised a brow at that question. "I beg your pardon?"

"You were quite clear that unless I *needed* to bring some-thing to your attention because I couldn't handle it otherwise, I was to deal with everything. *Act* as the boss, being that's what you wanted the men to see me as. Because you can't sit a new boss down while the old boss is still making the calls. Am I wrong?"

His father said nothing.

Marcus continued on with, "So do you really want to step back here, Papa, or do you just want to tell me how to do my job from the wings? I mean, if that's what it is, at least let me know so that I understand what's really happening here."

"Marcus—"

"Right now, my duty is to this family first," he interjected before his father could say anything else, "and everything else second. I'm doing my job, and I don't need you to tell me how to do it, Gian. You spent my whole life doing that. I think I'm good to handle it alone now."

The silence stretched on between the two of them.

Marcus didn't mind.

Finally, his father said, "Keeping me updated on a situation doesn't mean I would step in, or force you to make other choices. It concerned me, that's all. I worry you have too many plates spinning in the air, Marcus, and one is about to fall. If you can't, at the very least, keep me informed on the business side of things, then what else are you overlooking?"

"*Nothing*. I made a choice not to involve you in a situation I didn't think needed your hand. Nothing more, and nothing less."

"And when maple season comes up, what do you plan to do if you're still having these issues with the bikers? Specifically for the farm in Quebec, since I hear that's the one they've got a hard nut for and all."

"We're not at the season yet."

"But you will be."

"And I will handle it," he replied firmly.

Because if his father could use that *and that's the end of it* tone, then so could Marcus.

Be a boss, raise a boss.

Gian made this.

Marcus.

"And now I have somewhere to be," he told his father, standing from the table, "so if you'll excuse me, I would like to get back to that."

Gian sighed, nodding at the rear doors of the mansion. "Say hello to Cella for me."

"I will. Have a good day, Papa."

* * *

It took Marcus entirely too long to battle traffic and get home to the house in the suburbs. The clock on his dashboard said it was a little past noon—far later than he expected to get back. With his mind running a million miles a minute, considering all the shit his father said because what if Gian had been right?

What if he was fucking up?

Missing something …

He was so distracted, in fact, that he didn't even notice the vehicle he parked beside in his own driveway. That's what people didn't realize when it came to Marcus. When someone second-guessed him and made it known, that had him checking *himself*, too.

He couldn't have that.

Couldn't expend the energy.

Or the problems it might cause.

His flustered mind quickly cleared as he walked up the front steps to the house, and the door flung open. It wasn't that he'd forgotten about Cella coming, but all the other shit piled into his head and took over for a short bit. He finally realized he'd parked beside her car.

And that she was now standing in front of him.

Marcus smiled.

Light came back to his life.

"Hey," he said.

Cella's grin blew wide before she came out the door. His arms were already open, ready to catch her as she darted forward. The second she was in his embrace, nothing else but her mattered. Those painted-red lips of hers pressed against his, and all he cared about was getting her inside his house and closing out the rest of the world.

Between his kisses, she managed to mumble against his lips, "Missed you. Tiffany is having a nap because she was too excited to sleep much last night, and she can't sleep in the car. So, if you are *really* quiet, then we might be able to—"

"You mean, if *you* can keep quiet."

His lips traveled down her throat, and he kicked the door closed behind him.

Cella laughed. "Well, *yeah*."

Perfect.

He could work with that.

And what better way to spend an afternoon than fucking this woman?

CHAPTER
15

Cella hummed out a soft moan as Marcus's fingertips glided down her naked spine with a soft, tantalizing touch. As though her clit weren't still throbbing with every grind of his hips upward into her. His still-hard cock jerked inside. He'd already fucked her crazy and came once before getting her like this, too.

"Well," she breathed against his hard chest when her lips pressed down to kiss the damp skin there, "at least we made it to the bedroom."

His laughter coated her with something sinful and wicked. God, that sound alone could turn her into a woman she didn't recognize, but one that she loved nonetheless. She could never be *this* woman with someone else. No one allowed her to be wild and free and *loved* like she could be when she was alone with Marcus.

"After what, the *second* round?" he asked, still chuckling.

"Hey, what matters is we made it here."

"*Right*, that's what matters. Not that you've still got my cum across your back."

She was quite sticky.

Cella didn't really mind.

It felt like another mark he'd added to her, really. Another piece of him that she would take with her, even if she washed it away, and would feel long after he was gone.

Their silence stretched on while his arms circled tightly

around her. On top of him, with her face tucked against his chest, she watched the light from the sun dance through the slat between the pulled curtains. She couldn't remember the last time she spent an afternoon in bed with a man—that's how long it had been.

Tiff would wake up soon.

They'd have to get out of this bed.

Cella enjoyed it while she could.

"I needed you today more than you know," Marcus murmured.

Tipping her head up, she reveled in the warmth of his hard lines molded along her softer curves. She met his gaze, the gold flecks in his eyes more noticeable this close. She could get lost in that swirling brown and gold as he watched her. Every single time.

"Why?" she asked.

"Too much shit on my mind. And then there you were … ripped me right out of it, and let me breathe for five seconds. I needed it. People get me in my head, and then I second-guess *everything* I do. It makes me think I should be doing things more like they would, maybe, or just different from how I want to do them."

"Seems … not like you."

At all.

The Marcus she knew always seemed to be in control of everything. The people around him, even himself, and whatever else he could extend his hand to, he did. At times, he almost came off as cold because he only really showed emotion with those that he cared about and more often than not, she knew he was put in situations where he couldn't *be* himself.

He had to be a version of it.

She wished that didn't have to be.

"Business is always tricky for me," he said, shrugging one

shoulder. "I walk a fine line between the boss I would like to be, and the one others expect me to be because of where I come from. There's a balance I haven't found yet, and I feel like it shows when I hit a wall."

Oh.

That made Cella stiffen a bit.

Marcus didn't miss it. "What?"

"I just ... didn't realize that's what you meant."

"Business?"

"The mafia," she replied quietly, avoiding his gaze. "It's easy for me to put a distance between me and that, I think. I've done it for most of my life, and spent the last five years blaming the mafia for taking my daughter's father from her, and my husband from me. I thought, if I kept a distance between me and it, then it wouldn't affect me again like it had before."

"Cella, that's impossible. You are who you are."

Yeah, she knew.

That didn't make it easier, though.

"Look at *me*, yeah?"

Her gaze turned on him, a reaction she really couldn't control when it came to Marcus. He just had that kind of power, but especially over her. He demanded something, and she felt helpless until she gave him what he wanted.

It didn't make any sense.

It felt *crazy*.

She still loved it.

"I am who I am, too," he murmured, holding strong to her gaze, "so if that's gonna be something you need to work out here, I'm going to need you to do that, Cella. Not later, but *now*. Before we get deeper into this thing than we already are."

God.

How much deeper could they go?

The man was still fucking *inside* her.

His cum still painted her back.

She couldn't tell him she loved him enough times when he'd been fucking her just minutes ago. She was *here*. With her kid who seemed just as attached to this man as she was at the end of the day.

Her whole head was filled with stupid, silly things that girls who were new to the game of love thought when they found *the one*. Hell, she thought she'd already found that once, but look at her, here doing it again with Marcus.

Not that she regretted any of it.

She didn't.

But how much deeper could they get?

Look at them.

"I trust you," she told him.

Marcus swallowed thickly. "Good—that's all that matters to me. And there's no business this weekend. It's all about you and her for that, I promise."

Cella grinned, nibbling on her bottom lip before she pushed up to straddle his hips again. With her hands flat to his chest, she leaned down to get another taste of his mouth. He still tasted like her pussy that he'd *loved* eating after painting her back with his cum. She started a slow rhythm riding him that had Marcus groaning in the sexiest way against her lips.

There was nothing better than this man moaning.

Hard inside her.

His hands found her hips, and he started grinding back with her rhythm. It had his groin dragging against her clit in the best way. She let him fuck her deep like that, those harsh circles of their bodies hitting her G-spot with each one.

He'd make her come hard like that.

She figured, *surely they could fit one more round in?*

"Keep making promises," she whispered into his kiss, "as long as you keep them."

* * *

"Look at all these *maple trees*!"

Cella couldn't help but laugh at how high pitch Tiffany's voice became in her excitement. Her girl knew nothing about Marcus's plans for her that weekend, but Cella knew *just enough* to be well aware that her kid would go crazy.

Like a walk through the forest where a particular farm actually harvested their maple trees. It might not be in season for maple syrup, but that didn't detract from her daughter's enthusiasm at seeing things up close and learning about it all.

Plus, Marcus seemed to be enjoying it as well. How could Cella not love that?

"We'll have to come out again when all the pipes are put up, and the trees have been tapped," Marcus told Tiffany who darted further ahead in the forest. Orange ties on the trees helped to direct them, and would get them back out without them getting lost. It made her realize just how much Marcus thought about leading up to this day.

She appreciated the effort. That's all people needed to do. *Make an effort.*

"Will it be very cold?" Tiffany asked, looking back over her shoulder at them.

Next to her, Marcus shrugged. His fingers woven with hers kept her close to his side, and if Tiffany minded the affection between the two, she didn't say. Then again, after that conversation in the car the week before, Cella figured her daughter had a good idea what was happening between her mother and Marcus.

By all appearances, she liked it, too.

"A little cold—the season for harvesting here runs from

February to April. Sometimes we might start a bit later, if the weather stops us from starting normally, but once we start, it's a three-month window to do the harvest and have the syrup ready to be packaged for the year's exports and sales."

"And I can see that?" Tiffany asked. "You'll bring me back, so I can watch them make it?"

Marcus smiled wide. "I absolutely will. We'll even go out to one of the maple shacks, put some fresh, hot syrup in the snow, wrap it around a stick, and make suckers. They're the best."

Tiffany let out a *whoop* that echoed in the forest, followed by a statement of, "This is the *best* day of my life."

Cella shook her head, saying too low for her daughter to hear, "I'll remind her that she said so when February rolls around, and she incessantly asks to come out and see the trees being harvested."

Marcus tugged Cella closer to his side, letting go of her hand just so that he could wrap his arm around her waist. Dropping a kiss to the top of her head, she closed her eyes and soaked that all in. The smell of him. The noise of the forest around her. And even her daughter's happiness as Tiffany began to sing one of those songs she'd learned at pre-K.

Even with her eyes closed, she could still see the foliage on the rough ground, the strong trees towering high above them, and the bright green leaves that made a canopy to block out of the hot sun from the summer day. Although, she knew that one could still see a bit of the bright blue sky peeking through the leaves, too.

"You know," Cella said, sighing as she opened her eyes to stare at Marcus who smiled back at her, "even though she's going to like what comes next for this day more than us because let's admit it, the next bit is mostly just for her, this is perfect."

"You think?"

"You, me, and her? This place? Yeah, that's perfect for me."

Marcus reached up to push one of her wavy strands of hair back behind her shoulder. Then, those soft fingertips of his drifted along the line of her cheekbone. "Easy to please, hmm?"

"With just a little bit of effort, sure."

"I'll keep that in mind."

Good.

She hoped he did.

Lost in her moment with Marcus, she didn't even hear her daughter come up in front of them until Tiffany's small arms circled one of Marcus's legs, and one of Cella's. Without a word, he dropped one hand from Cella's lower back, and cupped the back of Tiffany's curly head. Smiling down at the girl, he couldn't have looked happier.

Tiffany looked back at him in the same way.

Cella thought … *like she could be his.*

"Can we play tag around the trees?" Tiffany asked.

Marcus nodded. "We can do whatever you want to do, *dolcezza*. That's what today is all about. Just you and your ma."

Tiffany grinned wide.

Then, she smacked Marcus on his leg.

"*You're it!*"

Her kid darted away from them with pealing laughter.

Marcus gave Cella a look. "She totally planned that, didn't she?"

"Most definitely. Stop looking so proud of her."

He shrugged. "Can't help it. That was a good one."

* * *

"Is that where all the syrup is made?"

Cella stood back as Marcus opened the rear door of the SUV and helped Tiffany from her booster seat. Of course, as soon as the girl's feet hit the parking lot, she practically danced on the spot from her excitement.

"It's a very *small* plant where some of the syrup is brought to be bottled and stored for shipment," Marcus explained, keeping a hand atop Tiffany's head like that was going to keep her in place. "And in the summer, there are often tours that come through this particular plant, and we also have a big play place for kids to go crazy. Today, I had the whole place shut down to the public, although there's no production happening anyway, so that you could get to see all the machines, where everything is stored, and have full run of the play place. There's someone in the restaurant portion to make you whatever you want to eat, and there's no time limit for whatever you want to do. Wanna see?"

"*Yes!*"

Cella laughed because the very second Marcus released his hand from the top of Tiffany's head, the girl darted toward the large tan-colored building with the big bay windows covering the entire entrance. Through part of the glass, some of the play area Marcus spoke about was visible. It reminded her of the play gym they had gone to in the city. At the other far end, a sign for a gift shop had been turned off, signaling the place was closed for the day.

Sliding glass doors opened when Tiffany came close enough to the movement sensor for it to sense her, and only then did she stop to glance back at them.

"Can I go in?"

Marcus nodded. "Trina, she's the manager of the place, will be waiting inside for you. Whatever you want to do first, she'll be there to help and keep you safe."

"Okay! Thank you, Marcus."

"You're so welcome, sweet girl."

Tiffany darted into the building, and Cella turned to face Marcus with a shake of her head. "This was way too much. Just seeing the maple trees and all that would have been far more than enough for her, but thank you."

"It's a little thing, really. And I could do it, so why not?"

Cella sighed.

Happy.

She couldn't remember when she'd been this happy.

Marcus leaned in and pressed a kiss that lingered just long enough to have Cella's heart beating a little faster in her chest. It took every single ounce of self-control that she possessed not to wrap herself right around this man. Public be damned.

There was just something about him.

It called to her.

"Now, I have to feed you, too," he said, pulling away from the kiss far too soon for her liking. "Other than break-fast, you haven't eaten. They'll whip up whatever you would like in there as well."

"Thought of everything, did you?"

Marcus winked. "I try."

She patted his cheek with her palm, and then caught his hand with her own. Once their fingers were woven tight together, and she was close to his side again like they had been walking through the forest earlier, the two headed for the entrance of the building.

And all she could think was *it's going to be a good day*.

Nothing could ruin it.

* * *

"It's so high, Ma."

Her daughter didn't lie. The play gym inside the plant

reached high enough that it actually went up along the metal rafters of the building. Of course, all the netting around the gym made it perfectly safe, and the kids couldn't go outside the many tunnels, slides, and stairs. The floor where they could walk was made up of thick rubber to make playing even safer, all things considered.

"Does it make you dizzy to look down?"

Tiffany shook her head, those golden curls of hers flying every which way in the process. "Nope!"

With that said, she pushed away from the small porthole window that was too small for kids to climb through where she had been calling out to her mother. Cella saw a pop of her daughter's curls before Tiffany jumped into the biggest slide in the play gym, the one that took the kids all the way from the top to the very bottom in seconds. Her daughter came out the other end with the skirt of her dress flying everywhere, and a big smile on her face showing off the one tooth she had missing on the bottom row of teeth.

Her first lost tooth.

"I'm doing that again," Tiffany said, laughing.

"Her poutine is almost ready," Marcus said from behind Cella. "So, whenever you think you can pull her out of there to sit down for ten minutes."

Right.

"That's going to be easier said than done."

Marcus chuckled. "No doubt. I'll leave that job to you."

"Well, thanks."

He winked her way.

The sexy bastard.

"Marcus, about the little girl—you said she wanted to see the floor of the bottling plant, right?"

The manager—Trina, Marcus said her name was—came to stand in the doorway of the playroom. It allowed parents to keep their kids separated from where the tour groups came through, and the small restaurant portion where everyone sat down to eat. There were a few small tables in the play area as well, which was where she figured Tiffany would probably eat.

"*Oui*," he answered. "She'll need the small sanitation suit, but even that will be too big, likely. We'll roll them up."

"I'll grab one from the storage at the back. It'll take me a bit—she'll have time to eat her lunch, and then we can show her the floor."

"*Merci*, Trina. You know I appreciate this."

"Yes," Cella said, "thank you for helping with this."

The woman smiled brightly, the lines around her eyes making her features seem even more welcoming. The few employees that were actually inside the plant seemed to enjoy the woman's presence, and Cella understood why. "No worries. I love seeing the kiddos light up. It's not very often we have just one in here to focus on. Usually, it's more. But anything for Marcus—he treats us well."

Cella gave Marcus a look, and he grinned right back. "Yeah, tell me about it."

Once the woman had left the doorway, Cella turned back to the play equipment to watch Tiffany climb back through the bottom large tunnel before her mother could tell her to come out and get ready for lunch.

"One more time," Cella called, "and then we have to eat!"

"Okay, Ma!"

To Marcus, Cella said quietly, "Okay really means *I will take my slow ass time*. Just for reference."

He smirked. "Kids will be kids."

"Mmhmm."

"I'll go get the food."

"Thanks," she said.

He pulled her in for a kiss that wasn't nearly long

enough for her liking. Not that it mattered. She would have that man all to herself later. Surely, she could wait for that.

"Let her have fun," Marcus told her, "no rush. We have all day."

"Right."

"Love you, hmm?"

Cella smiled at that.

How could she not?

"Love you, too."

By the time she watched Marcus head out of the play area, admiring those broad shoulders of his covered in a fitted blazer, she found Tiffany wasn't even at the middle section yet. Shaking her head, she couldn't help but laugh.

"You know, Marcus said there was no time limit on playing today, Tiff, so you don't have to *try* to be slow going back up."

Her daughter looked out a porthole near the middle. "Promise?"

Damn kid.

But she loved her.

More than she loved herself, honestly.

"Promise, baby," Cella said.

"Okay!"

Tiffany had climbed, crawled, and jumped her way to nearly the top when a piercing noise cut through the air. Cella cringed, covering her ears as she looked up to the speakers where the sound was coming from.

"What the hell is that?"

In a blink, Marcus came to the doorway. "You okay?"

Over the noise, his voice was still faint.

She pointed at the speaker. Even Tiffany couldn't be seen in the play equipment, probably covering her ears, too.

"What is that?"

"An alarm. A door must have been open in the back. Someone will shut it off in a min—"

The place went black.

Well, partly.

The power cut off before Marcus could even finish his statement. They had a bit of light from the windows, which helped, but beyond the doorway of the play section, it was quite dark.

Marcus looked behind him, and then back to Cella. "I don't know—"

It all happened so fast, then.

The roar of motorcycles.

How Marcus went from confused to *horrified*.

Glass breaking.

The smell of gasoline.

It happened *so fucking fast*.

Cella's scream for her daughter to get down became drowned in the noise—the shatter of glass as something *else* was thrown in through the window. She barely caught sight of the items, and her gaze swung from the breaking bottles with burning rags stuffed down the necks to the bikers outside in leather that roared past the now-broken windows.

Fire spread instantly.

It caught the netting.

The ribbons hanging down from the play equipment.

The flames licked up the side of the wall where her daughter was high in a tunnel. Or, that's where she'd just been a couple of minutes ago.

"Tiffany! *Tiffany!*"

CHAPTER
16

"*Tiffany!*"

Marcus rushed into the space, only managing to be barely one step ahead of Cella as he moved past the bit of netting that covered the majority of the play gym. Flames from the goddamn Molotov cocktails—*bastards*—climbed higher. As he ran for the equipment, scared to death for the little girl that was now screaming up above as she realized flames from netting were climbing to her, he cursed those fucks in every language he could speak.

"*MA!*"

"Come down the yellow slide!" Marcus shouted.

"But the fire—"

"Down the slide, Tiffany! Don't look at the fire. We're just going to come down the slide, okay? Come down the slide, *dolcezza!*"

Though his voice was raised, he still somehow managed to maintain some semblance of a calm demeanor. Although how, he had no fucking clue. Instinct, maybe, because the fear clawing at his throat was enough to damn near put him on his knees.

"Hurry," he shouted, "jump right in the slide and I will catch you as you come down, sweetheart!"

"Marcus," Cella whispered.

God.

She sounded in pain.

Like this hurt her.

He understood that all too well because at the moment, it felt like his fucking chest was going to explode from the pressure building inside him.

"We got her," he assured—although it felt like he was promising too; he'd yet to break one of those for her, and he wouldn't start now, either.

"Tiffany!"

Marcus swore he saw the heavens when Tiffany replied, "I'm coming down!"

He actually heard the sound of her thumping against the slide when she jumped into it. He cringed from knowing how hard she must have hit the thick plastic. Not that he had time to think on it for long because the black smoke from the burning netting was enough to make him choke when all he wanted to do was focus on the little girl flying down through the slide toward him.

"Catch her!" Cella cried.

He thought he might have to coach her out of the situation, but Tiffany proved to be smart and quick on her feet like every other Marcello he had ever met in his life. Including her goddamn mother.

Tiffany flew into his waiting arms first. He had already turned to run with her before he even had a proper grip on the girl.

"Just go out through the lobby," he yelled at Cella's back.

Like him, as soon as he had a hold of Tiffany, Cella turned to run. It was time to get the heck out of there.

"What happened?" Tiffany asked.

Had she not heard the bikes?

Well, she wouldn't know what that meant, he supposed. Nor why the bottles with burning rags they tossed through the broken windows had the place lighting up in seconds.

"Stupid people happened," Marcus muttered.

Cella shot him a look over her shoulder, the narrowing of her gaze darkening her pretty features before they exited the playroom. It brought them right out to the small lobby of the plant which also split off into hallways that led to work areas, the receptionist's desk, and a gift shop.

All which faced those same big windows that the play area sported. Each one that was now also broken out by the same gas jugs and crowbars from before. The gift shop had flames licking out of the door. Not a surprise considering the goddamn thing was mostly made up of *very* flammable items like plush toys, flags, T-shirts, and other knickknacks for people to buy.

And in the lobby, fire danced across the black and white checkered tiles on the floor from the little lakes of gasoline that had snaked across the room.

"Oh, my God," Cella said behind him.

The thing about old buildings?

They were fucking *old*.

This was one of the oldest maple syrup farms and plants in Canada. Not a lot about the place had changed over the past seventy years but for some modern upgrades. Part of the draw to the place for tourism was the fact it was so old and had great history for the province and even the country.

But it was still old.

And that meant it went up in flames as though it were a firework going off against a dry Christmas tree.

"What do we—"

Cella didn't even finish her statement before Marcus turned, grabbing her shoulder to shove her backward, too. "The exit down the hallway leading to the bathrooms—we'll go through there!"

He caught sight of a couple of workers going down that way, too. Hell, there were only maybe twenty on staff during an *open to the public* day. But with just him there, only a handful of people were on staff to keep the place lit up and useable. He figured those ones he saw were the only ones in the front. The two in the back inside the actual bottling section of the plant would have exited out a rear door.

Marcus kept that calm demeanor even as he kept up the pace of a jog with Cella right at his side. Panicking wouldn't do him any good, and he didn't want to scare Tiffany any more than she probably already was.

Tiffany coughed, making her crying sound even more miserable than it already did. "Why does it smell so *bad*?"

He didn't know how to tell her, but that was just what happened when shit burned. Especially when that stuff was *everything*. Plastic decorations on the wall. All the stuff inside the gift shop. Even the play equipment. Those weren't things that *should* be burned, so when it did, the smell and smoke could be both dangerous and overwhelming.

"Turn your face to my jacket," he told her, "and breathe into it, okay?"

She did.

Beside him, Cella *tried* not to seem panicked.

He could still see it.

"It's just down the hall," he said to Cella, "the next door on the left."

She made it to the door before him, shoving it open which just allowed the slight breeze from the outside to come barreling into the back hallway. The bit of pressure release went away and the black, tar-like smoke billowed out behind them.

He handed Tiffany to her mother. "Take her."

Cella did, but her wide eyes turned on him with fear. "What are you *doing*?"

The smoke behind him smelled *so fucking bad*.

Like poison.

Death.

And yet, all it took for Marcus was a quick look at the few people who had gathered at the side of the building for him to know they were missing someone.

"The plant manager," he said, "she went into the back storage to get the suit for Tiffany. She should have come out already, and if the power is out, it'll be dark."

Because the goddamn place needed a lot of upgrades. There were no safety measures in place other than a few scattered emergency lights, a few of which he knew had been busted out by the forklifts in the backrooms.

"Marcus," Cella hissed, snagging his wrist in her trembling hand before he could disappear into the building, "you can't go back in there—it's not safe!"

"Ma, my throat *hurts*," Tiffany mumbled, hugging tight to her mother, and hiding her face in Cella's neck. "It really hurts."

His gaze darted between the girl, and her mother. "Just look after her. I'll be right out. And if someone hasn't done it already, call for help."

"Marcus—"

"I'll be right back—I promise."

He let the door close behind him, and headed back into the dark, smoky hallway. Above the crackling of the flames, he could hear the phone in his pocket buzzing. He ignored it as he pulled the lapel of his blazer up over his mouth to cough into the fabric and try to give him some sort of filter to breathe without as much smoke.

Not that it helped.

Fucking pointless, really.

Marcus came back into the lobby, but quickly realized the space was far darker than it had been just minutes before. No, that was wrong—it was black from *smoke*. The heat from the flames felt like they were licking far too close to him as he used his knowledge of the area to head for the swinging double doors that led into the bottling plant on the right side of the receptionist's desk.

Not that he knew if he was going the right way by sight because he couldn't fucking see at all. The phone in his pocket kept ringing.

And *ringing*.

"Trina!" Marcus shouted into the bottling section of the plant.

The storage was at the back of the plant where it would be easy for the workers to move pallets of bottled syrup to the rooms at the rear. While there were exit doors *in* the plant, and cargo doors for trailers to back up, in the rooms where they kept things for the tours and the general public, there were none.

And chances were, Trina hadn't even known a fire started if the power had been cut. Which was exactly why the alarm stopped.

But why had the alarm been set in the first place?

She should have been out by now.

That alarm was for *break-ins*. Pushing those double doors wide to enter the main floor of the plant had been a mistake because the second he did, it took the place all of ten seconds to fill with smoke.

More smoke.

The fire had traveled.

"Trina!"

In the quick moment it took for the place to fill with all that toxic smoke, Marcus found the plant manager. On the other side of the conveyer belt at the far end of the plant near one of two exit doors, apparently, the one that had its glass smashed out at the top which explained the alarm, the plant manager rested face down in a puddle of her own blood.

The wires leading into the main breaker box for the plant had been cut.

Marcus didn't need to check to know Trina was dead.

And now he couldn't breathe, either.

He moved for the door with the broken window, coughing harder into his jacket. The smoke crawled out of the hole leading to the outside in thick plumes, and while he tried his hardest not to breathe it in, he couldn't help it.

How did the bikers know he would be here?

Who gave them that information?

It was all Marcus could think about as he pushed open the exit door and rushed outside into the fresh air. He thought taking in huge gulps of the outside would help, but his throat burned. His eyes watered from stinging so bad.

All he could taste was that *smoke*.

And then the coughing started again.

Until all he could do was cough.

Marcus managed to make it a good fifteen feet *away* from the plant before he passed out.

* * *

"Sir, please, you have to keep the mask on your face."

Hard plastic was shoved over Marcus's mouth as his vision cleared, and he came back to reality. He took in the chaos around him. No, that was a lie. It wasn't chaotic inside the ambulance. In fact, the paramedic working on him did so with a calm demeanor and steady hands.

He dragged in a lungful of the oxygen pumping through the mask, but it didn't feel like it helped to actually give him air.

"Breathed in too much of that smoke—your lungs are going to feel like hell for a while," the man explained.

From the front of the ambulance, a new voice called back, "Did you hear the other guys back there?"

"Yeah," his paramedic replied, "guess there was a body

inside, and all the windows were busted out with crowbars and gas jugs. It's a fuckin' *maple farm*, eh? What happened back there?"

He swallowed the roughness in his throat.

He knew what came after this.

Marcus blinked.

The white ceiling of the ambulance stared back at him.

"Cella—Tiff?"

The man passed him a look. "We're almost to the hospital. I'm about to give you a shot. It's going to calm you down, let you relax for a bit."

Fuck.

Marcus didn't *want* anything.

He just wanted to know if Cella and—

A sharp prick in his arm followed the sensation of something cold rushing through his veins.

And that was that.

* * *

"Marcus! *Marcus!*"

"Sir, please step back from the gurney—"

"That's my fucking brother, *back off.*"

"Sir, he's going to be fine, but he needs better oxygenation and—"

All at once, Marcus's brother colored his vision. He wasn't sure what had been in that *shot* the paramedic gave him, but it knocked him out good. Whether or not that was the medication's intended purpose, he couldn't really say.

But it worked.

"Cella called Ma," Chris explained fast, "and we're working on it, okay?"

Marcus opened his mouth to talk, but it fucking ached.

His throat killed him.

"I know," Chris said, "you don't gotta talk, man."

Marcus shook his head, his thoughts running a million miles a minute. The mask pressed tight to his face fogged with every breath he took, and while it hurt to do it, he couldn't help the need to breathe.

"The enforcer," he mumbled under the mask.

Was the gurney still moving?

It felt like it.

Strange how nothing more than inhaling smoke could lay somebody out.

Damn.

"What?" Chris asked.

Marcus's gazed darted to the paramedics wheeling him toward what he suspected was the emergency room of the hospital, and his brother seemed to understand. Chris leaned down, still walking just as fast as they moved.

"Tell me, Marcus."

"The enforcer," he croaked out, "at the tribute. He's the only one who heard us talking about this weekend, Chris. He's the only one that knew I'd be at the eastern farm."

"Marcus—"

"Pull him in. Get the fucking info."

The next thing Marcus saw was the ceiling of the hospital.

CHAPTER 17

The thing about trauma?

It never goes away.

A permanent scar on one's soul and psyche, it stayed dormant until a trigger came along to make it flare back to life.

Muscle memory, some called it. Like a person's body and mind just *remembered* what it felt like in the moment when they experienced their worst trauma, and instinct took over. It became impossible to act rationally or really comprehend what was going on when every single part of someone was screaming to survive.

Just fucking *survive*.

Cella barely remembered anything after Marcus went back inside the building. Just flashes of moments that led her to sit in the hospital's emergency waiting room with her sleeping daughter tucked into her lap.

The sirens.

Smoke.

Paramedics checking her.

Someone asking Tiffany's name.

Other details were foggier like the police that quickly came on the scene after the firefighters arrived to battle what had turned into a very dangerous blaze in only minutes. The paramedics who took her to the hospital, assuring her that she and Tiffany were fine and suffered very little smoke inhalation.

Right.

Yeah, she remembered all those details.

But not how she responded.

Not what her child said.

Just the flashes.

The moments.

So, as she sat in the hard, plastic chair of the emergency waiting room, all Cella could do was become lost in the rushing tidal waves of her past trauma. Memories thick with fear that tasted the exact same as what she felt like right now. Brief, short snapshots of a time that she hadn't thought about in a long time because that's also what trauma did to someone.

It made them forget.

Until it made them remember.

Cella didn't want to go back to that time—the day when she lost William—and yet, she was thrust there all the same. No warning. No help.

No escape.

Her mind was hell.

"*No, Daddy.*"

She screamed at her father when he told her. Fought his hold—the hug he offered. At some point, she'd hit him. More than once. Begged for him to be lying. Puked all over the floor when they finally got her out of a hotel hallway and into the privacy of a room where they could explain more.

She could still taste the vomit.

Or maybe that was because she wanted to puke *now*.

Cella couldn't be sure.

Muscle memory, again.

"Wait, what the fuck do you *mean*?" she heard someone ask sharply to her left.

Cella glanced in that direction, recognizing the two men huddled together in the corner of the room as Marcus's brothers.

Christopher.

Bene.

She heard their conversation.

In her mind, though, she saw her father. He'd come to her room that morning to ask if she wanted to have breakfast with her mother. They'd been at the hotel overnight for her cousin's wedding. Someone in the hallway had said something to her father. That horrified look on his face when he turned back to Cella in the room …

She would never forget that look.

That moment when she *knew* something happened to William.

Tiffany had been in the car when they shot it up, and run him off the road. He wasn't really the target, he was just *easy* for them to attack. A way to make a point to the Marcellos because that was how the fucking mafia worked.

Her husband hadn't needed to be the person who started the war between her family and another one. He didn't even need to be *made*. He just had to be an easy fucking target and connected to their family in some way.

"It's definitely the bikers, then?" she heard Bene ask.

"All the witnesses, the few people that were at the place," Chris replied, "all said the same thing. They heard the bikes —the two at the lobby actually saw the bikers go past and throw the shit through the windows. So, yes."

"*Fuck*. Dad is gonna—"

"Let Marcus handle it," Chris said fast. "That is what Dad needs to do."

"Yeah, I know, but … whatever, how the fuck did they even know Marcus was there today? And why the hell didn't he just put those assholes down *months* ago when they first started causing problems?"

Wait …

Had this been happening for a while?

Were the Guzzis having issues with rivals that had turned violent?

The thought made Cella sick because she hadn't *known*. If she had, then she very well might have made different choices for her daughter's safety. She'd trusted Marcus to keep them safe. That's what he told her he would do, but how was keeping information like that from her making sure they *were* safe?

"Because it's *Marcus*." Chris blew out a hard breath, adding, "It's Marcus, Bene, and he knows better than to just answer violence with more violence. It's the last resort —*always*."

"Yeah, and look where it fucking got him."

"You don't even know what you're fucking talking about, man."

In her lap, Tiffany shifted in her sleep. Cella should wake her daughter up, and get her something to drink. She was sure her throat was probably still dry and aching. A lot like hers in that moment, although only partly caused by the smoke she'd inhaled. The rest of that pain was from all the tears she kept holding back.

She couldn't cry.

Not now.

Not *here*.

Once she started, she was not going to stop.

As it was, she had barely held it together for this long. Dragged back through the memories of her husband's murder while being terrified for her child today, and a man she fell in love with, allowing herself to be vulnerable to this very thing *again* … she couldn't cry yet.

"We pulled the enforcer in," Chris said, "because that's what Marcus asked for us to do thinking it was him who gave the bikers the information about where to find him. Little late to apologize to the guy because his fucking brain matter is all over a cement floor in the west end's warehouse, but it wasn't even him. This wasn't even meant to be an attack on *Marcus*, okay? So you don't know what you're fucking talking about, Bene, just shut up."

"What?"

"Yeah. Seems the fucking farm notified everyone on their social media that the place would be closed down to the public for the day because they had a *special guest* coming in. Marcus probably wouldn't even have known they did that. I bet the fucking bikers just thought it would be an easy hit—it might not even have been the Quebec chapter of the Riders that did it. It could have been any one of the chapters that rode in thinking they'd let the Guzzis know they were in town. Marcus being there was just *circumstance*."

"Fuck," Bene breathed. "Where's Ma and Papa?"

"On their way. I called Corrado, too."

Bene cleared his throat. "I sent Beni a message 'cause he had some shit to do today, but I'll call again."

Cella heard it all, of course.

Her heart ached for a man who lost his life for reasons she didn't even understand. Her soul hurt for the child in her lap who had cried herself to sleep.

And as for *her*?

Cella?

She still couldn't fucking breathe.

Still couldn't get those memories to *leave*.

* * *

A person connected to the mob knew how events like these

went down once police became involved. Of course, the *say nothing, saw nothing* approach was always best and the only thing acceptable to *la famiglia*.

However, she found it disgusting how the second the police realized the maple farm and plant were attached to the Guzzi name, and the second victim of the fire who actually needed medical attention—Marcus —was identified as a Guzzi, their entire demeanor changed.

They were no longer victims.

They were just *connected*.

For a bit, Cella had the benefits of Marcus's family deflecting the police attention on her and Tiffany—who had finally woken up from her nap—while they waited for the doctor to give the okay on Marcus, and allow visitors into his room.

She was pissed.

Terrified.

Mad like nothing else.

But *God*, she stayed there. Through her flashbacks, and the ache in her throat from a lump that formed and wouldn't leave no matter how many times she tried to swallow it down. She stayed even though her heart raced so fast it felt like it was going to explode out of her chest. She didn't move out of her chair even when all she wanted to do was hide away and cry because of the horrors this day dredged up for her.

She stayed.

For him, she stayed.

She had things to say to him, and she was mad, yes. Because clearly there had been a lot of things going on in the business side of his life that he hadn't at least given her a fore-warning about, so she could make her own choices, none of that mattered. She loved Marcus, and so she stayed through her fear and her pain because this was where she needed to be.

Even if this hurt her, too.

"Hello, what's your name?"

"Tiffany Gagnon-Marcello."

Cella blinked out of her stupor to find a woman—one she didn't recognize—had come to sit in the chair next to Tiffany's. Cara had brought the girl a sandwich and juice from the cafeteria on the second floor, but where the rest of the Guzzis had disappeared to, Cella wasn't sure. A quick glance around the waiting room let her know they must have slipped out for a moment because the only people left were faces she didn't recognize filling the chairs around her.

Including the woman talking to her daughter.

"And how are you doing today, Miss Tiffany?" the woman asked.

Her daughter frowned. "Well, I'd be a lot better if I could see Marcus."

"I bet. Do you remember what happened today?"

Always polite, her daughter seemed *far* too willing to talk to woman and answer her questions. Had that been a man, Cella bet Tiffany would have kept her lips tightly shut. Before her daughter said another thing to the woman dressed in a cheap-looking pantsuit, she spoke up to find out just what this person wanted and who they were.

"I'm sorry, who are you?" Cella asked.

She didn't even *try* to tamper her tone.

The woman with brown eyes that *seemed* warm looked to Cella with a smile that was just as welcoming as her stare. "Emilia Denesry, but most people just call me Constable—"

A cop.

That was all Cella needed to hear. In a heartbeat, she reached into the next chair and pulled her daughter right out of it and slightly further away from the woman sitting too close to her. Tiffany looked up at her mother, eyes wide with confusion, but Cella just held tight and didn't bother to hide the glare she leveled on the cop who rolled her eyes.

"They thought it would be better for *me* to get your statement, and one from your daughter, Ms. Marcello. It's Cella, right?"

"What task force are you on?" Cella demanded.

The woman just smiled. "No one said anything about a task force."

"Right, but I bet you're on *something*. Something specific to watching the Guzzi family, and since you're looking at me as though you know who I am, you should already know what's going to be said to you. We saw nothing at the farm. My daughter was in the play equipment when the fire started, and we were too focused on getting her out to see anything else."

"Ma," Tiffany started.

"Quiet, baby."

She kept her tone happy for Tiffany.

Not so happy for the cop.

"You should understand, Cella, that being you're an American on Canadian soil, if you choose not to cooperate with the investigation here, we can take action against you to have you removed back to your country. All it takes is the filing of some paperwork and a couple of calls. Are you involved with Marcus Guzzi in some way? Is that why you want to protect him here?"

"He was a victim of today," Cella replied.

"Or an instigator," the woman said back.

Cella's jaw ached from clenching her teeth so hard.

Then, the woman's eyes turned on Tiffany. "As for her … well, if we have reason to believe your daughter is a valuable witness to this investigation—"

"She didn't see *anything*."

"*Ma*."

Tiffany's whisper had Cella's panic rising higher. Like her daughter could just tell something was wrong here, and her mother was two seconds away from snapping. It had all been just a little too much. The day had started out beautifully but ended *horribly*. From the fire to the fucking hospital, and now these cops.

It was all just too much.

And with the way her daughter fisted her shirt as though she didn't want to let her mother go, the tiny tremble of Tiffany's hands obvious to Cella, all she wanted to do was protect her child. Take her away from this, and let her breathe.

"But she might have seen something," the female cop replied, "and that's another phone call and a few signatures away from getting her pulled into the station for a proper interview. So, would you like to talk now, or later?"

"Are you threatening me?" Cella demanded.

"Oh, I'm sure you know how this game is played, Cella. Your father—Lucian. How many times was he arrested during your childhood?"

Fuck you.

"My official statement for you is *no comment*," Cella hissed.

The woman's threats were useless, albeit scary. If only because Cella knew it would take her an hour to get to Marcus's place, get in her car, and then drive two hours to be back on American soil where this bitch couldn't do fuck all.

"How about—"

"No comment," Cella repeated.

That time, she stood from the chair as she spoke. She'd said what she said, and she had nothing more to add. Grabbing her bag from the chair, and keeping her daughter on her hip who was way too heavy to be carried, she headed for the exit of the emergency's waiting room with the cop still calling her name at her back.

She didn't turn around.

The only thing she *needed* to do right then was to protect her child.

Tiffany came first.

Always.

"Ma, what did that woman want?"

Cella dragged in a hard breath, remembering the interviews she'd been forced to go through with police after her husband's death. *Hours and hours* of interviews while someone else held and cared for her baby because the police just wouldn't accept that her husband had been an easy target, and not murdered for any other reason than his connection to her.

She wouldn't do that again.

Couldn't.

And there was no fucking way in *hell* Tiffany would experience it.

Cella would make sure of it.

"Hey, hey, where are you going? Are you *leaving*?"

Cella had barely made it out of the hospital before someone else decided to take her for another round like she was up for it today. This time, it was a familiar face.

Chris Guzzi.

"I have to go," Cella said, her tone short and her words *angry* when he stepped in her path to stop her from leaving. "Get out of my way."

"Where in the hell are you even going?"

"Away from here, now move."

Not that she expected him to understand.

She couldn't explain.

The memories were back again.

Killing her again.

"You can't just leave—Marcus is going to ask for you, Cella."

"I have to go," she repeated firmly.

Chris let go of her wrist, his expression disgusted. She hadn't even realized he'd been holding onto her. That's how *numb* she felt from the terror wrapping around her like a cobra ready to slowly suffocate her to death.

"Ma, I want to see Marcus," Tiffany said quietly.

Cella kept walking.

"Are you running?" Chris called behind her. "What, shit gets tough, Cella, and you have to run? Is that it?"

Fuck him, too.

He was probably just as pissed as she was. Just as scared. Except he didn't know her fear.

This pain.

He didn't know it.

And she wouldn't explain.

"Ma, I want *Marcus*," Tiffany said, watery eyes staring up at her.

Tiffany had been too young that day to ask for her father as they sat in a hospital waiting room while they cried for a man who was already gone. Today, she could ask.

How was Cella supposed to deal with that?

Cella still couldn't talk.

Her own tears had finally started coming.

* * *

Cella made it across the border a little past twelve at night. It took her longer than she expected to grab all of their shit at Marcus's place. She barely managed to get her composure to face the border agent who asked for her passport and reason for coming back into the states, along with the request to declare if she had purchased anything in Canada that she was bringing back.

Somehow, she kept her tears at bay.

While still dying inside.

At some point, Tiffany stopped asking for Marcus. Maybe because she noticed that the more she asked for him, the harder Cella would cry.

Yes.

God, yes, she wanted to turn the car back around and give her daughter exactly what she asked for. She wanted nothing more than that man who she was sure had finally been granted visitors, which he expected to be them, amongst many others. They wouldn't be there.

Because Chris had been right.

Cella *ran*.

Tiffany, the sweet girl she was, so fucking loved by her mother, forever Cella's very best friend because that kid sometimes felt like all she had in the world, decided to try calming her mother down. As though that was her job.

All it served to do was make Cella feel like a shitty fucking mother.

Her kid fell asleep just before the border.

Cella cried until her eyes burned. Until her throat constricted around every sob she tried to hide, so it wouldn't wake her daughter up in the back seat. Knowing she couldn't go one more mile without a worse breakdown than she was already experiencing, she managed to pull off on the side of the freeway and get her phone from the bag in the passenger seat.

She called the only people that would understand.

Those who had been there *that day*.

That day when she lost everything.

It felt like Cella was living in that day again.

She didn't move after she made the phone call. Didn't

pull back on the highway, and couldn't be bothered to watch the cars speed on by without even considering stopping to see if the woman in the black BMW needed help.

She did need help.

Not from strangers, though.

Her father got to her in *four* hours.

Just the drive to her place would have taken him at least six. From Rochester to her current location, another hour or more. She didn't even want to know how fast he drove.

Her brother came with him.

John took Tiffany from the back seat and let Cella give her daughter a hug and a kiss.

"Uncle John is gonna take you home, okay?"

Tiffany sniffled, so confused and tired.

Cella hated herself more.

Why couldn't she do this?

Why couldn't she breathe through this?

"Cella," she heard John say.

She met her brother's gaze.

He nodded like that was a whole battle won right there. "It's okay to need a minute—she's going to fine when you are. It's *okay* to not be okay."

Of course, John would be the one to say that.

Of course, because he would know better than anyone.

"Take her home, John," Lucian murmured.

"Say bye to your ma, Tiff," John told her daughter. Tiffany tried to smile, and wave.

Cella managed the same.

"Bye, Ma. Love you."

"Love you, too, baby."

John moved Tiffany to the other car. She watched the taillights of her father's Mercedes disappear on the freeway.

Lucian sat in the passenger seat next to Cella in the BMW, saying nothing, and letting her scream it out.

Just scream.
It felt like she'd been doing that for so long.
Screaming without sound.
Inside, where no one knew.
Now it was all coming out.

CHAPTER

18

"It wouldn't hurt to stay in the hospital for another day, *fils*," Gian said even as Marcus continued to heave himself from the uncomfortable bed. Honestly, what did Canadians pay all their taxes for if that was the piece of shit they had to *rest* on? "The doctor said—"

"I could leave or stay. I'm leaving."

Jesus.

Marcus felt like the floor wobbled under his feet when he stood from the bed, and he was sure that wasn't supposed to happen. He didn't acknowledge the dizziness because it would only make his family worry more, and he had other things on his mind to handle.

"I'll get the walking papers," Chris muttered near the door, turning to leave right after.

"Has anyone else arrived?" Cara asked. "Corrado was coming in, right?"

"Lands around noon."

Marcus let out a hard sigh. The only show of his annoyance, really. "Why? He doesn't need to come—he has enough things to handle at home with Les and Ginevra, and the kids. I am *fine*."

"Beni will be here Tuesday," Bene spoke up.

"Great, are we just having a fucking get well soon party, or …?"

He appreciated his family's efforts, certainly, but he didn't want or need everyone to gather around him like he was about to die. He hadn't even *almost* died. Well … that depended on who you asked, but Marcus felt how he felt. Simple as that.

His mother and father shared a look. Then, Gian nodded his head at the door and without needing told verbally, his mother said she was going to step out of the room for a moment. That left Marcus alone with his father, and Bene.

"I'm checking out," he told them.

"I'm not going to argue with you if it's what you want to do," Gian replied, "but we should also go over some of the information we've gathered since yesterday regarding the bikers and their attack, don't you think?"

"What I'd really like to know," Marcus replied instead of answering his father's question, "is why no one has told me where Cella and Tiffany are despite the fact I've asked at least a dozen times since I woke up this morning."

Shit, whatever medication the paramedic gave him knocked him clean out. It was possible—very likely, really— that the doctor had given him something to help him sleep and relax through the night once they figured out he wasn't suffering from burn injuries, and mostly just needed oxygen to help his lungs.

He woke up to a room full of people.

All people he loved, yes.

Except for two.

Cella and Tiff.

Where was *she*?

The silence that coated his hospital room wasn't lost on Marcus. He let his father and brother chew on whatever they didn't want to say as he shedded the fucking awful, scratchy hospital-issued gown to change into the three-piece suit someone had brought him. He recognized the clothes as his own, so someone must have gone to his house.

Cella?

He doubted it.

A part of him just *knew* …

"Well?" he asked, yanking the pants up around his hips.

A look passed between his brother and father.

"Business first, *oui*?" Gian shrugged, trying to keep a calm disposition, but Marcus could see right through it. "Business always comes first, Marcus, and then we'll deal with the rest."

Fine.

If that was the game he had to play …

"What did the enforcer have to say?" he asked.

"It wasn't the enforcer who gave the biker gang any information about your whereabouts this weekend," Bene spoke up, clearing his throat when Marcus's sharp gaze turned on him. "We brought him in, questioned him, and nothing came from it. Believing he was lying, the man who did the questioning chose to kill him. In vain, because again, wasn't him."

Marcus's jaw was beginning to ache from how hard he clenched his teeth. "I'm not following."

"The social media accounts for the maple farm," Gian put in, crossing his arms over his chest as he spoke, "had announced it would be closed for the day to the public due to a *special guest*, as they put it. The guest wasn't specifically named, but it makes sense they would post about their change in hours. We have it on good faith that the bikers were following the accounts, and thought the farm would be an easy hit."

Really?

Fucking really, though?

"And a very publicized one," Bene added, "considering how popular that particular farm is, and the number of tourists that come in and out of it on a yearly basis. The bastards probably thought to hit you where it would really hurt. Force some of this into the public spotlight, and—"

"Maybe I would have a change of heart about business with them," Marcus interjected gruffly.

The harsh flood of irritation through his bloodstream was enough to have Marcus's vision swimming all over again. He pushed aside the dizziness to throw on the pressed dress shirt before he took his time doing up the buttons. All the while, he cursed in every fucking language he knew inside his head.

A boss didn't *overreact*.

Not when others watched.

Not even if those others were family.

"It was circumstance," his father said finally, breaking the silence between the three, "and nothing more. They had no idea you were going to be there, and I have no doubt they're trying to rally now that they know there has definitely been a line crossed."

"Oh, you think?"

Marcus didn't bother to tamper his attitude, but if his father felt any sort of way about it, the man didn't say. He finished getting dressed, slipping on socks, then shoes, and finally the blazer resting over the foot of the hospital bed.

"Where is my goddamn phone?"

"Cops took it," Bene muttered, "*evidence*, they said."

"Of course, they did."

"Yeah, but the fire ruined it anyway because they couldn't even turn the fucker on, so."

"And if a program can successfully pull info *off* it?" Marcus asked sharply.

"Man, since when do you do *that* kind of business on your personal phone?"

"Marcus, relax," Gian murmured.

How?

How should he do that?

"I'm done with the bikers," he said, settling himself on that fact. "I'm not playing their games anymore, and I have let this go on for too long. My next step for them will be to permanently remove them from the situation."

"If that's—"

"Where is Cella?"

He hadn't turned around to face his father or brother. The person who answered his most important question wasn't Gian or Bene, however.

"She left yesterday. Packed her kid up, walked out of the hospital, and wouldn't explain shit to me when I tried to talk to her."

Marcus turned to find Chris had come back to the room, only now he leaned in the doorway. The blank expression on Chris's face belied the anger he found in his brother's stare.

"She left?" he asked.

"I tried to—"

"She's gone."

That time, it wasn't even a question.

A million and one things raced through Marcus's mind in those few seconds where no one around him had anything to say. He wanted to demand answers, although it was clear no one would have any for him. He wanted to ask for someone's phone so that he could call Cella himself and find out why she felt like she had to leave at a time like this. The rational part of his brain knew he couldn't make a scene, certainly not one over a woman, and he also knew Cella …

Her history.

This *life*.

"All right," Marcus said thickly.

Chris cleared his throat. "Sorry, man."

Right.

"Did you get my walking papers? I'm not staying in this hospital like a sitting duck for one more second."

"The doctor said you really should stay," Chris said with a shrug. "Even for just the day, Marcus."

"Absolutely not."

Not with this giant fucking hole in his heart.

Nobody would fix that.

* * *

The voices of Marcus's family filtered up through the stairwell as his brothers discussed what their next move would be in between phone calls. Those calls had to be made, if only because any made Guzzi man with sense would be currently wondering about the state of their boss. No doubt, word of the attack would have traveled through the grapevine, and now they needed updates. Not only that, but they needed direction.

A *stand down* until otherwise notified.

A *lay low* from all the media and police.

Fucking hell.

Marcus's next couple of weeks would be full of dodging interviews with officials while also trying to plan his next, and *final*, move against the biker gang. Not to mention, the media attention that would be all over this fucking story.

Things he didn't need …

Bene and Chris took care of *la famiglia's* side of things, which took something off his list to worry about for the moment. Chris would also be handling the personal side of things for Marcus while he was at it. All phone calls that weren't from his immediate family would go through his personal assistant, who he still hadn't spent more than five minutes with, but Chris assured the woman could handle it all. Everything else, he was told, would be only details.

He needed to focus on *work*.

Business.

The bastards in Quebec.

Or, that's what he should be doing.

Marcus, on the other hand, paced in his upstairs office as he listened to the conversation happening downstairs. A conversation he should absolutely join because his voice, as the acting boss, was really the only one that needed to be heard. And yet, he didn't go down to join his brothers.

Or his father.

Gian accompanied him home, too, but was currently quiet downstairs.

As for Marcus, well, he couldn't stop looking at the goddamn phone on his desk. With every pass he made by the phone at the edge of the desk, the need growing inside his chest to just *call her* became more and more prominent. He couldn't seem to ignore it no matter how hard he tried. The bigger problem was the other shit he felt.

Bitterness.

Betrayal.

But how should one—someone like him—feel when he allowed someone like Cella into his life, gave her the parts of himself that he kept most protected, and then she was so quick to throw it aside when the inevitable happened.

Because that was the thing ...

This had been inevitable. Whether it happened yesterday, or four months from now, it *would* happen. That was just this life of theirs. Something was always right around the corner waiting to show them that one couldn't escape the legacy following them.

He understood this life had already taken from her, and no doubt, the thought of it taking more scared her away but that didn't change how he felt.

This heaviness.

The *loneliness.*

It didn't answer his *whys.*

"Are you going to call her, then?"

Marcus had been reaching for the phone—his inner desires making themselves known without his physical permission—as his father asked the question from the doorway. He dropped his hand back to his side and spun on his heels to face Gian.

"You don't know how to knock?" he demanded.

To his father's benefit, Gian barely blinked at the attitude. Apparently, there was a first for everything. Maybe it was the circumstances they currently found themselves in as to why his father was letting things slip that he normally wouldn't, but Marcus couldn't be sure.

"Sorry," Marcus quickly said, "I'm just ... in a mood."

Gian shrugged, leaning against the doorjamb. "I have decided you are allowed to ... do whatever you would like to do, attitude included."

"I beg your pardon?"

"You said something to me that made me think. Was I letting you do your job the way *you* should do it, or was I putting too much of my expectations on you to behave as I would? Maybe you didn't say it in those words, but that's what I considered. I'm making an effort not to do that anymore, *fils*."

Huh.

"I appreciate it," Marcus replied.

"I actually wonder whether or not the fact you haven't already permanently taken care of the issues with the gang in Quebec had anything to do with me. And if so, does that make *me* to blame for what happened? I'm not sure, but it's where my mind is at the moment."

"Do you want an honest answer?"

Gian smiled. "I expect nothing less from you, Marcus."

"Yes," Marcus said. "*Yes*, I kept you in the back of my mind. I didn't want to do what you did—I remember how you told me taking over *la famiglia* in the midst of chaos made it harder to feel comfortable in your position. That your seat felt unsteady."

"You don't have to prove yourself."

Didn't he?

His father was *Gian Guzzi*.

Everything about his entire life felt like a moment to show up and stand out. The only Guzzi singleton without a twin. The one people said looked and acted *most* like their father.

"You should stop thinking like me," Gian told him, "and start just being you. They don't want the same boss they've had for the last thirty years. Because in case you haven't figured it out yet, you're not me and everyone knows you can't be. Your brothers are handling things downstairs for you, so don't feel like you need to join them until you're ready. They don't expect you to because like you, they know their place, Marcus."

"Tell Chris I want to go ahead with Plan B with a few extras for the chapters that have arrived into town so that everyone knows where the Guzzi family stands. He'll know what Plan B is."

"I think we all know what Plan B is, son."

Yeah, well …

His father turned to leave, saying over his shoulder, "And who knows, Marcus, maybe chaos will make your seat in this family a little more comfortable. Also, you won't know what the woman in New York wants from or with you unless you call her. Might it hurt? *Oui,* but is she not worth that risk? That's the important question. It determines everything."

Alone again with only his thoughts and misery to keep him company, Marcus went back to pacing the length of his office and ignoring the phone on the desk. No, that was a lie.

He couldn't *ignore* the phone when the entire time, he continued to stare right at it.

Call her, call her ... call her.

The mantra in his mind played on.

Nothing felt right.

Everything was *so wrong*.

Because she wasn't there.

Marcus hadn't planned for that.

He didn't know how to make it better when at the end of the day, he couldn't make Cella come back. There wasn't anything he could say that would be good enough, he knew. All her worst fears had just come true all over again.

Only this time, she had a child to think about, too. A child who was old enough to understand what had happened. So despite how he felt, so fucking wrong and turned inside out because the woman who had his heart hadn't given it back when she left, he decided that even if it killed him ... this had to be on Cella.

If she needed time, so be it.

She could have it.

Silence?

He'd not say a word.

She had to come back.

She had to want to.

For now, Marcus would focus on making Plan B a reality because if he learned anything over the last day ... it was that he didn't have time to waste. Tomorrow didn't seem to be promised.

* * *

One of the many good things that came along with being a Guzzi was their reach. The power they could extend when needed was unmatched. Marcus had never been more grateful for that if only because once he committed to Plan B where the bikers were concerned, things moved fast enough to satisfy his need for vengeance.

He wasn't the vengeful type. A desire for revenge had never been something that filled his days constantly. And yet, the moment the gang made a move against Marcus, and people he cared about ended up caught in the crossfire … well, all bets were off.

"Are you sure this is what you want to do?" Chris asked from the front seat as he navigated the vehicle into a parallel parking spot near a Quebec café just at the edge of a small town. "I know you're going to tell me not to ask you that, *but* I feel like I have to, Marcus."

In the backseat, Marcus frowned at his reflection in the mirror. "I know, Chris."

It's who his brother was.

They couldn't help who they were.

"And yes," Marcus added with a sigh, "this is what I want to do."

"The media—the police … I mean, have you seriously considered what today will do to our business? How much attention this is going to bring? The fact you won't be able to walk out of your house without a camera in your face, or a fucking cop on your heels?"

Of course.

He considered all of that, and much more.

It changed nothing.

"If it was Val," Marcus said quietly, "or your daughters … would you risk it happening again?"

"I'm not saying—"

"It's a yes or no answer. Either you would or you wouldn't."

"You already know the answer to that. I just wonder why you're allowing your final straw to be a woman who left you while you were recovering in the hospital without so much as a goodbye and still hasn't contacted you after a week."

"Because that doesn't change the fact that I love her." Marcus reached for the door handle of the car when his brother put it into the park but hesitated before opening it to add, "And the next time, it might be your wife. Our mother. My godson, or any other one of my nieces or nephews. The next time they try to come for us, it could be someone you love. So, if you think that I am choosing *this* route just for her, you're mistaken. I am not, nor have I ever been, that self-ish. All I ever did before today, and after, is look out for this family. I don't know how to do anything different, Christopher. And don't act as though you didn't know that."

"Marcus—"

"He makes a stop at the café every afternoon—I need to be in there, yes? I'm sure we can pick up this conversation where we left it when I get back. Make the calls and have everyone in position. Understood?"

Chris nodded. "Yeah, I hear you."

"Thank you."

Marcus pushed open the back door and stepped out of the car. Before he closed it back up, however, he hesitated just long enough to bend down and say to his brother, "And I know you want to protect me—business aside, we're speaking on *family* here. I get you don't want shit to fuck with me, including a woman, Chris, but you don't need to keep reminding me that she left. I know what she did. I am *alone* because of her choice, but it was hers to make. You have not lived her life or lost the things she has; so have your opinions, feel whatever way you need to about what she did, but it changes nothing for me."

"I'm trying," his brother muttered.

Marcus dragged in a breath that hurt.

It all hurt lately.

"Try harder."

His piece said, Marcus shut the car door and headed across the street to the small café where the first part of his plan would be put into motion. As the boss, he couldn't be directly involved in the main portion of his plan—a bit too dangerous, all things considered. He could still make it known that every single thing that was about to happen to the chapter of the Riders in Quebec had been done by his hand to people who needed to know.

Under *only* his direction.

Once inside the café, Marcus ordered a black coffee just to give him something to do although he had no intention of drinking it. He found a seat near the front windows which would allow *his* men to see him, and with his back facing the glass, the man he was currently waiting on wouldn't know Marcus was inside until it was too late.

Which was entirely the point.

Marcus palmed the mug, watching the steam rise and curl around the rounded edge. Across the quiet café high on the wall, a clock ticked down the minutes. Not that he particularly liked having time to himself to get lost in his thoughts lately, but he did exactly that as he waited.

Thankfully, he didn't have to sit in that pit of hell for very long. The ringing of the bell above the entrance door had Marcus turning his head to find Glen Cote standing on the café's welcome mat. In his leather and patch, a beard that touched his chest, and jeans that looked as though they had seen better days, he was sure the man came off as formidable to anyone standing up against him.

To Marcus, the man was a fucking nuisance.

Had been since the beginning.

Glen, comfortable in the café as he believed this part of Quebec to be *his* territory alone, especially since he'd taken over as the chapter's president for the Riders, the man didn't even bother to look around the business before he headed for the front to order. Marcus bided his time, knowing better than to cause a scene when as it was, this entire day would be exactly that in a *major* way.

Once Glen had a coffee in a to-go cup ready in his hand, the man turned to leave. *Finally*, his gaze landed on Marcus sitting at the two-person table near the door. He took great enjoyment from watching the way the man's face morphed from surprise to confusion in a blink. Sure, he attempted to appear unbothered, but it was still there.

Marcus liked that a lot.

"Don't know what you're doing in these parts, Guzzi," Glen said as he neared Marcus's table, "but that's a mistake— I've got enough Riders in Quebec to make a call that will promise you won't get out of town before they kill you."

"Right to the threats, huh?" Marcus smirked and waved at the chair across from his. "Take a seat."

"I have other things to do."

"Yes, like your twice weekly visit to the previous president's old lady, right? That's what you all call those women you keep close. Does she know you fuck her stepdaughter on the weekend, too?"

Glen's jaw clenched.

Marcus shrugged. "Just curious."

"Leave."

"No can do," Marcus replied, "because we still haven't had the chance to chat after that little mistake of yours with the maple farm in eastern Ontario. See, I know you all weren't aware I was there that day, but I was. With people I cared about, too, and when you put them in danger for your cause … well, I had to draw a line, Glen. I'm sure you understand, or shit, maybe you don't. I really don't give a fuck anymore."

"What does that mean?"

"Are you going to sit down?"

"No."

Marcus nodded. "Didn't figure you would. See, that's where your problems first started with me. You couldn't give me respect, Glen. You thought you were going to *take* respect from me like I just owed it to you. My only debt is to God and Cosa Nostra. Before you try to play with the big guns, you really should learn a bit about men like me."

Before the asshole across the table could say anything, Marcus stood up. He still hadn't drunk a drop from the coffee, but he left it on the table, unconcerned. Pushing in the chair, he then fixed his blazer and gave Glen a nod.

"Currently," Marcus explained as he figured it was time to just get this over with, "your clubhouse is being attacked by a group of assassins my brother called in that he works with. I hear your people like to meet up every morning, and only a couple stay at the clubhouse, right? They were dead before the others arrived. And no worries, Corrado promised to make it fast for the rest of the bastards that came in this morning."

Clearing his throat, Marcus smiled thinly, continuing with, "As for the other chapters of the Riders who came into town over the last month … each one is being approached today, and they'll all be given a reason *not* to stay here to help you or your club. For that, you can thank the last thirty years of my father helping to supply the majority of cocaine to organized crime across Canada through his contacts. Because here's the thing, Glen—the bottom line is all anybody cares about in this business, and nobody fucks with someone who can fuck with that. I'm sure you understand."

"You can't possibly—"

"Oh, it's not time for you to talk," Marcus interjected calmly, "as I gave you plenty of chances to do that with me, and each time, you shit all over it."

"You little *cocksucker*."

Marcus frowned. "The better man always knows when the lesser one no longer feels valid because insults are all he can afford. And as for *you* ... well, I had a couple of choices. I could have killed you myself. Possibly had someone do it for me while you rushed back to your clubhouse to find out if everything I said here today was true, but that didn't feel *good* to me. It wasn't enough. So instead, we made a few calls. See, we've been watching you for a while and given our reach, nothing is off limits to the Guzzis when we can make anything happen."

"I will fucking kill you, Guzzi."

A smile curved Marcus's lips. "But will you? Or is the better question, *can you*?"

"I—"

"You haven't asked what my plans are for you, Glen. Don't you care to know? See, the shipment of illegal cigarettes you have coming across the border this morning? Oh, it was picked up by the Canadian officials. I know your supplier because he works with us, too. Thing is, the Guzzis can make it worth his while to lose your business, and so we did just that. By the time you get home, RCMP will be waiting to arrest you for smuggling contraband into Canada. Your freedom will only last you as long as it takes you to finish your coffee on the way home. Have a good day; we won't be seeing each other again."

Marcus might have taken the time to revel in Glen's distraught expression, but he couldn't be bothered. He had other things to do, now. Before the asshole across the table could react, Marcus slipped out and headed for the door. Glen was fast on his heels, but by the time Marcus exited the café, Chris was already waiting with the back door open.

And a gun pointed at Glen.

Chris kept the gun pointed at the biker as Marcus

climbed in the back seat. Never lowering his weapon or looking away from the biker, his brother rounded the front of the car and slipped into the driver's seat. Tires screeched against the pavement as they pulled away from the café.

"Did he fall for it?" Marcus asked, never looking away from the blank screen of his phone that he'd pulled out after getting in the car. The lack of calls or messages mocked him. This emptiness was not something he would ever become used to feeling, but that's all he was now without Cella, it seemed. Entirely fucking empty. "Did he?"

Marcus looked up to see Chris peer in the rearview. The sound of a motorcycle's engine gunned behind them, muffled from the distance they had already put between themselves and the bomb that a friend of a friend had been paid good money to place on Glen's motorcycle while Marcus kept him distracted.

Everything else he said in the café?

All true.

The clubhouse would be gone.

The other chapters would leave soon.

Glen, however, would die today.

And then came the *bang*. The bomb finally blowing. The pressure hit the back of the car a couple of seconds later. Chris pursed his lips and nodded.

"Yeah, man, he fell for it."

"Good," Marcus murmured, going back to stare at his phone, "now we can get back to normal."

Well, *they* could.

He was still alone.

Failure had never been an option before when it came to Marcus, and yet this felt more like that than anything ever had.

CHAPTER 19

"Knock, knock."

Cella quickly hit the pause button on the remote for the television inside her office. The news that had been playing silenced instantly. The second her sister, Lucia's, gaze turned on the television, Cella had already hit the power button.

"What are you doing?" Lucia asked.

"Taking a break before I get back down to finishing these designs for the final rooms of the Toronto job."

"Ah." Her sister rocked on her heels a bit, eyeing the black screen of the television on the far wall before she took a couple of steps further into the room. "Just thought I would run over and see if you wanted to maybe have lunch with someone instead of alone in your office again."

Sure.

Cella heard what Lucia didn't want to say. Her family had been so worried about her that for the last week and a half, they rotated traveling to Rochester to help her with Tiffany, and give her company. She pretended like that wasn't what they were doing because they worried she might send them away, but really …

She needed them, too.

"Lunch sounds good," Cella said, standing from the desk. She tossed the remote for the television to the far edge and gathered her purse hanging on the back of her chair. "What are you feeling like? The little Mexican place, or—"

"Well, what I really want to do is ask you how you're doing since that seems to be the thing we're all avoiding right now, but I could go for some Mexican food."

On another day, Cella might have laughed at Lucia's attempt at being forward. Well, she supposed it wasn't so much an attempt seeing as how she succeeded. In fact, it caught her off guard, and the first thing that slipped out of her mouth was not what she expected.

"I wish I didn't leave like that, but I still don't know how I could have done it differently. I couldn't very well stay when I was having a nervous breakdown. And here we are a week and a half later, but he's not called me. Maybe he's waiting for me to call him. I'm not really sure, but every time I think of picking up the phone again, I get another flashback. I shouldn't have to do that again, Lucia. I don't want to lose what's left of this heart of mine. I'm not sure I can take that a second time."

Actually, she felt as though she'd said more than she wanted to. From the moment that she crawled out of her bed after her father safely tucked her in when they arrived home, she kept shoving all of this down.

Her regrets.

Everything she did wrong.

How she probably hurt Marcus.

Even the parts that were harmful to her, she ignored to the best of her ability. She refused to speak her dead husband's name lest she be thrust into another round of memories she couldn't handle and panic attacks that put her on her knees. She slept with the lights on because that was the only time she didn't dream, and she was sick and tired of the nightmares.

Of Marcus dead.

Her daughter, gone.

Her life over.

This wasn't just about what happened in Toronto for her. Nothing could be that simple because her life wasn't that easy. The events in Toronto had simply been a catalyst to the reopening of her trauma from William's death. Only now, it felt worse because she couldn't only consider herself here when she had a child old enough to understand what was happening around her.

"Grief is funny, you know?" Cella asked, rounding her desk as she shifted the strap of the purse onto her shoulder. "It has a way of warping and changing. It's ever-changing. Just when you think you might have a handle on it, well then it comes back around to remind you that really, you were never in control. It's always going to be there feeding off you until you have nothing left to give."

"He's not Will—"

"I know Marcus isn't William," Cella interjected fast, not quite ready to move away from her desk, "and that's never even been a question for me."

"Do you *want* him? Isn't that really what it comes down to, Cella? Either you want him, and being with him is worth the risk, or you don't?"

"Is *can't* not an option?"

Lucia shrugged. "Not with love, no. You'll love him today and tomorrow and five years from now even if you don't speak a single word to him in all that time. Shit, maybe you get out of a cab someday and look across the street to see him standing there staring back at you. And you know what? You're still going to love him then, too. So no, *can't* is not an option, but I think you already knew that."

Yeah, she did.

"What do I even say?" Cella asked, feeling the tears starting to fill her eyes even as she tried to blink them away. "What do I tell him when I call—I'm sorry that I ran, but I basically had a nervous breakdown. Oh and then I couldn't convince myself to pick up the phone and call you because I spent the last week and a half trying to convince myself that maybe we shouldn't be together even though I know that isn't true?"

Lucia blinked. "*Well* …"

"Lucia."

"Is that the truth?"

Cella let the first tear fall, although she quickly wiped it away. "All of it. As stupid as it is, yes."

"It's not stupid. And yes, that's what you tell him. *The truth.*"

How simple that seemed.

Lucia cleared her throat and nodded at the blank television. "I'll let you finish watching the newsreel—I saw it this morning. You only have a minute or so left. I don't mind waiting in the car."

Shame might have filled Cella at being caught watching a newsreel highlight of current events in Ontario and Quebec, but she couldn't even muster up that, honestly.

Her sister gave her a shrug before she turned to leave the office. Cella shook her head, but the urge to finish watching the news program was also too much for her to ignore. So, she didn't and grabbed the remote to resume where she had left off.

Which just happened to be where the reporters had caught Marcus leaving the police station after what they reported were several hours worth of interviews regarding the attacks on a biker gang in Quebec.

Or rather, the *slaughter* of an entire chapter.

"Mr. Guzzi," a reporter called to him, "we have it on good sources that you had a direct hand in the bombing and fire that killed several Riders in Quebec. Do you have anything to say on the matter?"

Marcus, in his three-piece suit, not looking at all worse

for wear, smiled at the man as he passed him by on the steps of the police station. "I'll tell you the same thing I told the cops."

"And what is that?"

He smirked at the camera. "*Prove it.*"

* * *

"You know, I can just run in and grab us food to-go," Lucia said.

Cella glanced up from the phone in her hands, realizing for the first time that they were currently parked outside of the little Mexican restaurant. Her distraction clearly wasn't missed by her sister, and even Lucia made a pointed look at the phone she held.

"And why don't you make a phone call?"

"You don't know that's what I wanted to do," Cella muttered.

"I do when you look at your phone like it's your whole world."

"Every teenager does the same thing."

"But you're a twenty-nine-year-old woman, so … "

Cella frowned. "Sometimes, you could just let people have their pride, Lucia."

"What is *that*?"

Of course.

She wished she was surprised.

"And," Lucia added, "now is the time you fight for what you want, Cella. I don't think you've ever really had to do that before. Back then, everything was just taken from you and nobody gave you any choice at all. You have a choice now. *Fight* for it."

Lucia winked at her sister and climbed out of the car while muttering about take-away food. That left Cella alone in the car to watch as her sister headed into the restaurant, and she still sat there with a phone in her hands.

It should be easy.

All she had to do was *dial*.

Except it scared her to death.

Lucia was right, though.

Can't would never be an option when someone asked if she loved Marcus. She wasn't a liar either, so she couldn't say she didn't love him. And though she fell in love once, and had that man ripped away from her by things outside of her control … she would not lose her second chance to be happy because of her own doing.

Yes, it terrified her.

Yes, he was also worth the risk.

Before Cella could overthink it for even one more second, she turned on the screen of the phone, unlocked it, and dialed a familiar cell number. It had never taken Marcus more than two rings before he picked up a call of hers, but this time?

It took five before someone answered.

It wasn't even him.

"Ashley Marcey speaking."

Cella blinked. "Um, I think maybe I called the wrong number. I was looking for Marcus—"

"Oh, yeah. I'm his personal assistant. All his calls for this old number and his home office now come through me. What can I help you with?"

What?

When had that happened?

Cella quickly came back to her senses, replying, "It's Cella Marcello, I was hoping to speak with Marcus."

"Right, the woman who is heading the team at the penthouse. I guess I am to put you through to Chris if you need anything regarding the penthouse because Marcus is busy handling other … things, at the moment. Is that going to be a problem?"

Um, yes?

And now she was just *the woman heading the team*?

Cella cleared her throat, regaining whatever sense of professionalism she had left as she replied, "No, that'll be fine. I'll just … take his number down, thank you."

For nothing, she added silently.

* * *

"Ma, have you seen Marcus yet?"

Cella did her best to smile at her daughter through the video chat as she walked through the Toronto penthouse. A week after her attempted phone call, and she didn't have a choice but to make the trip to give her final okay on a few of the rooms. In a couple of weeks, the rest of the rooms would be finished, the project would be done, and that was that.

Hard to believe, but the penthouse—despite everything else that had gone wrong and crazy since she started this contract—turned out beautiful. Not that she honestly expected anything less when it came to seeing her designs come to life.

"Well?" Tiffany asked.

In the background of the call, someone cleared their throat. Either her mother, or father, Cella couldn't really be sure. They'd agreed to watch Tiffany while Cella made the trip to Toronto, all the while *trying* to find out if she was going to see Marcus while she was there.

If only she could have said yes.

Really, she didn't know.

The assistant still took her calls, and Cella had little to no desire to explain to the woman that she wanted to speak with Marcus because their relationship was more than just this fucking penthouse. It wasn't the woman's business so what did it matter?

"I haven't seen Marcus, no," Cella said quietly. "And I am leaving tonight to fly back home, so I can pick you up as soon as you open your eyes tomorrow. How does that sound?"

Actually, she'd arrive in New York around midnight, drive to her parents', and sleep there for the night, but those were details that weren't important for Tiffany to know. She hadn't even bothered to drive to Toronto this time when she wouldn't be staying for longer than the couple of hours it would take to give her final approval on the majority of the rooms.

"I miss Marcus."

Cella went back to the conversation with her daughter, wishing her heart didn't feel like the entire organ had broken into a million and one pieces inside her chest. She kept trying to fix it, but nothing worked.

Nothing but him would do it.

Tiffany helped, though.

"Me, too," Cella replied.

On the screen, Tiffany frowned. "Well, if you do see him, will you tell him I said hi?"

"I absolutely will, baby. Now, I gotta go so I can finish up here before the team comes in for our meeting. I will call you back to say goodnight, okay?"

"Okay, Ma. Love you."

"Love you, too."

Cella hung up the call, and slipped the phone into her bag as she turned around to head for the kitchen of the penthouse. One of the first rooms to be fully finished and ready for her final approval. She didn't make it more than a step toward the kitchen because as soon as she turned around, she came face to face with a Guzzi she hadn't expected.

Chris stood at the end of the entry hallway, leaning against the wall as though he had been standing there for a while. Cella let out a gasp, her hand coming up to press against her chest where her heart suddenly felt like it was about to race right out of her chest.

"You don't make noise?" she asked him.

The man shrugged. "Was taught not to, actually. It's better this way. I often hear things people don't intend for me to, and I like that."

"*Spying*, you mean?"

He didn't reply.

Cella had another thought. "Were you listening to my conversation with my child?"

Chris cleared his throat. "Maria asks about her a lot— Tiffany, I mean. Always wants to know when she's coming back so they can play hide-and-seek again. Mia Cara is still too young to really play it right, and all, so …"

"That doesn't answer my question."

"I know." Chris let out a hard breath, tipping his head to the side as he surveyed her. "You just took off that day—and I was right, you were the first person he asked for when he came out of the sedation."

Ouch.

The man didn't pull any punches.

That one hit her right in the heart.

"Tell me," Cella replied, "between the flashbacks I was trying to get through of my husband's murder, my terrified daughter, and the police officer who was threatening to deport me while also file paperwork to make sure my daughter stayed in their custody because she was a witness … how I should have *handled* that day, Chris?"

The man said nothing.

Cella nodded, scoffing under her breath. Not caring if he had anything more to say to her, she decided that she didn't have to stand there and wait for him to figure it out. She headed past him in the hallway, determined to just wait in her rental car downstairs until the team showed up for her final directions.

Chris's next question had her hesitating halfway down the hallway. "Have you even tried to call him?"

She swung right back around. "Excuse me?"

"Marcus. Have you tried to call him at all, or are you just going to pretend like you didn't leave him hanging here wondering if his mistakes were too much for you?"

"His mistakes—"

"Are you going to answer my question?" Chris demanded. "Or is your next move to run away again because you can't *deal*, Cella?"

"You got a lot of fucking nerve, huh?"

That seemed to make the man do a double take.

Cella nodded, pointing a finger at him. "I get it—he's your brother, right? Your oldest brother, so I bet he's spent his whole life looking after you and the rest of your siblings. I get why you want to protect him, so your only way of doing that here because you can't possibly understand the complexities between him and me is to strike out at the person you think is hurting him ... but fuck you, Christopher. For believing anything about me that you didn't have the balls to ask first, for thinking you know what it's like to live my life, and for assuming you could make any of the choices I need to make. Fuck you."

"Cella—"

No, she was done here.

Entirely done.

Spinning back around in her five-inch heels, Cella headed for the elevator that was still open from when Chris entered. It spoke to her distraction because a bell rang throughout the penthouse whenever the elevator opened to the place, but she hadn't even heard it when she was talking to her daughter.

"Cella, wait!"

Footsteps caught up to her before she could reach the elevator. She'd tried her best to keep all those tears at bay while she stormed away. It never helped a woman when she cried ... it only made people feel bad for her, or worse, think she was weak.

Cella didn't want pity.

And she was *anything* but weak.

"Just *wait*," Chris said.

His hand snagging her wrist before he turned her back around was enough for the floodgates to finally be opened. She didn't even bother to wipe the tears away as they fell down her cheeks while she faced the man. He sobered at the sight of her tears, swallowing hard and apologizing though she didn't care to hear it.

"*There*," she snapped at him, "take a good fucking look at me. Because this is what I look like when I go to bed, and when I wake up. This is me when my daughter can't see me. When I don't have a client to deal with. Whenever I'm alone, this is *me* now. So fuck you for thinking running away was the easy choice. I know it was wrong, but I did what I had to because I didn't have another choice."

Chris opened his mouth to speak.

Cella was faster to say, "And yes, I have called. Apparently, he's got an assistant now, huh? As far as she knows, I'm just the woman doing this job here ... certainly not important enough to get a direct line to him. Is that the answer you wanted? Let me go, please."

Chris did, saying, "He had to get a new phone—the old one was ruined in the fire, so he switched to a new number. While he handled everything happening here in Toronto, the assistant I hired to take some of the load off his shoulders was just given the bare minimum information about people who might call through to the old number. That was my fault; she only had to deal with your team up until now, and I never thought to update her to give you the new number. I thought maybe he would have called you from the new one or whatever but I should have known better. He told me this was on you—whatever you wanted, he would let you decide."

That sounded *exactly* like Marcus.

"He's not ignoring your calls, Cella."

Jesus Christ.

Why did her heart hurt again?

Why wasn't it easier to breathe?

"He's *waiting* for you to call," Chris said quietly, "and I'm sorry. You were right. Marcus has always been the one looking out for us. That's his number one job, and he does it pretty well. I guess we're not nearly as good at doing it for him as he is for us."

Cella's bottom lip trembled.

She *tried* to stop the tears.

They just kept coming.

"I want his new number."

Chris nodded. "I'll give it to you."

"I also just want to talk to him. Face to face, but I have a flight to catch and—"

A whole fucking life in New York waiting for her.

Wasn't that the story of her goddamn life?

"He's got a lot going on. His next week is full of interviews with investigators and hours spent with his lawyers. We're trying to keep everything else around him at a dull roar while he handles the legal shit, you know?"

Yeah, she did.

"I'll give you the number," Chris said again, "and you can decide the rest. Whether you want to call, or you want to wait until you can see him. That's up to you. I'm done assuming like I know what you should do, Cella."

The lump in her throat was back.

"Thank you."

"And my daughter really does miss Tiffany," he murmured, "so if you plan to bring her around some time, Maria would be happy to see her."

"I'll keep it in mind."

CHAPTER 20

"Since when does Marcus drive us *anywhere*?" his mother asked from the backseat.

Marcus smiled to himself, knowing neither Cara nor Gian could see it. "Just for tonight, Ma. It's a special night."

"Yes, but *why*?"

"Would it be a proper surprise if I explained all the whys to you?" Gian asked.

Cara sighed dramatically. "This seems like a lot of effort for a *little* surprise, Gian."

Oh, was that what his father told his mother?

Marcus shook his head.

She was really going to be shocked.

"We're almost there," Gian murmured, "now hush up, and enjoy your night, *cara mia*."

While Marcus enjoyed his parents' conversation in the back of the Mercedes, and he kept his attention on the very busy city street in front of him, he couldn't help but let his mind and focus wander elsewhere, too. Like to the phone in his pocket, and a voice message he had yet to listen to from Cella if only because he was a coward.

Yes.

Marcus was a fucking coward.

She'd sent him the message about a week or so ago. He missed her call because he had been in the shower, and jumped out too late to grab it. By the time he did get to it, she was already leaving the message. Just seeing her name on the screen of his phone after weeks of no contact had been like a punch to his gut.

Was that it, then?

He had to wonder …

Was she calling to say goodbye?

Since he was such a goddamn coward, he decided not to listen to the message because right then, he didn't want to know. After all this time of no contact, he figured there couldn't be any other reason why she was calling except to tell him this was over between them. So, a day turned into two, and then another and another until it had been a little over a week since she left the message.

He still didn't have the courage to listen. He was going to turn thirty at the end of the month, in a week, actually, and here he was acting like a teenage boy who was afraid of a breakup. What was that bullshit?

Whatever.

Fuck my whole life.

But tonight was not about his personal problems, so Marcus pushed the thoughts to the side and decided to focus on his father's surprise for his mother. Peeking in the rearview mirror, he found Gian smiling at Cara while she tried to pry yet more information from him about the evening. Gian wasn't giving her a damn thing. Not that it mattered because soon his mother would know everything anyway.

They were almost at the penthouse.

Tonight was the *big reveal.*

As it was, the rest of his brothers and a few close friends of his mother and father were already waiting at the penthouse to celebrate with them when they arrived. A cold-plate lunch had been set up for everyone to enjoy while they walked around and admired the newly designed rooms and all the hard work that had gone into this surprise for Cara.

He knew his mother would love it.

Of course, she would.

For him, though, the penthouse didn't bring very many good feelings for him. Oh, there were certainly *good* memories. That was the place which really started it all for him and Cella despite the fact he'd met her years earlier, but that didn't matter.

It was there that he really *saw* her.

"Almost there," Marcus murmured from the front seat.

"Almost where?" his mother asked. "This is the way to the old penthouse—did that sell yet?"

Gian simply chuckled. "No, it didn't."

"What?"

"I said, it didn't sell yet, Cara. In fact, I never put it on the market."

"Why not? I thought that's what you wanted to do?"

"No, that's what you seemed to settle on when nothing else satisfied you when it came to the penthouse. I had … a different idea," his father said.

Marcus smiled again.

His mother had gone silent.

Soon, Marcus had pulled the Mercedes into the underground parking garage of the building where his parents' penthouse was located at the very top. Putting the vehicle in park, he couldn't help but shake his head at the million and one questions that his mother started to ask after her short bout of silence. All it took was a look from his father from the back seat for Marcus to step out of the car.

Everybody needed their privacy, after all.

He also felt like his father was due a moment with his mother before this whole day really began for Cara. While Gian hadn't been the one working on the penthouse behind the scenes, he did expend great effort to make sure this all happened just the same.

Outside the car, Marcus fiddled with the phone in his hand. He didn't pay much attention to the other vehicles parked in the garage, or even the passersby on the street just beyond the cement walls. His mind was too distracted; his heart was still fucking empty.

He had no reason to decide *that* moment was the one when he would finally listen to Cella's message but for whatever reason, he decided to just do it. Get it over with, and if the message was what he thought it was, then today could be the point where he started over. Not that he wanted to do that, but this had always been about her from the beginning anyway. What she wanted, he would be there to give.

Even if that meant she didn't want him.

Marcus hit the number one on the screen, holding it until it dialed through to his messaging service. Putting the phone to his ear, he listened as the recording played through its standard message before he hit one again to play the only message on his phone.

"Hey, Marcus, it's Cella," she greeted in his ear. "I'm sorry it took me this long to call. At first, I just didn't have the right number but then I wasn't sure if what I needed to say would be better said on the phone or face to face. Anyway, if you call me back, we can chat. If you'd rather wait until we can see each other, that's okay, too. Your father invited me to your mother's surprise party for the penthouse. It's just me coming. I wish I had better reasons for why I needed time, but I don't. I just needed it. I hope you understand. Tiff says hi, by the way. Asks about you all the time. Talk soon, okay? Bye."

He pulled the phone away from his ear, suddenly feeling like his feet weren't even on the ground. *She's here.* That's all he could think about—it was the only thing that seemed to make any sense at all to him.

She was there.

Upstairs in the penthouse.

But what for?

To say goodbye?

Or to stay?

Marcus didn't know if he was ready to find out.

"Son?"

Glancing over his shoulder, he found that his father had stepped out of the car with his mother. Cara had a hand tucked in Gian's arm, and the two stared at him expectantly.

"We're heading up there," Gian said.

Marcus nodded, not at all ready. "Yeah, sure, let's go."

* * *

The first thing Marcus should have noticed when the elevator doors opened to the penthouse was the many guests waiting inside to greet and surprise his mother. Or maybe even the way the entry hall had been changed to include walls covered in portraits of his mother's favorite people. Her husband, children, and grandchildren. He could have taken note of the way his mother lit up at the sight of her guests, and the realization of just why his father hadn't sold the penthouse like he said he would.

Instead, Marcus looked for *her*.

Cella.

And he didn't see her. Not in the crowd of people already starting to move their way, or even behind them where a few friends of his parents lingered to allow their sons, the wives, and grandchildren to come forward first before inserting their presence, too.

Had she changed her mind?

Did the fact he hadn't called make her think he didn't want her at all?

Unfortunately, Marcus didn't have time to focus on the

heaviness coming to rest upon his chest because people crowded around him, and while they were his family, he still had a part to play here. A mask to put on so that he could be who he needed to be when he needed to be it.

The oldest Guzzi son.

Always steadfast.

Forever in control.

"And you helped to make this happen, Marcus?"

He turned to his mother, putting his smile firmly in place to nod for her. Reaching out, he hugged his mother with one arm, and drew her into his side so that he could press a kiss to the very top of her head. She smiled up at him, a line of water in her eyes that she couldn't quite blink away.

"You love this place," he said, "and Papa knew you didn't want to give it up. You just didn't want it to stay the same."

Cara dragged in a shaky breath. "That's why Cella—"

Her name had his smile faltering.

His mother didn't miss it, and she stopped herself from saying more. Her hand came up to pat his cheek, that motherly touch of hers taking away all his worries for a brief second. Of course, it couldn't last too long, but he appreciated it all the same while he had it.

"Don't be sad," Cara told him as though she just knew, "it's not over until you say so, Marcus."

"I don't think that's how it works. And tonight is about *you*, Ma, not me."

"Well …"

"Come on," he told his mother, turning her around so that they both faced the rest of the people while he moved them further down the hall, "let's go see all that Cella had done to the place. There's one room for the grandkids I think you're really going to love."

Speaking of which …

"Uncle Marcus!"

Little Marcus Gian, although they all called him Marc, Bene and Vanna's only child—thus far—broke past his mother and father to rush his uncle. All of two years old, the kid was like a hurricane. When Bene asked Marcus to be his godfather, it forced him to fix the bridge he almost burned with his brother and Vanna.

"Playroom?" his godson asked.

Marcus laughed, reaching down to pat Marc on the head as he hugged his uncle's legs. "That's where we're going right now."

"Come play?"

"Sure will, buddy."

"You know," Beni said, staying close to his wife's side, "if Papa is still thinking about selling this place, I might be—"

"Definitely not selling it," Gian cut in fast, "so don't even ask."

Laughter colored the room.

"So, we're eating, drinking, and … what are we celebrating tonight other than this place?" Ginevra asked.

Alessio gave her a shake of his head, while Corrado on the other side of her wrangled their two kids as best he could, one in each arm.

"This family," Gian said, smiling. "We're celebrating the legacy of this family tonight, and how much you all have changed it for the better."

Right.

Marcus had to wonder as he lingered behind to stand at the end of the entry hall while his family went forward to admire the rest of the place with his mother … what exactly had he given to this legacy so far?

The fact he didn't have an easy answer bothered him. Far more than he was willing to admit. For a long time, he simply assigned his purpose to being there *for* his family. Taking care of them. Looking out for all of them, whether they thought he needed to or not. He understood all the things he had to show for it, but that didn't change the fact that at the end of the day …

Well, at the end of the day, Marcus still went home alone.

A familiar ding ringing throughout the penthouse had him turning around to see who was being let off the elevator into the penthouse. In the few minutes since he arrived with his parents, it certainly had time to go back down and bring someone else up. However, all the guests should have already *been* at the party.

Marcus froze in place when the elevator doors opened, and there stood Cella looking down at the floor in a black dress that hugged the hourglass shape of her curves perfectly. Gold thread detailing had the dress contoured down the lines of her body. The pencil thin skirt fell a couple of inches above her knees. In her hands, she held tight to a black clutch with a gold chain that was also wrapped around her wrist. The black pumps on her feet did the best fucking things for her legs.

The sight of her wearing a dress with gold detailing reminded him of the first time she'd accompanied him to his parents' mansion. The gold dress she'd worn that night made her look *draped* in it. Tonight, the gold on her seemed to show *Cella* off. She pulled it off either way, and both had him as hard as a fucking rock.

She didn't know about the Guzzis love of gold, but *he* did. Everything his family owned had their mark of gold written all over it. Kind of like their signature, really.

Jesus.

She moved forward one step, looking up at the same time. Their eyes met from fifteen feet away, her at the elevator and him at the far end of the hall. For a second, the world stopped moving as her familiar blue met his brown gaze. Under the lighting in the hallway, her tanned skin gleamed. Painted red lips curved into a smile that had him standing a little straighter and taking in another breath of air. Her winged eyeliner and loose waves had him crazy in an instant.

God.

Why was she so beautiful?

Why did it have to hurt?

"Traffic?" he asked.

Kind of stupid.

It was the first thing out of his mouth, though.

Cella nodded. "Yeah, and my Uber took the wrong exit."

"Ah, well—"

"Uncle Marcus, come *on*!"

He looked over his shoulder to find his namesake was jumping up and down on the spot, waiting for him. Marc was a lot of things, but patient wasn't one of them. He quickly turned his attention back on Cella, still unsure what was about to happen between the two of them, but she smiled at him and shrugged her shoulder.

"We can chat later," she said, "I'll be here."

"Yeah, sure."

But what would happen then?

* * *

Marcus had been wrong. For one reason or another, more guests began to show up to the small gathering as time went on. Mostly a few family Capos that he knew his father considered friends with apologies and excuses already on the tips of their tongues for as to why they hadn't gotten there sooner.

It didn't escape Marcus how Gian was quick to accept the apologies but also turned each man to him as though they also owed *him* an apology. *Should speak to your boss*, his father would say before turning his attention back on his wife.

For now, with the party in full swing, Marcus had the chance to stand back and observe the rest of his family the way he liked to do. And currently, that included his mother who stood in the middle of the playroom with her grandchildren running all over the place shouting at the top of their little lungs with Cella beside her.

"Here I was," Cara said, "trying to sneak my way onto your waiting list, and you already had a whole project going on for me."

Cella smiled. "Well, thank your husband for that."

"Oh, I will, but that's not the point."

"I couldn't *tell* you. That would have ruined the surprise."

"I suppose."

"Do you like it?" Cella asked.

Cara took a moment before answering that question, but only as long as she needed to look around the playroom with the huge jungle gym that reached the ceiling and allowed the kids wall to wall play space. "This room scared me for a long time."

"I was told that, yes. I hoped you could make better memories in here now."

"I will, thank you. And yes, I love it more than I can explain. Then again, Gian does have a way of outdoing himself every time he tries when it comes to showing his love for me. It seems like an extra gift for me in this that I was able to properly meet you, too."

The two women quieted, and Marcus felt a presence come to stand next to him in the doorway of the playroom. Beside him, Chris crossed his arms over his chest and smiled at Maria who helped her two-year-old sister, Mia Cara, climb to the second level of the jungle gym.

"Have you spoken to her?" he asked.

Marcus shook his head. "Not yet."

"Doesn't seem like you to avoid—"

"Not avoiding, Chris. There are just other things to handle first."

"*Right.*"

His brother didn't particularly sound like he believed that statement, but he didn't press. Marcus was grateful because honestly, now just wasn't the time. He hadn't lied.

"I spoke to her when she came into town a little while back to do some last-minute things here," Chris said.

Marcus took in a deep breath. "Oh?"

"Seems her lack of calling was a miscommunication on my part. Sorry about that."

"Huh."

Maybe that was what she meant in her message.

Did it even matter?

He still wasn't sure what she wanted from him. So, whether or not she had called during their time apart didn't really make a difference to the fact everything about them at the moment was still hanging up in the air.

Unsteady.

Completely uncertain.

The conversation between his mother and Cella drew Marcus's attention back to them for the moment, and thankfully away from the thoughts filling his mind. He didn't want to feel that doubt—for her, he wanted to be sure of *everything.*

Even if right now, he knew nothing.

"And what gave you the idea for this room?" Cara asked. "It's a bit unconventional, as everyone has said to me tonight at least once. Not that I care what they think because *I* love it. Gives the babies something to do with me when we're here."

Cella grinned. "Well, exactly that—your grandkids. How

much you love them, I guess. Marcus took Tiff and me to an indoor playground in the city while we were here, and I thought something like that might be just right for a room this size with as many grandkids as you have. Not to mention, whatever other babies might come along."

Cara laughed. "I've been told to stop asking for more because it might be off-putting."

"Oh?"

"Apparently, I ask too much. Speaking of your daughter, why didn't you bring her?"

At that question, Cella hesitated.

Not for long, though.

"I had some other things to handle here, and I wasn't sure that it was the right situation for her to be around, that's all. She's young ... adult issues aren't meant for children."

That felt like a punch to the gut.

Not that Marcus hadn't thought about Tiffany or considered her since the maple farm incident because he did. All the time. A lot like her mother. Thing was, he wasn't her father. He had no say in what happened in her life. There was nothing he could do about the fact that even though he'd fallen in love with that little girl and her beautiful soul, her mother took her away, too.

That was Cella's choice to make. It still fucking hurt, but he understood.

Like his mother just knew he was standing in the doorway, Cara peeked over her shoulder to glance his way. Cella followed, looking his way as well.

Instead of just standing there seeming more foolish than he already felt, Marcus turned on his heel and headed into the hallway.

So, maybe Cella wasn't the only one who liked to run sometimes.

CHAPTER
21

Cella's heart seemed to drop into her stomach as she watched Marcus turn on his heel and leave after hearing her say that she chose to leave her daughter behind because of unfinished business here. Of course, she understood that probably hadn't been what he wanted—or even expected—to hear, but it was the truth.

Sometimes, that was a hard pill to swallow.

That didn't mean she wanted for him to hear it like that. It would have been far better had she been able to take Marcus aside, have the conversation that had been weeks in the making for them, and then explain why she hadn't brought her child along for this.

Nothing could be easy, though.

Before Marcus could disappear out of Cella's sight, his father stepped in his path with another man at his side. Just like that, Marcus's disposition changed from an expression of sadness to one that held no emotion at all. He nodded at whatever the man said while the guy waved between Gian, and himself.

It looked like business as usual.

She was reminded all over again how no matter where Marcus was—as long as he wasn't alone, or just with her where no one could see—he still had a part to play. A man who constantly wore a mask, and didn't allow anyone to know there were things happening in his life that they had no idea about.

He didn't allow them to know.

It didn't matter.

Not if he hurt.

Not if he wanted to *go*.

He was who he was, and he needed to be that person even when it was the last thing he wanted to do.

The clearing of Cara's throat brought Cella's attention back to her. With the kids making a ton of noise and having all sorts of fun while ignoring their parents' pleas to *be careful* it was easy to be distracted from the handsome man just twenty feet away who still had her whole heart, even if he didn't know it.

"I was you once," Cara said quietly.

"I'm sorry?"

"Walls so high. I couldn't let anyone over those walls. That meant I might get hurt again. This life … it might take from me again. And if it did, would the next thing it took from me be something I couldn't afford to give?"

Cella's inhale rattled in her chest. "You had a twin, didn't you?"

Marcus told her that once when she noticed a picture in his home. He'd never explained in detail about how Cara's twin died, just that she had when she was young.

Cara nodded once. "People couldn't tell us apart unless they knew us very well. We lived together from the time we were born up until the day she died right beside me on marble steps. Every time I look at marble now, I see blood in the grain. It's not the same, I'm sure, as losing your husband because of this life, but it still felt like a piece of my soul was taken from me until I met Gian."

The woman shook her head, turning to watch the kids

come down the big red slide one by one as she continued with, "People called me silly—naïve. They expected me to just understand I couldn't *not* be who I was. I couldn't walk away from this life, and this person it turned me into. And so it terrified me. I was scared to death of what it meant to want a man like the one I have. He stayed, though. Just like a pillar in a hurricane. Nothing moved him, and I kept going back for safe shelter."

Cella didn't quite know what to say to that, so she opted to say nothing at all. Cara didn't seem to mind because the woman turned to her with another one of her soft smiles. The one that felt like a *mother's* smile. It spoke of a woman who had watched life evolve around her, and she was proud of all that had become of it.

God.

Cella wanted to be that woman.

Ready.

Unafraid.

Strong.

"There came a time," Cara said quieter, "where I began to realize that I needed to stop looking at Gian as though he was the one who had to be worthy of *me*. He'd already been that. Stood by me when I turned him away. Loved me when I swore I didn't love him. And I didn't need to be worthy of him, either, when he already showed me that I was. See, it's once you start demanding that this life be what you deserve that it starts to give back to you, Cella."

"I think I knew that," Cella replied, fingering the thin shoulder strap on her dress just to give her something to do. "From the start, he was just *there*."

"When you didn't expect him to be?"

"Exactly like that."

Cara nodded. "And falling never felt so natural, hmm?"

"Easy, really."

Because it had all been easy with Marcus. Maybe so

much so that she found it just as easy to run away. Things that didn't take work could sometimes be the simplest things to leave behind. It was only now that she had learned maybe it had been this way for them together because life was finally starting to give her something back after all it had taken from her.

He was what she deserved and that's why she was here. Because Cara was right. Lucia had been right. She wanted to be happy. *Would be*. And she was ready to fight for it.

"Go," Cara told her as music started to play from somewhere else in the penthouse, and Gian called out for the woman of the hour to come dance, "and take what you deserve, Cella. Don't you think it's time?"

She did.

* * *

"You know, gold really does suit you."

Cella felt those words just as much as she heard them. Strange how that worked, but then again, it had always been like that with Marcus.

In her determination to find him after everyone gathered in the large sitting room to dance and share drinks—because he seemed to just disappear—she hadn't realized he'd done that purposely. He left the crowd to hide in the shadows, and it was almost disconcerting how well he blended into them as she nearly walked right on past. She figured maybe he'd slipped away from the rest of the party to take a phone call, but considering she found him standing there as though he were waiting for *her* … well, that changed everything.

She admired the sight of him in his three-piece suit, the red vest and tie he'd opted to wear bringing out the golden tan of his skin even more.

"What are you doing back here?"

In the doorway of one of the spare bedrooms, Marcus shrugged. "I think you know the answer to that, Cella. This seemed like the perfect time to *chat*—isn't that what you came here to do? Talk to me?"

"More than anything."

She could tell just by the fleeting surprise that quickly left his expression as fast as it came that her response wasn't the one he expected to hear.

"What?" she asked. "Did you think I would try to save my pride here—act like you're not everything I want, Marcus?"

The strong line of his jaw worked as he chewed over his next words. Cella let him have those moments, knowing he probably needed them as much as she had needed these past weeks without him. Space to breathe, and time to think.

Sometimes, it brought everything into focus.

Everything that mattered, anyway.

"I wondered," Marcus said, tipping his head to the side as he reached out to finger the low neckline of her dress, "if you came all this way today just to tell me you were done here. So I avoided hearing it—I was sure that's what you were going to do."

"You think I still might?"

He grinned just a bit.

Sexy and sly.

"Not in that dress, no," he replied. "I don't think you'd look this good to just tell me that, *bella donna*. You don't seem like the type to step on my heart in heels before you walk away."

"Oh, I'm exactly that type, but I just don't intend to say goodbye, Marcus."

"I'm sorry for what happened."

She nodded. "I know."

"I wish you didn't leave."

"Me, too."

"Did it help?" he asked.

Cella stared down at the floor between them because God knew that was easier than the weight of this man looking at her when he was this close and touching her at the same time. He still did that to her. Made her lose her train of thought while at the same time, causing the rest of the world to disappear around them.

It was just her and him.

The hallway.

Them *together*.

Like she wanted it to be.

"The distance helped," she admitted.

"Look at me."

Cella didn't hesitate to meet his gaze, and there she found the same thing that always waited for her when Marcus stared at her. Understanding. *Patience*. Sympathy.

His love.

At the same time, his mask from earlier was gone. Because of that, she found the man who had made her fall in love with him so easily staring back at her. All his passion, the parts of him that made her heart race and her lungs ache. This man, who felt entirely like hers and no one else's.

Cara was right.

Cella could be the hurricane.

Marcus would be her safe haven.

Always.

"It helped," she repeated, "because it reminded me where I wanted to be the most. It didn't matter that I was scared, or that it felt like every fear I had was coming to life all over again. None of that mattered because I was still willing to take the risk. I still wanted to be here. I needed to figure that out, but I couldn't do that here with you. I'm sorry if you thought differently, but I didn't know how to explain this over a phone call."

"Well," he drawled, pushing away from the door jamb to stand at his full height. It made her have to look up at him, even in her heels. His head tipped down as he moved closer to her, the small bit of distance between them becoming nothing at all in a blink. "You could have started by saying *I love you* because that was the thing I thought I had ruined that day."

His body molded against hers, but Cella didn't move away. Like this, his lips were close enough that all she needed to do was lean up for a kiss, and she would have it. Instead, she waited, asking, "And then what could I have done?"

"You could have let me apologize," he murmured, "for trying to do too much; for letting my feelings cloud my judgment in a way that I put you and her in danger; for failing because I've never done that before, but I felt like I did with you."

Cella shook her head. "No, you really didn't."

Down the hall, the music became louder.

"Except you couldn't tell me that," he said, "because you weren't here."

And she hadn't called.

"But you waited," she whispered. "For me to figure this out ... to come back, you waited."

"Of course, I did."

"Even when you thought—"

"You're mine, Cella. I will wait for you forever."

"Promise?"

Marcus reached up to pinch her chin between his forefinger and thumb. Not that she wanted to look away from him, but like *this*, he didn't give her a choice but to stay still. "I'm kind of tired of making promises of what could be because I'd really just like to give you whatever you want. If you ask for the world, woman, I will give it to you."

"I really just want you."

"I'm yours."

That was all she needed to hear to propel her closer to him, taking away the little bit of distance so that she could finally do what she had wanted from the second the doors of that elevator opened and she found him standing at the end of the entry hall.

Kiss him.

Her lips found his, and it was like coming home again. Like finding the one place that would always be hers and was forever safe. The world around them that had felt like it was entirely off-axis suddenly tilted back into place. His lips swept over hers, soft and slow at first, tasting with soft flicks of his tongue against the seam of her mouth, urging her to open up for him. And when she did, when she took his kiss deeper, she tasted heaven.

Cella, still feeling as though she were floating, grounded herself by fisting the lapel of his blazer. She drifted the pad of her fingertips down his jaw as the kiss slowed, and his next words whispered over her lips.

"Say it—I've missed hearing it."

She knew exactly what he meant.

Felt what he wanted in her soul.

"I love you," she told him.

Marcus kissed her again. "*Sempre*—forever, Cella."

Laughter echoing down from the hallway had Cella wishing she could catch her breath. "We better get back to the party."

"Just long enough to say goodbye."

"*Marcus.*"

He smirked. "*Fine.*"

His fingers wove with hers, and his dark laughter—

sending sparks shooting through her bloodstream—chased them out of the hallway. No one seemed to notice them rejoining the party, or that they slipped onto the middle of the floor to dance a slow waltz as a few others were doing.

Or maybe that was just them.

Maybe *they* didn't notice the others.

After all, Marcus was still watching her like *that*—all heavy and intense, and ready to drown in her. She'd missed that. *Him.*

Everything about him.

* * *

Her hotel was closer. And that was really what it came down to for Cella when Marcus asked her where she wanted to go for the night after leaving his parents' penthouse party that ended up going a bit into the evening. That was the thing about life when someone had the chance to be with people that made their days better and brighter—one could lose track of time.

Then, the moment someone mentioned the time as they decided to leave, the atmosphere between Cella and Marcus changed in a blink. Oh, they certainly took their time saying goodbye, and playing their part. She'd kind of realized that to stand *beside* Marcus—as she chose him—that she needed to be what *he* needed her to be. The same way she knew he wanted nothing more than to pull her out of there and fuck her against the closest flat surface, but he played his part, first.

Stepped into his role.

The dutiful son. A Made man. Rising crime boss, if what the news had to say was to be believed.

So she turned into the person he needed her to be while she stood beside him, until she could finally get him alone, and then Marcus became the man she knew best. Who took what he wanted from her, and made sure she loved every damn second of it, too.

Cella didn't even get more than four steps inside her hotel room before the hard slam of the door had her stomach clenching in anticipation.

"Turn around."

She did, spinning in those *too-high* heels that she knew damn well would make her legs look good, and have Marcus watching her everywhere she walked during the night. She hadn't been wrong on either of those things. The shoes did both.

Marcus hadn't even moved away from the door he'd just slammed shut; his gaze nailed to her, and she got the best sight of him licking along his bottom lip as he tipped his head to the side. That stare of his traveled up her body, appreciating the way her dress hugged every curve she had before he finally met her eyes with his own.

His stare had her wet.

The intensity.

How he arched his left brow *just enough*. That strong jaw of his clenching every so slightly when he swallowed. Even the way he flicked his wrist over to undo the buttons of his blazer.

He was perfection wrapped in a fucking *suit*.

"How fond are you of that dress?"

Cella's breath caught in her chest as she replied, "Fond enough that as long as a dry clean will fix it, I don't care."

Marcus nodded. "Good to know—give me your panties."

"Like, *to* you?"

"Off, in my hand, and then they're going in my pocket."

"I don't get them back?"

"Not the pair you have on tonight. Did you think I wouldn't see them when you bent over to *fix* the strap on your heel in the elevator? Since when do you hike a fucking skirt up to damn near your thighs to bend over, Cella? They're mine to keep after you tease me like that. *Off.* Now."

She grinned because, yes, she had done that.

No shame.

"That's how it's going to be tonight?" she asked.

Marcus let his tongue drift along his teeth, sucking in air as he did so before saying, "Seems so—keep that sass up."

Oh, she would.

He liked that, too.

Even conversation could be foreplay with this man. She bet that had been hell for him, too. Seeing her bent over, the way her panties hugged her ass and hid that sliver of her sex, as they left through the elevator from the penthouse. If that wasn't bad enough, he had to drive six blocks before they arrived at the hotel.

"You told me once you like to break the rules."

Marcus made a thick noise under his breath. "I did say that."

"Well, maybe I like to *make* you break them. Or I just like to see you try *not* to."

"I'll keep that in mind."

Cella winked. "You should."

"*Panties,*" he drawled as he began a slow process of removing his blazer. "They're mine."

Right.

"Of course," she simpered, winking.

Marcus shook his head, but Cella still hurried to do what he demanded of her. She did, however, take her time to bunch her skirt up to her hips before she pulled those panties down her legs until she could step out of them entirely. At the same time, she was careful to not even give him even a quick peek at her pussy.

Just to make him wait more.

He'd make it worth it.

His teeth nipped into his bottom lip as she crossed the room with those panties in her outstretched hand, ready to hand them over. He took the flimsy scrap of white lace from her grasp with a quick jerk of his hand that had her thighs clenching together to soothe the sudden ache now pulsing between her legs.

Sure enough, he tucked the panties into his pocket.

Marcus hummed his approval. "Show me what's mine."

"How?"

"Any way you want. For as long as it takes me to get what I need off, anyhow, and then I'm going to bend you over the edge of the bed and fuck you until my goddamn cock aches. I don't care how you do it, just *show me*. Oh, and keep the damn dress on. After watching you walk around in that all night, I feel like it owes me and so do you."

Cella laughed, feeling breathless already, as she walked backward until her thighs hit the edge of the bed. Sitting back, she hiked her skirt up all over again, this time not bothering at all to tease Marcus as she spread her thighs wide for him. Nothing was sexier than the way he groaned when she showed him just how wet she was with two fingers sweeping through her slit.

He, on the other hand, took his sweet time getting undressed. One goddamn button at a time while she continued toying with her sex, alternating between fucking herself with her fingers, and then rubbing circles into her clit.

"Want to come?" he asked.

Her air came out in a shuddering exhale. "I *could*."

His blazer was long gone. His vest, tie, and then dress shirt followed the same path. Her thighs started to tremble when she rubbed the circles a little faster into her clit, and he worked his belt apart far too slowly for her liking.

"Do you like that? Getting teased like you did to me, I mean."

Cella smirked. "But look at what it's getting me, Marcus."

He grunted low.

"Say it again."

"What?" she breathed.

"My name—just before your orgasm, it sounds like a prayer."

"Can I come?"

"When you say it again."

She did, her eyes squeezing shut and head falling back while his name passed her lips. Her body seemed to shatter into a million little pieces at the same time.

Marcus loomed over her when she opened her eyes back up again. He'd finally pulled that belt apart and shoved his pants down just enough to free his cock. In his hand, he stroked his length, leaning down to tease his kiss along her quivering lips.

Those hot kisses of his trailed lower. Over her skin, and then down her throat. Across the expanse of her breasts, lower to her tummy, and then where she wanted him the most. He took his time tasting her, licking the taste of her orgasm straight from the source until she was shaking and begging again.

"Marcus, I'm going to … let me—"

He lifted a hell of a lot faster than he had gone down on her, taking away her oncoming orgasm with nothing more than a chuckle before he kissed her. Cella whined into his mouth, frustration curling deep in her gut until those dark words of his reminded her of what would be quickly coming next.

He could eat her later.

She wanted to be fucked right now.

"*Bend over.*"

She did, making sure to let every inch of her body mold against his as she moved, so he felt all of her. He pulled her to the edge of the bed with a rough tug of his hands on her hips that had her moaning. When he filled her full of him, taking his time to let his cock stretch her out in the best way, her body felt taut and ready to snap all over again. He shoved her dress up around her hips again.

Then, he was fucking her.

All at once.

Long, deep thrust.

A hand in her hair.

Another on her ass, leaving fingerprint bruises.

His brutal pace had her grabbing for support against the bed with one hand while she reached back for him with the other. His hand on her ass left to grab onto hers, his fingers twisting with hers as she cried out against the bed sheets.

He fucked her harder, then twisted the loose strands of her hair around his fist to yank a little firmer until her throat was taut. All those sounds of hers had the muscles in her throat vibrating. A lot like the rest of her body that met his thrust for thrust.

"Fuck, this *pussy*, woman."

"Oh God, *yes*," she gasped. "Like that … *just like that.*"

She was sure he'd make her work for that orgasm. After all, she *had* teased him … and he'd only gotten her back a little for making him suffer, but he didn't do that at all. He fucked her until she was shouting with her second orgasm, and then he let go of her hand to slip a hand between her thighs. His pace stayed the same, he rubbed swift circles into her tender clit, and kept it up until she sobbed his name against the bed while she came again.

Only then did he slow down.

Only then did he let her breathe.

Barely.

Marcus leaned down over her, his wet fingertips trailing over her inner thigh while his mouth ghosted over the back of her neck.

"Not done," he told her, that husky tone of his making her anticipation grow all over again. "Not even close to being done, Cella."

"Before you get started again," Cella mumbled against his kiss after he'd pulled out of her just long enough to roll her over on the bed and fit right back between her thighs again, "do something for me?"

"Anything. Just ask."

It was *not* the right time.

It was, however, late.

Cella might miss her chance, and she didn't want to do that. It wasn't just her that had been waiting for a chance to have this man back.

"Call Tiff," she said. "Say goodnight."

He leaned back a bit, his gaze softening from the heat that had been there just a moment before. She shrugged at his unspoken question. Yeah, it was a total fucking cock-block, but they could get back to this moment. Soon, her daughter would be asleep and Cella had promised she would try her best to get Marcus to call.

"She's asked about you every chance she had," Cella said, "and she knew I was coming to see you today—I didn't realize there was something missing in her life, even if we all did the best to give it to her, until she started acting like she might have found it."

A dad, she didn't say.

Thing was, Cella couldn't say that.

Neither could Marcus.

Only one little girl could say that—even if everyone around her saw the questions and behavior for exactly what it was when it came to Marcus—it was only for *her* to say. Just Tiffany.

"Yeah."

His simple *yeah* said it all. His understanding in a word.

He grinned.

She smiled back.

"Of course," he added, "let's get her on the phone, and say goodnight to her."

This man?

He truly was perfect.

For her.

"And then we'll pick this up where we left off, hmm?" Marcus asked.

"You know it."

A lot like them.

This wasn't a *restart*. Not from the beginning. They were just picking back up where they left off.

EPILOGUE

One Year Later

"Ma has a surprise," Tiffany blurted out in the back seat.

Marcus's gaze lifted to the rearview mirror to find the girl in the back seat currently red-faced where she sat in her booster seat. Her sense of embarrassment was cute, really. Car drives, but especially long ones, were always fun when it came to Tiffany because she never stopped talking from the moment they got on the road. It kept him entertained and awake, anyway.

"Does she?" he asked.

"Not supposed to tell."

He pressed his lips together, desperately trying to hide the smile forming. Tiffany was a lot of things, and each of those were special to him. He loved everything that made up this sweet child, and more. One of the things she couldn't seem to do, however?

Keep a secret.

It would be cute.

If someone meant for their secrets to be told.

"Do you feel better now that you told me she has a surprise?" he asked.

Tiffany sighed like a weight was off her chest. "*Yes.*"

"Don't tell me what it is, okay?"

"I won't."

"Good. That's what matters."

Well, not really.

He wouldn't break his girl's heart, though. He was pretty sure Cella hadn't intended for Tiffany to say anything about this *surprise*—Marcus had no fucking idea what it was; he was curious now—but he wouldn't make the girl feel badly for it, either.

Besides, soon he'd arrive at Cella's mother and father's place where he'd meet up with her later in the day after she finished a consult with a client in Brooklyn, and surely, he would find out her surprise then.

This thing between him and Cella?

It took work to keep *working*.

Like weekends with her in New York, and then the next with him in Toronto. Or making sure Tiffany could visit her grandparents on a regular enough basis to make sure the kid never felt like she went without her family. He'd been lucky that for the past couple of months during the summer, Cella mostly took on jobs that were based in and around Ontario or Quebec except for this last one that came from a friend in Brooklyn who had apparently been waiting forever to get a design done. During that time, she even started looking for a place to move her Rochester office. He hadn't asked her to do it, but she brought it up one night and he didn't tell her to stop.

"Are we almost there?"

And just like that, as with most kids, Tiffany changed direction entirely.

"Almost," he said.

Then, he had another thought.

"You know, I have a surprise for your ma, too."

In the backseat, Tiffany threw her hands high. "Well, this is just *impossible*!"

Marcus laughed for the rest of the drive.

Man, he loved that kid.

* * *

"Marcus."

"Lucian."

The two men greeted each other with a quick shake of hands after Marcus helped Tiffany to remove her shoes and the backpack on her shoulders. The girl gave her grandfather a hug around his waist, and then ran deeper into the house. Probably in search of her grandmother.

"Remember, no telling secrets!"

"Got it, Marcus!"

He smiled, shaking his head.

"Oh, we have secrets, do we?" Lucian asked.

"Apparently."

"Good ones, I hope."

Marcus shrugged. "Have to ask Cella about hers, but as for mine … give me a few minutes."

Pocketing his Mercedes keys to his pocket, Marcus tried to shake off the strange nerves that crawled around his throat. It wasn't like him to get *nervous*, but here he was. Doing exactly that, it seemed.

"You said you wanted to chat?" Lucian asked.

Marcus nodded at Cella's father. "Yeah, before Cella gets here, if you wouldn't mind. And of course, if you have a minute to spare for me."

"I was taught never to shun a boss, Marcus, even if that boss isn't *mine* and he's decades younger than me. A boss is a boss …"

Ah.

Yeah.

"Is a boss," Marcus finished for the man.

Cosa Nostra rules never changed. It didn't matter if a man was no longer active in the life—like Lucian because as far as Marcus knew, the man had stepped out of his active role in the family *years* ago—he was still expected to follow the rules.

"You know, I've never publicly confirmed that," Marcus said, twisting the ring around his index finger that his father had worn for years. The *Guzzi* ring—the one that signified the boss. Men had kissed that ring for years. *Wished* they could be the ones wearing it. Now, it belonged to him and surprise, it was a perfect fit. Not that he expected anything less. "The fact I took over the Guzzi family, I mean."

Lucian smirked from the side as he turned in the hallway with a wave. "Ah, but you don't have to. The Marcellos hear *everything.*"

Right.

Marcus wouldn't forget it.

On the way past the kitchen, Marcus peeked in to find Tiffany was telling her grandmother all about the friends she had made in Toronto over the summer during their many outings and trips to parks near his home. She seemed content, so he didn't bother her. A quick smile from Jordyn, Cella's mother, had him nodding hello back before he continued following Lucian to the upstairs where the man's office waited for them.

Once behind the closed doors, Lucian took a seat behind his large desk dominating the far end of the room. Marcus stayed standing, if only because life had taught that when inside another man's office, he didn't prefer to *sit*. Lucian didn't say anything about his choice to stand, so he didn't think the man was too offended.

"You know," Lucian said, "the last time Tiffany was here, we were having Jordyn's birthday party. She called you her dad to one of her cousins."

He spun fast on his heels, eyeing the man from where he currently stood near the windows. "Did she?"

"I take it that's not a regular thing, then?"

"I think she's feeling out the idea … testing it," Marcus said, shrugging. "Seeing how it sounds, and if she likes it. How other people react when she says it. She's a smart girl, and she acts like it, too. If people pay attention, they would notice it more often. Instead, people tend to overlook children because they *are* children."

"Smart like her mother."

"Exactly."

"But how do *you* feel about it?" Lucian asked.

Marcus smiled faintly. "Well, that's not really about me, is it?"

He didn't get a say.

That was all on Tiff.

"Doesn't mean you can't feel a certain way about it."

"You're right, and I do feel …"

Happy.

Proud.

Pleased.

Honored.

"Well, I'll keep that for me," Marcus finished quieter.

Lucian nodded. "I get it. So, that chat you wanted to have—what was it?"

"I want to marry Cella."

Marcus wasn't really sure what he expected after that declaration. He thought, perhaps, he might just *warm* Lucian up to the idea of what he planned to ask the man. Not that Cella's father didn't like him, or anything, but he didn't want his request for her hand to come off as a demand.

Yet, it did just that.

Behind the desk, Lucian laughed. "Took you long enough."

Marcus met the man's gaze. "Pardon?"

"My bet was six months. You made it a year. I owe my wife a grand."

Well, then …

"Is that a go-ahead from you?"

Lucian sighed, lifting one shoulder. "You didn't really need to ask."

Yes, he did.

"It's who I am, Lucian."

* * *

"So, I hear you have a surprise for me."

Marcus glanced up from the sink basin to find Cella was currently leaning against the master bathroom of her bedroom. "Well, at least she made it a day before telling you. And from what I hear, you have a surprise for me, too, hmm?"

Outside the bedroom, fast footsteps pattered down the hall followed by Tiffany's very loud, "*I regret nothing!*"

Cella grinned.

Marcus just shook his head.

"*Also*," he added, pointing his razor at her in the mirror, "I had the decency to know you had a surprise—whatever it is—not to tell you I knew that you had one. And look at you … you couldn't even give me the same."

"I'm too impatient for that."

His laughter colored up the bathroom.

"Maybe you should wait," he added.

"Do you want to wait for your surprise?"

That made him hesitate.

"It's not a tit for tat, Cella."

Goddamn this woman.

He loved her.

"So, you're not going to admit it's killing you to know I have a surprise for you?" she asked.

Jesus.

"Well—"

"Technically, it's *two* surprises," she added.

"Cella, if you give me yours, I'll have to give you mine. Maybe I was trying to do something for you. Have you thought of that?"

"Yes, and I still want it."

No shame.

She had *none*.

He loved that, too.

"So, are you going to give me the surprise?" she asked.

"How about you read Tiff her bedtime story, and we'll revisit this later?"

Cella sighed. "*Really?*"

"Patience is a virtue, *bella*."

"In *your* world."

He chuckled.

She still left him to his business, though.

Marcus took his sweet time shaving what remained of the facial hair on his throat before moving onto the rest of his face. When he was in New York for a week with Cella, he could get away with having a bit of scruff on him. It also helped that he still had to use a faked passport, one with his brother's identification information but *Marcus's* picture, to get across the border because he still wasn't supposed to leave his country. While the investigations had died down because the cops still couldn't prove he had a hand in taking out the Quebec chapter of the Riders, he still had a lot of legal issues that seemed to keep coming up one after the other.

Nonetheless, the facial hair helped because Corrado was going through a whole phase of growing out a beard—which his spouses hated—and he and Marcus looked far more similar when his grew out, as well. Not that anyone at the border seemed to know the difference, and the bribes he paid to keep a couple agents quiet certainly helped. But tomorrow, he had to head back to Toronto, so he'd shave tonight and cross the border clean-shaven so that when he had his meeting with the made men of the family in the evening, they didn't think their boss was pushing the rules by not shaving.

By the time he finished his business in the bathroom, Marcus found Cella's Rochester home to be quiet as he walked through the upstairs hall. Tiffany's bedroom door was firmly closed which meant the girl had finally allowed her mother to tuck her into bed for the night. He went in search of Cella, quickly finding her downstairs in the kitchen where she stood against the island with her back slightly turned to him.

He could still see the small smile playing on her lips, though. Not to mention, the way that smile of hers grew wider when a sound started to echo from the phone in her hands. He said nothing, leaning in the doorway as she listened to what sounded like the hooves of horses beating to the ground on top of white noise. Then, the recording went straight to white noise with no other sound before the hooves came back again, a bit slower than the first time. He was sure he'd heard that before but where, he couldn't quite place it.

"What's that?" he asked, when it finished.

Cella turned fast, that phone of hers dropping to the counter at the same time. Her wide eyes met his, and he grinned back. "God, you *need* to make noise."

"Okay—but answer the question."

"Heartbeats."

Marcus took a second.

Then, two.

"As in, more than one?" he asked. "Wait, whose heartbeats?"

Cella smiled.

In that moment, Marcus understood *everything*.

Her passing comment—*technically, two surprises*.

He knew exactly where he'd heard that sound before. Each of his brothers had sent him similar recordings when they first had the chance to hear their babies' heartbeats during pregnancy exams.

"You're pregnant?" he asked.

Even as he asked that, he wasn't sure he actually said it. His legs moved on their own accord, taking him across the kitchen as Cella nodded in response to his question.

"Nine weeks," she told him, "and I'm not even sure *how*."

"Nine weeks," he echoed.

Right.

Because birth control.

Her *shot*.

"Twins?" was all he managed to ask.

"Apparently. There are two heartbeats, and even though they're very small, the doctor found them on an ultrasound. Same sac. I had a bit of spotting, some cramps. I went in to my gynecologist last week just to do a—"

Cella didn't even get to finish explaining how she found out she was carrying his children before Marcus had her in his arms. All he wanted to do was *kiss* her. So, he did exactly that, his mouth crashing down on hers as his hands slid under the hem of her night shirt to push it higher. His palms laid flat to the very small curve of her stomach that seemed warmer against his touch for some reason.

This was *not* the surprise he expected.

It was still perfect.

"I know this isn't the *best* time," she whispered when their kiss slowed, "we're not married, we're still living in two different countries, and—"

"None of that even matters to me, but I was working on one of those anyway."

Her stare met his.

"What?"

"Your surprise, Cella."

Marcus wanted to propose in a totally different way. He wanted to plan something *huge*—give this woman everything she deserved and more. Besides, he was a fucking Guzzi, and they never went halfway on *anything*.

Not even a proposal.

This seemed better, though.

The right time.

Kneeling to the floor, Cella's hands drifted from his jaw to rest overtop his palms still resting flat against her stomach. He did take one hand away, although that was only to pull out the item he'd been keeping a hold of ever since his father gave it to him when he asked for it. A ring his mother had worn for years. It meant so much to his family. Passed down for generations. It felt appropriate that he could put it on Cella's hand, now.

Glancing up at her, he twisted the white-gold band with the oval-shaped diamond surrounded by a crown of small, blue sapphires between his fingertips. A line of water wet her lashes, but she didn't move to wipe the tears away.

"*Ti amo. Vita mia.* My *life*, Cella. You've become that to me now. Because my life certainly wouldn't be the same without you. I don't ever want to be without you. Or Tiffany. Everything else, we'll figure it out. Right now, though, this is all I want to know. Will you marry me?"

She leaned down with him, her kiss finding his as she gave him everything that he wanted all over again with nothing more than a simple, "*Yes*."

AUTHOR'S NOTE

I have the immense honor of knowing someone, who, far too young lost her husband not longer after she had given birth to their son.

It is such an honor to me to know her because I could never imagine losing the person I consider my soul mate and still be able to show as much strength and courage that she did during the period that followed his death and her pain. And then a few years later, I had the privilege to watch from an outside perspective as a new man came into her life, and she slowly, very naturally … fell in love again.

I often thought back to that someone and her real-life happily ever after when I thought about how I wanted to tell the story of Marcus and Cella. No, the stories are not the same—this is not "based on" anything, but I felt like because I had been lucky enough to see someone have their second great love in such a real way, that I wanted Marcus and Cella to feel the same.

As for the rest of this series … I always thought that The Guzzi Legacy would be my last books in the Commission world, and for a long time they were. But then I decided for one more—Cory Rossi from Chicago, and we added that, too. Then Pink came into my mind, with a book, too. But it still does feel like an end of an era still for me to know this world is basically finished now, I have closed it out with them.

And what a trip this was—*what a ride.*

I never imagined a family I saw in my mind calling themselves the Filthy Marcellos would turn into … all of this. I didn't know that when I started writing Lucian, it would grow into something huge as I wrote more and more. This has been one of the greatest experiences of my life becoming an author and sharing my talent and stories with the world. Or my world, anyway.

I hope that something in your life gives you as much joy and pride as writing does for me. And if you haven't found that thing yet … please, never stop looking for it.

Thanks for being on this journey with me, loves.

I am far from finished. This world, which I know you all will miss so much, was just the beginning for me. I can't wait to show you more.

—BK

BETHANY-KRIS

Bethany-Kris is a Canadian author, lover of much, and mother to four young sons, two cats, and three dogs. A small town in Eastern Canada where she was born and raised is where she has always called home. With her boys under her feet, a snuggling cat, barking dogs, and a spouse calling over his shoulder, she is nearly always writing something ... when she can find the time.

Find Bethany-Kris at her:
www.bethanykris.com

BOOKS BY BETHANY-KRIS

The Guzzi Legacy

Corrado

Alessio

Chris

Beni

Bene

Marcus

Renzo + Lucia

Privilege

Harbor

Contempt

Andino + Haven

Duty

Vow

John + Siena

Loyalty

Disgrace

Cross + Catherine

Always

Revere

Unruly

The Companion

Naz & Roz

Guzzi Duet

Unraveled, Book One

Entangled, Book Two

DeLuca Duet

Waste of Worth: Part One

Worth of Waste: Part Two

Donati Bloodlines

Thin Lies

Thin Lines

Thin Lives

Behind the Bloodlines

The Complete Trilogy

Filthy Marcellos

Antony

Lucian

Giovanni

Dante

Legacy

A Very Marcello Christmas

The Complete Collection

Seasons of Betrayal

Where the Sun Hides

Where the Snow Falls

Where the Wind Whispers

Seasons: The Complete Seasons of Betrayal Series

Gun Moll Trilogy

Gun Moll

Gangster Moll

Madame Moll

The Chicago War

Deathless & Divided

Reckless & Ruined

Scarless & Sacred

Breathless & Bloodstained

The Complete Series

Maldives & Mistletoe

The Russian Guns

The Arrangement

The Life

The Score

Demyan & Ana

Shattered

The Jersey Vignettes

Standalone Titles

Dirty Pool

Effortless

Inflict

Cozen

Captivated

Dishonored

Find more on Bethany-Kris's website at www.bethanykris.com